John Bew

American Husbandry

Containing an Account of the Soil, Climate, Production and Agriculture, Of The

British Colonies

John Bew

American Husbandry
Containing an Account of the Soil, Climate, Production and Agriculture, Of The British Colonies

ISBN/EAN: 9783741185571

Manufactured in Europe, USA, Canada, Australia, Japa

Cover: Foto ©Andreas Hilbeck / pixelio.de

Manufactured and distributed by brebook publishing software (www.brebook.com)

John Bew

American Husbandry

AMERICAN HUSBANDRY,

VOL. II.

AMERICAN HUSBANDRY.

Containing an ACCOUNT of the

SOIL, CLIMATE,

PRODUCTION and AGRICULTURE,

OF THE

BRITISH COLONIES

IN

NORTH-AMERICA and the WEST-INDIES;

WITH

Obfervations on the Advantages and Difadvantages of fettling
in them, compared with GREAT BRITAIN and IRELAND.

BY AN AMERICAN.

IN TWO VOLUMES.

VOL. II.

LONDON,
Printed for J. BEW, in Pater-nofter-Row.
MDCCLXXV.

AMERICAN HUSBANDRY.

CHAP. XXV.

GEORGIA.

Climate — Situation—Soil—Productions — Agriculture—Exports—Observations.

GEORGIA is in many respects the same country as Carolina, differing very little in climate, but generally in favour of it. Upon the coast it is not above sixty or seventy miles from north to south ; but in the internal country the distance is upwards of one hundred and fifty miles. The climate upon the coast is hot, damp, and unwholesome, like Carolina, though there are hilly spots which form strong exceptions. The flat country extends in general about two hundred miles from the sea, and the interior tract, which reaches from thence to the Apalachean mountains, and is about one hundred miles

        B   broad,

broad, ranks in every refpect among the very fineft in all America. The climate at the fame time that it is hot enough to produce the moft valuable ftaples, is healthy and agreeable to an extraordinary degree; free from thofe fudden changes and violent extremes that are felt in the maritime part of the province, and which are fo pernicious to health wherever found. In this country the foil is of a fertility that even exceeds the back parts of South Carolina, efpecially on the river Savannah, and its branches to the weft and north-weft of Augufta, and indeed all round that town : no flat lands are found, no fwamps, no marfhes, but high, dry tracts, waving in gentle hills, and the vales watered with numerous ftreams. The foil a deep black loam, fo rich that there is fcarcely any exhaufting its fertility : it was for a long time unknown that fuch a country exifted here; but upon firft fettling Georgia, and for many years afterwards, the flat fandy coaft was the only part of the province attended to or known ; and as long as this has been the cafe with any of our colonies to the fouth of New York, they have languifhed, and emerged from their languor as foon as they penetrated into the rich and healthy

part

part of the country. Georgia was a very inconfiderable province as long as the people confined themfelves to the coaft; but the efforts fince made here have been by means of removing backwards, where filk, indigo, and other commodities of great value, are cultivated with a fuccefs far greater than was ever found in any of the maritime parts of our colonies. But however clear the excellencies of thefe interior parts of Georgia may appear, to fuch as have viewed them with an underftanding eye, yet are they not one tenth peopled: it is but a few years fince any attention at all has been given to this province by American or European fettlers; but after the arrangement of the American governments in 1763 had confined all the colonies to as narrow bounds as the encroachments of the French before the war, and their operations in it, they then found good land, unpatented, fcarce; which pufhed them upon a more induftrious fearch: this was the caufe of Georgia receiving fince the peace fuch an acceffion of people, that fettled in numbers in the back parts of it; and it was the fame caufe that contributed to the peopling feveral diftricts in North Carolina, which had been long neglected.

B 2

The

The foil and face of the country in the maritime part of the province, refembles South Carolina; it confifts of a flat territory, very fandy, and in general either pine barrens or fwamps; the flips of oakland are not large or numerous: the fwamps are inferior to thofe of Carolina in the production of rice, and in general the country is not fo good for the whole breadth of the flat part; but this inferiority is not great; all the fea-coaft of America, from Jerfey to Florida, has a ftrong fimilarity.

The vegetable productions both of trees, fhrubs, roots, flowers, &c. are the fame as thofe of South Carolina; nor is there much difference in the growth, for though Georgia lies to the fouth of that province, yet is the climate not hotter than that of Carolina; and there are fome parts of the latter, particularly Charles Town, much hotter than moft in Georgia. Relative to a further account of the foil, climate and products of this province, I fhall here infert an extract from a letter written by a planter, who went from England and fettled not far from Augufta, and has refided there eight years.

" I muft freely own, that in fome inftances I was much difappointed in my expectations

pectations of this country,—I thought the
foil had been more generally good, and the
climate I was taught to imagine was more
agreeable to an English constitution; but
in summer I find the heat very oppressive,
and gives one, for two or three hours in the
afternoon, a languor which I never experienced in England even in the hottest days;
going out is then disagreeable, and the
only way to be tolerably at ease, is to keep
one's self perfectly quiet, to sit still in rooms
that admit much air but no sun, and to be
cautious in diet: this season lasts through
July, August, and most of September. The
way to enjoy the agreeable parts of any a-
vocation during those months, is to rise
early in the morning, and to transact whatever business requires your being abroad,
by eleven o'clock, or at most by twelve
(unless the days are cloudy), and then to
keep the house till five in the afternoon: in
the evening the air is cool enough to render the fields pleasant.   What I have now
told you is not general with all constitutions; I have a servant, who came from
England with me, that feels no more inconvenience from being exposed through
the heat of the day to the sun, than the
very negroes themselves, who generally

B 3   delight

delight in the moſt meridian beams; and among my neighbours, I know two or three who are of the ſame temperament. But my own conſtitution is very different, for a fever would be the leaſt conſequence I believe; and indeed I partly know it from experience, which would enſue from my uſing any fatiguing exerciſe, from one to three o'clock in the afternoon in ſummer, when the ſky is clear; for with a ſouth wind the ſun's beams are ſo intenſely hot, that the only pleaſure I feel, is to be perfectly at reſt.

" But at the ſame time, Sir, that I deſcribe theſe inconveniencies, let me remark, that I ſhould uſe very different terms if I lived near the coaſt : I have been often at Savannah, when I have longed ardently to be at home ; the climate is there beyond compariſon worſe than at Auguſta, and the farther weſt we go, the better it becomes. This will doubtleſs appear very ſtrange to you, as there is ſo little difference in the latitudes of theſe places ; but that is a circumſtance which has little to do with climate in this part of the world. I attribute the great contraſt there is between the ſea-coaſt and the weſtern part of the province, to the flatneſs of one, and the varied

ried

ried furface of the other—alfo to one being full of fwamps and marfhes, and the other being entirely free from them. Flat countries have always lefs wind and agitations in the air, which render it far more pure and wholefome to breathe in, as they carry off fpeedily every noxious quality; there is fcarce an inftance on the globe, of a hilly or a mountainous country being unhealthy; even under the line or the troprics fuch are always inhabited by a hardy and robuft race of people. The other circumftance is of yet more confequence; the effluvia of ftagnant waters in a hot climate, and efpecially of fuch as rice-fwamps, which are fhallow, fometimes fields of mud, at other thinly covered with water, cannot but prove prodigioufly injurious to the health of the human body, at the fame time that it renders the heat not only burning, but clofe and fuffocating: fuch a thick heavy atmofphere, in a country fo flat as not to be windy, muft neceffarily make the maritime part of this province far more hot than the internal part, creating a difference greater than what many degrees of latitude could occafion.

" In the obfervations have made on the climate's being uncommonly hot, I con-

fine

fine myfelf entirely to the hotteft part of the fummer, July, Auguft, and part of September, and perhaps, but not always, a week the latter end of June.   As to the reft of the year, you have no idea in England of the charms of this climate at a diftance from the fea.   March, April, May, and June, are a warm fpring, in which fcarce a day offends you : the fky is a clear expanfe, clouds rarely to be feen, and the heat nothing offenfive ; the beauty of our country is then enjoyed every hour of the day—in fhort, no feafon in any part of the world can hardly be more agreeable than thefe months in the back country of Georgia.   The latter part of September and October are alfo perfectly agreeable, in being fufficiently warm without a melting heat. But this is not all I have to fay in our favour ; for to me the winter is a moft pleafing feafon here ; the degree of heat is that of a warm fpring, with fome days as hot as a common fummer; but in fome months in the latter country I have felt days as hot as are generally experienced in Jamaica : ideas of heat fhould not therefore be taken from the height to which the thermometer rifes in certain days, but to the mean height when every day is re-

giftered.

giftered. In the winter feafon, and alfo in fpring, we have extreme cold winds, particularly the north-weft; and alfo fharp frofts; but the fudden changes from heat to cold, which are fo much complained of on the coaft, are rarely felt with us in any fuch degree as is common there. I have heard many of my neighbours complain of thefe frofts and cold winds, but to an European conftitution they are natural, and are certainly wholefome whenever the changes are not fudden from heat to cold; and even in that cafe they are better than conftant heat, if any caution is ufed in drefs. I muft fay for my own part, that neither froft nor wind have ever proved difagreeable to me; and that upon the whole, I much prefer the climate to any in which I have lived before; and yet I have refided at Cadiz, Naples, and the Weft Indies, not to fpeak of Bofton and England. But whatever I have mentioned on this head is relative only to the country to the weft of Augufta, that is, the weftern half of Georgia; for the other part does not by many degrees enjoy fo good a climate."

In another letter was written as follows. " The foil in this neighbourhood is good; in general, we have very little that is bad; and

and none that will not produce some useful crop or other. Like you in England we have wastes uncultivated, which spread almost over the whole province; but our wastes are such only for want of people to accept their property, whereas yours are such from being of a poor and almost worthless soil. I have travelled over parts of Scotland, and even the northern counties of England, which carry such an aspect of barrenness, and are so dreary and waste, as nothing in all this country can be opposed to them. All land here that is uncultivated, is either a very rich and valuable forest, or a meadow, which in its natural state would be worth ten or twelve shillings an acre in England. On the coast they have swamps, which produce nothing, tho' not many, but here swamps are rare; the low grounds on some of the rivers are more properly marshes; they are small, and such as are found in the best and most beautiful counties of England; low meadows on rivers, wherever they are found, were (in a state of nature) marshes: we have none but what might easily be drained, and would then be the richest meadows in the world, especially if kept as watered ones.

Even

Even thefe marfhes are with us found full of tall and beautiful cedars and cypreffes.

" Our flat tracts, or more properly the furface of gentle waves of country, rather than levels or hills, are of a rich loamy foil ; the furface from twelve to eighteen inches deep of a fine light, black, fandy loam, which has the appearance of being the earth which has been formed by the rotting of vegetables ; and yet, which is extraordinary, we have this foil where no trees are found.   Under this loam we find another of a reddifh brown colour, three, four, or five feet deep, and then meet with clay, and in fome places rock; this under-ftratum of loam has the appearance of being admirable land.   Other tracts of this fort, and efpecially the fides of hills, are covered with a reddifh loam, with many ftones in it, from one to two feet deep, and under it rock : the appearance of this foil is not fo good, but on experience we find it to be very fertile. In fome vales, between gentle hills, we find the black loam three or four feet deep, a foil which I am perfuaded might be applicable to any purpofe in the world.   A true clay on the furface is fcarcely ever found in thefe tracts; but in the low lands on the river fides the

foil

foil is a very ftrong loam, near the clay. Some of the rivers, however, run among the hills, with high rocky fhores. For 150 miles from the fea the country abounds with what they call a *pine barren*, which is a light white fand, very poor, covered with pines; it is reckoned the worft part of that country; we are not entirely without it; here and there is a pine barren, but they are rare. There are other varieties of foil, but not in confiderable quantity; we have fandy tracts, which though light are very rich, and of a nature entirely different from the pine barren fand. Some fpots on the rivers and the higheft hills are rocky, and fo rough as not to admit of culture; but thefe are covered with foreft trees, and add very much to the beauty of the country.

" Uncultivated tracts of country in this part of America are very different from fuch in other parts of the world; the plenty of the fineft timber is aftonifhing to an European upon his firft arrival. We have feveral forts of oak which come to a prodigious fize, twice or thrice as large as oaks in England; and fome of thefe are much more excellent for fhip-building than is commonly imagined: an injudicious choice

of

of the fort of oak, was for fome years the
caufe of this idea; but later trials have dif-
fufed a more correct knowledge of the value of our timber, for fome has been found
fuperior in duration even to Britifh oak.
This wood is alfo cut into various articles
of lumber, which are exported to the Weft
Indies; pine, cyprefs, and cedar, are likewife appropriated to the fame ufe: this is
a vaft advantage annexed to thofe parts of
the country which have a good water-carriage, fince thefe forts of woods converted
into lumber will pay the expences of clearing the thickeft forefts in this country, even
if a proportion of the timber be of other
forts, and not ufed in building: when this
is the cafe therefore, a man enters not only
into the poffeffion of an eftate without expence, but even an eftate that is ready to
cultivate.

" Our forefts are generally open, confifting of large trees, growing fo thin that
you may generally ride through every part
of them, rarely having any underwood, and
in fome tracts they are wide enough for
waggons to pafs every where: the labour,
therefore, of clearing, when the wood is
not of a proper fort for lumber, is not great.
We have immenfe numbers of wild mul-

berry

berry-trees, upon the leaves of which we feed our silk-worms, without forming any plantations for that purpose. Walnuts and hiccories are also very plentiful upon the best lands, and grow to a very great size."

A third letter contained the following particulars. " My plantation is situated on a small but navigable creek, which falls into the river Savannah, about thirty miles west of Augusta; when I first came, I had a very large tract of country to chuse in, for the settlements to the west of that town at any distance from it were not numerous; had I then been as well acquainted with agriculture as I am now, I could have made choice of a plantation, consisting more entirely of rich land; but as it is, I have no great reason to complain, and what I lose in soil, I gain in the extreme beauty of the situation.

My house is on the side of a hill; behind it is a fine spreading wood of oak, walnut, hiccory, &c. before it a large tract of grass which I have cleared, and which is bounded by the river, whose course I command from almost every window, for three miles on each side: on the other side of it, and all round the lands adjacent to my house, are the fields which I have in

culture. The whole plantation, which is my property, confifts of 6340 acres, at leaft, in the rough manner in which the furveyor-general's people reported the furvey, that is, the quantity regiftered; the only fence which furrounded it for fome years, was trees market with a hatchet, or croffes dug in the meadows, with here and there a poft fet up; but other fettlers having fince fixed near me, who have taken up fmall grants of land, their fences have been made in fome places in my boundary line, which have faved me the trouble. In fome places I am yet open to the country not granted away; for this tract of land containing a large proportion of excellent foil, I paid not quite one hundred pounds, including every charge and fee incurred in order to procure it.

" The method here taken, is for the perfon who wants land to fix upon a fpot and take what he likes, under condition of peopling it in a given number of years : I had twenty allowed me, but they are now giving only ten or fifteen years. It is not common to fee people fixing by each other ; they generally plant themfelves at a diftance, for the fake of having an uncultivated country around them for their cattle to

range

range in : all the country not granted away belongs to the king, and is common for every man to turn his cattle upon, but not in the manner such right is enjoyed in England, where the same thing is done not by permission but by right; for here every new comer has a liberty of fixing in this common part of the country, and inclosing his property immediately if he pleases; so that the lands on which we turn our cattle farther than our own bounds, are continually decreasing: the consequence is, the planters who on this account have not range enough for their large flocks, take up new grants of small quantities of land farther to the westward, for the sake of sending their cattle thither, by which means they are enabled to keep very great flocks, even so far as a thousand head. I have four hundred and forty head of cows, oxen, bulls, heifers, &c. but their value is far from what it would be in England.

" The plenty of timber in this country is a great advantage to new settlers, in rendering their buildings and many of their utensils of no other expence than that of labour, tools, and a little iron. My house, a barn, a stable, and some other conveniencies, cost me no more at first than one hundred

dred

dred and seventy-four pounds in cash, and the labour of ten negroes during three months; this was done by hiring carpenters, and paying them by the month; and two of the slaves learnt so much of the art in that time, that by working since with them occasionally, they are become good carpenters enough to raise a shed, or build any plain outhouse, such as you see common in England in little farm-yards: our wood is of so little value, that their making waste is of no consequence. I have made many additions to my house since, at a small expence, so that it is now a very convenient and agreeable Habitation.

"When I consider that for one hundred pounds a man may in this rich and plentiful country buy an extensive tract of land, that for two more he may raise a good house and offices; that he may buy slaves for thirty or forty pounds a-piece, or hire white labour a very little dearer than in England; and that he may settle himself with as few as he pleases, and increase them as he can; when this is considered, it surprises me to think that more people of small fortunes do not come among us, but that they should prefer the narrow way in which they must live in Europe. The plenty of this country is much greater than you can think of; a little planter, that is a good gun-man himself, or has a flave that is fo, may in half a day kill much more game than two families will eat in a week; and in parts of the country where it is comparatively fcarce, an eafy walk will yield him a day or two's fubfiftence of this fort for a moderate table. By game we here underftand deer, rabbits, wild kine, and wild hogs, turkies, geefe, ducks, pigeons, partridges, teal, &c. Our rivers are equally abounding with excellent fifh, which is an advantage not inferior to the other; and the two together in hunting, fhooting, and fifhing, affording a diverfion equal to what is met with in any part of the world, and fuperior to moft. Sporting here is carried on with unlimited freedom, and in a ftyle far fuperior to what I have any where elfe met with; and whoever keeps houfe in this country muft prefently find the immenfe advantages attending the great plenty of thefe articles, which reduce all expences of this fort very low. And now I am giving you the information you want on this head, I fhall add, that our great plenty of fruit is another point in which this country is very fortunate; we

have

melons, cucumbers, water-melons, peaches,
pears, apples, plums, &c. &c. in any quantity we pleafe, almoft without trouble or
culture. The climate is fo favourable, that
to plant them is all the attention requifite.
Upon a new fettler fixing, one of his firft
works is to inclofe and plant a large orchard. Peaches are the moft plentiful of any
kind of fruit : a ftone fet, becomes a bearing tree in three years, and the fruit that
drops from it rifes in young trees ; fo that
a fingle tree would become a wood of
peaches in a few years, if they were not
grubbed up. ·

" You fee, Sir, from this account, upon
the truth of which you may abfolutely re-
lie, that you want for nothing in this
country that nature can give us. Rich land
is plentiful ; building no where fo cheap ;
game, fifh, flefh, fowl, and fruit, in the
utmoft profufion ; labour by flaves very
cheap, by fervants not dear. And to this
may be added a government mild and e-
qual, in which more liberty is no where to
be found ; taxes too trifling to be mentioned, and where neither tythes nor poor's
rates are to be found : may I not therefore
conclude, that if mere living well, plentifully, and at eafe, be confidered, no country can

 exceed,

exceed, perhaps not equal, this. In refpect of fociety, we are deficient; but this
is made up to a ftudious perfon, or one
who does not diflike retirement, by the a-
mufements of the field, by the employments of agriculture, and by reading; not
however that we are without company; I
have eight or nine neighbours within twenty
miles of me, with whom I vifit; and fome
of them are families in which a rational
converfation is by no means wanting!"—
In a fucceffive letter the fame perfon gave
the following particulars.

—" Refpecting the agriculture we purfue, about which you enquire, I fhall give
you the beft account I am able: the objects moft attended to are Indian corn,
wheat, and provifions, which long occupied this country chiefly; but for a few
years paft filk and indigo have made great
ftrides among us. The country near the
fea is not near fo fertile in corn and provifions as that about us; we therefore not
only fend great quantities for the Weft India export, but alfo to feed the towns and
rice plantations in part. I am much in
doubt whether the common hufbandry of
raifing corn and provifions be not as profitable as that of indigo or rice; the beft

planters

planters we have, and it is the fame in Carolina, do not reckon they make in total product above 20l. or 25l. each for their working hands: I have exceeded this fome years by Indian corn, wheat, &c. and fome of my neighbours have carried it much farther than me, by more fkill and clofer application.

" The firft bufinefs in our hufbandry is clearing the ground, which is for corn, generally done by grubbing the trees up by the roots in order for the plough to go: this method I have followed in all the land I have cleared: the expence is fmall, from the eafe of ftirring the light foil; and after raifing my houfe, offices, and negro camp, with lengths and pofts for fences, &c. the refidue I have fent down the river in feveral forts of lumber, as boards, planks, ftaves, pieces, cafks, &c. to Augufta and Savannah, but not with fuch advantage as others lower down on the river, who have not fuch a diftance: after clearing, I have planted the land with Indian corn, for three and four years fucceffively, and got from thirty-five to fixty bufhels an acre, and at the fame time from twenty-five to fifty bufhels of Indian peafe an acre. Of wheat my crops are not fo great; but from

C 3

thirty

thirty to forty bushels an acre is 'my usual crop. Barley we also sow, usually after wheat or Indian corn; I get the same quantity as of wheat; I have some fields, the soil of which is so rich, that I have got for six years successively crops of these kinds of grain, and all equally good, and I do not now find that the soil has much abated of its fertility; but in some of my fields, it begins to wear out; but fine grass will come, and soon yield nearly as good profit as middling crops of corn. I do not think our farmers in England grow quite so many successive crops of corn as we do here, yet I imagine our products to be much the largest. I have never laid on any dung or other manure for corn.

" My black deep loams, which were covered with wood, yield kitchen plants of very fine flavour and an extraordinary size; I allotted a piece of it near my house for a garden, in which several articles of common product much exceed what I remember seeing in England, and yet I have never manured it : this, however, is much owing to climate. I have raised cabbages of 60 lb. weight, and turneps of 25 lb. Potatoes thrive astonishingly in it; I have had 300 bushels from a bed, which in size

did

did not exceed a quarter of an acre ; and
several of my neighbours having found their
great increase in this soil, have begun to
go pretty much into them as an article of
sale : they find a ready market at Savannah
for the West Indies.   I design taking the
same hint, and believe they will be as profitable as any other article.

   " There is one circumstance in this
country which is very valuable in planting ;
it is the warmth of the climate rendering
it unneceffary to houfe or otherwife attend
cattle in winter more than in fummer ;
they find their fubfiftence in the woods and
natural meadows, and return home of
nights only for the fake of food given them,
not fo much through neceffity, as to induce them to be regular.   Our fwine fare
yet better, for the woods abound greatly
with maft and fruit of various forts, which
they are greedy in finding, and keep themfelves fat on ; but we ufe them to come
home in the fame manner as the kine.
The number of hogs kept in this country
by every planter is very great ; they who
begin only with a fow or two, in a few
years are mafters of fourfcore, or an hundred head ; I have above three hundred of
all forts and fizes, and in a few years, if the

country does not settle very fast, shall have twice or thrice as many. Pork and beef barrelled make a confiderable article of our product; and hides are not the moft inconfiderable part of the product of our cow kine.

" Befides the articles I have mentioned, we cultivate indigo, filk, tobacco, and hemp, but not in fuch large quantities (filk excepted) as they do in Carolina; I have them all upon my plantations; indigo and tobacco require the fame foil, which is the richeft and deepeft we can give them, but it muft be dry; tobacco is but juft coming in, but we make as good, if not better than any in Virginia; and I am of opinion, fince the price has rifen, it will be as beneficial as any article we can go upon. Hemp is fown in the low lands on the rivers and in drained marfhes, where the foil is a ftiff loam, upon clay: we do not reckon it fo profitable as either indigo or tobacco; but as the land which fuits it is not the right fort for thofe crops, it is cultivated in fmall quantities. I cannot fpeak with any precifion of the products which my neighbours gain of thefe commodities, but I can tell you pretty accurately what I have done myfelf. When I had increafed

my

my ten negroes to twenty, from that number, eight of whom were women (who I should observe do as much field-work as the men) they made me, with the help of five white labourers,

	l.	s.	d.
36 acres of Indian corn, the produce of which sold for in sterling money,	146	13	8
26 acres of wheat, the produce of which sold for in ditto,	93	8	0
12 acres barley, the product of which sold, yielded	18	10	0
40 barrels of pork at 1l. 12s.	64	0	0
26 ditto of beef at 1l. 2s.	28	12	0
16 acres tobacco yielded 12 hogsheads	96	0	0
33 pounds silk,	30	0	0
420 pounds of indigo from 4 acres and a half	52	10	0
Hides, live stock sold, and small articles,	47	18	0
	£. 577	11	8

This product from 25 hands is above 23l. each; but the two following years I had not such good success. You see, by this account, that I made 33 pounds of silk: this is an article which deserves more attention than has been given it, either by the inhabitants of this province, or in encouragement from the mother-country: the number of hands who made this 33 lb. in a season was but eleven, which is 3 lb. a-head. This appears to be a very considerable object; among them were four of

my

my children (who did it by way of amuſe-
ment, and indeed a very rational one it is),
and three women; they did not employ
ſeven weeks in it, and I need not tell you
that in this buſineſs it is but a part of the
day that is employed.   Georgia has, proportioned to its inhabitants, made a greater
progreſs in feeding ſilk-worms than any of
the other colonies, but yet her people do
not make near the quantities they might;
ſuppoſing they made but two pounds a-head,
and leſs than this I have never made for
every perſon I have employed in it, this
would be a vaſt acquiſition for all the women, many of the children, the old men,
and diſabled perſons, with proper aſſiſtance
from others; and in Carolina, where the
people are ſo much more numerous, the
importance of the object would in a national light be ſtill greater.   This is ſo fa-
vourite a theme with me, that were I to
trouble you with all I could ſay on the ſubject, I ſhould go near to exhauſt your pa-
tience.

    " Hemp has been too inconſiderable an
article with me to come to market, but I
hope next year to ſend two or three tons
down to Savannah.   It may be to your ſatisfaction alſo to know, that I have made
                                                ſome

some trials of wine, not yet as an export, but have used several small casks in my own family, which have proved better than I expected. Four years ago I planted about a quarter of an acre of a dry rocky spot of land, hanging on the side of a hill, to the south of which I thought promised well, I used setts of our native grapes, having no others ; these are so plentiful all over the country, that you can scarce go an hundred yards without meeting with numbers. This little plantation, which, for want of better knowledge than I could gain from one or two treatises on the vineyard culture, was not managed near so well as it ought, has turned out much better than I expected. I have made wine from the same grapes growing wild, and have the satisfaction to find that the produce of my cultivated ones is beyond comparison of a finer flavour, which shews that we have much to hope from attending well to our native vines ; were they managed with the skill that is exerted in the wine countries of Europe, they would perhaps turn out among the profitable articles of our husbandry. One of the neighbouring planters, a Frenchman by birth, has written to France to a relation, to send a vigneron,

well

well experienced, with some setts of the
Burgundy grape: this is to be done at my
expence, and I have good expectations from
the scheme; though my neighbour is quite
of a different opinion, and thinks that
(farther than our own consumption) if I
make it succeed, the culture will not prove
near so profitable as indigo: how far this
will prove true, I am not yet a judge. Ma-
deira, which is the only wine we import,
comes very dear to us. If we could make
a sort sufficiently good to be substituted for
that, it would be a great acquisition. I
shall give you the account of my sale in a
year since the former, being nearly what
my present produce is.

	l.	s.	d.
50 acres of Indian corn, produce in ster- ling money - - -	187	14	0
35 acres of wheat produce in ditto -	132	0	0
20 acres of barley ditto - -	35	0	0
50 barrels of pork, - - -	82	0	0
40 ditto of beef, - - - -	50	0	0
Hides, - - - -	24	10	0
Live stock sold, - - -	30	0	0
Lumber, - - - -	36	0	0
47 pounds of silk, - - -	47	0	0
16 acres of tobacco, 11 hogsheads, -	88	0	0
Indigo, - - - -	87	10	0
	£. 799	14	0

The

The number of negroes 25, and 5 white labourers, 30 in all ; the total divided gives 26l. a-head ; and this I believe may generally be equalled by those who have any luck in fixing on tolerable land, without poffeffing great fkill in choofing the beft.

" This, Sir, is a very important part of the information you requeft me to give, as it explains to you what is to be expected from fettling in this country ; I have little doubt of your friend being able to make from 20l. to 30l. a-head annual produce, fold at market, for all the working hands he employs, befides fupplying the plantation with all the provifions confumed, both by the family, flaves, cattle, poultry, &c. this however is not profit ; for negroes coft at prefent from 40l. to 50l. a-head, if good ones are bought. Cloathing, phyfic, attendance, &c. come to fomething, and diftempers will now and then break out among them which prove very deftructive, though in general the increafe will keep up the number. Implements, tools, furniture, manufactures, &c. &c. are all much dearer than in England, except the articles which are made of wood. Wine, tea, fugar, and fpices, are fome of them dearer, and none of them cheaper, than in England. Re-

2   pairs

pairs of buildings is an article of some expence.   Negroes must have an overseer, at
the annual expence of from 40l. to 60l.
All these and some other articles are deductions from the planter's profit; nor should
I omit to add, Sir, that the nature of the
country, as it prevents many of the expences which are common in England, so
it brings on us others, of which you know
nothing.   Hospitality, to a degree totally
unknown in Europe, is the virtue of all A-
merica; and a man can hardly through inclination, but especially from example, be
niggardly on any occasions that call for it;
his great expence will be wine, rum, and a
few other articles of house-keeping; not
that this amounts to any thing very considerable.

   "In general, our planters are very much
on the thriving hand, yet few are rich,
though I have heard of some large fortunes
in Carolina; we have scarce one in the province whose circumstances do not improve.
As to making a fortune, I believe no part
of the world is better adapted for it, provided the planter is skilled in land, has a
good degree of knowledge in matters of a-
griculture, and is very industrious and attentive to his business : you may easily suppose

pose that all these qualifications are necessary; indeed I know of no business in which money is to be made without knowledge and industry: I must also add, that he ought to have his capital, especially if it is not considerable, free; for interest here is 8, 9, and 10 per cent. and money even on such terms very difficult to be got; he should therefore possess, or raise whatever he wants, in England, for no dependance is to be had on getting any here.

" There are very great advantages in the husbandry which is carried on in this country, of a nature not general in others, especially in Europe; the quantity of land to be had by any person that pleases, is a circumstance no where else to be met with on the globe, at least in countries where the religious and civil liberty of mankind is secured; and among all our colonies, none has better land or a more favourable climate than the back parts of Georgia. The expences of living are low, and particularly the necessaries of life so very plentiful, that subsistence is no where easier gained; on the contrary, the articles of merchandize produced here yield a large price, as it is the nature of mankind to rate luxuries much higher than necessaries, and not to

let

let the value of one depend on that of the other.   Thus the planter feeds and subfifts himfelf and family very cheap, while he fells his produce very dear: filk, indigo, wine, hemp, tobacco, &c. are by no means neceffaries, but their value is much greater: this is a circumftance of great value to the planter; how far you enjoy in the fame in certain articles produced in England, I am not a good judge; luxurious articles may be very dear, but the neceffaries which fupport the planters and their workmen are dear alfo."

Thefe extracts, from pretty long corre-fpondence carried on with a view of fet-tling a relation in Georgia (which is fince done), I am happy in being allowed to in-fert: it is true they principally concern only one plantation, but they abound with many valuable circumftances that concern the whole province, and as fuch could not but be deemed highly worthy of infertion.

The following is a ftate of the exports of Georgia, upon an average of three years fince the peace.

		£.
18000 barrels of rice, at 40s.	- -	36,000
Indigo, 17000 lb. at 2s.	- -	1,700
Silk, 2500 lb. at 20s.	- -	2,500
		———
	Carried over,	40,200

			£. 40,200
Brought forward,			
Deer and other skins,	-	-	17,000
Boards, staves, &c.	-	-	11,000
Tortoise-shell, drugs, cattle, &c.		-	6,000
			£. 74,200

But since this account was published the articles are most of them very much increased; the rice is raised to 23,000 barrels, and the price to 3l. 10s. so that this article alone makes more than the whole of the above articles; the indigo is proportionally increased, but the silk is declined: the Indian trade at Augusta is also thriven very much of late.

Before I take my leave of this province it will be proper to mention the large tract of country lately acquired by the government of the Cherokees, containing by estimation about seven millions of acres. This country lies to the westward of Augusta, and is bounded on one side by the Savannah's branches; from the description I have heard of it, I apprehend the plantation described in the above letters very nearly resembles it: the soil is as rich as any part of America; every article of spontaneous vegetation, luxuriant in the highest degree: the climate, like that of the western part of all our southern colonies which bounds upon the Apalachean mountains, as desirable as any in the world, both for the production of profitable staples and healthiness. It is further said to be as well watered with streams and rivers as can be wished, with three or four of them navigable for large canoes. Many are the people who have given in petitions for grants of land in it, so that it is expected in Georgia the whole tract, large as it is, will be settled in a few years: the articles of culture upon which the planters will go are particularly indigo, hemp, flax, cotton, tobacco, vines, and silk, not to speak of Indian corn, wheat, and other provisions: for all these, it is said, no part of America can be better adapted.

It is very much to be wished, that so fine a tract of country may be put to the most advantageous use, particularly in respect of silk, wine, and hemp. These are commodities which we want more than any others from our colonies, but for want of a proper soil and climate the nation has for so many years been disappointed in its expectations; but there can be no doubt of all these articles doing as well in this newly-acquired country as in any part of the world, provided the right methods are

taken

taken in the culture of them: Planters left entirely to themselves are apt to fall into the articles of husbandry to which they have been most acquainted, and not into those which will pay them the greatest profit, unless they have been before acquainted with them. But their chusing their crops well is a matter of vast importance to this nation, and therefore proper means should be taken to give them all the light and instruction that is wanting in any thing which it would be adviseable for them to undertake. Persons skilled in feeding silkworms and winding the silk should be distributed through every district of such a country; such might be got in America, and they should teach, gratis, every family that was willing to learn the business. The same thing should be done with vine-dressers from France, or perhaps better from Portugal, Spain, Italy, or Greece; these men should move from plantation to plantation, to shew the planters the culture of vineyards—to assist in planting them, and also in dressing the vineyard: it would not be very expensive to procure forty or fifty such; and that number would in a few years be able to train up many pupils, and spread a tolerable knowledge of the

 vine-

vineyard culture through two or three provinces. Hemp is better underſtood in A-
merica, the ſame means would not therefore be neceſſary. To theſe meaſures re-
wards, both honorary and pecuniary, ſhould
be added, for ſuch planters as produced
given quantities of the beſt wine, of ſilk,
and of hemp : a couple of thouſand pounds
a year beſtowed upon a province in ſuch
premiums, would be ſufficient to introduce,
in conjunction with the above mentioned
meaſure, any article of culture the government would have them purſue : and no-
body can doubt but the national intereſt
would be far more advanced by ſuch an
expenditure of public money, than injured
by the loſs (ſuppoſing it ſuch) of a few
thouſand pounds. There is ſcarcely any
thing in domeſtic policy but what may be
effected, and with profit, by means of premiums judiciouſly offered, and impartially
given, provided means be at the ſame time
taken to inſtruct the people, if the object
required be out of their knowledge. In-
ſtead of acting thus, the bounty on ſilk has
been ſuffered to expire.

Bounties and other encouragements of
this nature have been of long ſtanding for
hemp and other articles without effect ; but
this proves nothing in general. While the
colon iſts

colonifts were confined to the coafts of America, by which I mean the flat, poor, fandy tract of country which extends for 100 or 150 miles from the fea, no encouragement would ever make any thing of hemp, filk, or wine, for the foil and climate were equally unfit for all; but now they have fpread themfelves into the back or hilly country, where both foil and climate are effentially different, the cafe is different alfo; and much lefs encouragement would prove of high utility, than before was attended with no effect. For this reafon, the old inefficacy of fuch meafures fhould never be inftanced as an argument againft them at prefent.

Very many great and beneficial effects might be made to flow from the fettling and planting the internal parts of our maritime colonies. Hemp is an article which cofts this nation feveral hundred thoufand pounds annually: it is befides a neceffary for our royal navy, which ought not to depend on the good pleafure of any foreign nation, whatever friendfhip may be between us at prefent.

Flax is another import which we take from the Baltic, though our colonies would raife it as well, and parts of them perhaps much better,

D 3

I have

I have not feen public accounts of what our import of wines of all forts is, but certainly it amounts to an immenfe fum ; the wealth of the nation would be very different if fuch an import, chiefly from our own fworn enemies, was transferred to our colonies, and inftead of being paid for with cafh, as is the cafe with hemp, to be purchafed with our manufactures.

Silk is another article which we import from China, at the expence of more than half a million flerling ; yet our filk-mills are univerfal in affirming, that what we have had from America is equal to the beft we receive elfewhere : furely therefore it much behoves the government to promote whatever meafures have a tendency to render filk an article of confideration in the imports from America, inftead of fuffering old ones to expire.

Oil is another import which cofts this country great fums of money: none is or can be produced at home ; but the olive thrives well in the interior part of Georgia, and might be made a valuable article in the products of that province, efpecially the new acquired diftrict.

Madder we buy of the Dutch, to the amount of more than two hundred thoufand pounds a year ; thofe induftrious people
raife

raife it in the province of Zealand, that is, in a country far inferior in foil to the back parts of Georgia, where are tracts of rich deep black loam that would produce prodigious crops of it : no article of American hufbandry would prove a more profitable ftaple.

Wool we take in large quantities of Spain, becaufe it is of a kind we cannot produce in England : our colonies on the continent of North America, fouth of New York, produce a wool entirely fimilar to the Spanifh ; no ftaple they could produce would therefore be more advantageous to Great Britain. It is well known that a piece of fine broad cloth cannot be made without Spanifh wool ; it is alfo known that the Spaniards have of late years made great efforts to work up their own wool ; if they fhould fucceed, or if they fhould by any other means prevent the export of it, our woollen fabrics, though they might not be ftopped, would at leaft be burthened with a frefh expence and new trouble ; all which would be prevented by encouraging the import of wool from America ; and at the fame time that this good effect was wrought, another would be brought about

D 4

in

in cramping the manufactures of the colonies; of which more hereafter.

Cotton we import from Turkey at the expence of above two hundred thousand pounds a year; this commodity agrees well with the soil and climate of Georgia, especially those of the back parts of the province: I am sensible that our West India islands would produce it, but the land which is so occupied there would produce more valuable staples; there we want land, but on the continent is more land than we know what to do with; it is here therefore that it should be produced.

These imports might be enlarged to a greater number, were it necessary, but they are sufficient to shew that the nation takes from foreign countries, and from enemies, commodities to a very great amount, which she might have produced in her colonies. It is at present the opinion of many mercantile gentlemen, that the balance of all our trades, except America and the East Indies, is against us; if so, it must undeniably be owing in a great measure to the great consumption of these articles, many of which are taken from countries that take little from us: if our colonies produced them, we should, on the contrary,

pay

pay for them with our manufactures, a circumstance essentially different from having them in any other mode.

A writer who has taken great pains to be well informed, has given the following account of some of these imports.

	£.
Hemp and flax, - - -	400,000
Wine and brandy from France alone in 1663, 100,000	
Suppose the total - - -	1,000,000
Ireland alone in one article, claret, takes 150,000l.	
Silk, - - - -	1,825,000
Cotton, - - -	* 300,000
Madder other accounts make -	250,000
Let us suppose oil - - - -	50,000
And for wool - - -	50,000
Total -	3,875,000

Other imports, which do not concern so immediately our *southern* colonies, as iron, timber, &c. &c. would run this account up to a much greater height: but if the total did not amount to more than half of it, surely the sum is too confiderable to take from foreign nations, in articles which we might produce generally as well in our own colonies.

---

* *Political Effays concerning the prefent State of the Britifh Empire,* 1771.

CHAP.

CHAP. XXVI.

EAST FLORIDA.

*Falfe defcriptions of the country—Climate
—Soil—Productions—Obfervations.*

WEST FLORIDA.

*Climate — Soil — Importance of thefe pro-
vinces relative to fituation and commerce—
Obfervations.*

IN fuch a free country as Britain, new
acquifitions made at a peace will not be
well underftood for fome years. The party
who concludes the treaty will in the nature
of things extol the terms they have gained,
and for that purpofe magnify the acquifitions they have made : on the other hand,
the party in oppofition will be fure to condemn the treaty, and depreciate the value
of the territories acquired ; and what is a
great misfortune in fuch a cafe, is the almoft univerfal influence of parties : few men
that actually go to the countries in queftion, but whofe judgment or report will be
warped

warped by their connections or political opinions. Most of the people who frequent such countries are soldiers, sailors, governors, civil officers, or traders, and if any of these should publish accounts, not much strict truth is always met with in their descriptions; either from being fearful to offend their superiors, or from motives of interest. It happened thus with the Floridas. The ministry, upon the conclusion of the peace, sent a physician, who had no business to leave in England, to view and describe East Florida; though upon his return he found his employers out of office, and a new administration, yet as his was an official business, he dedicated his book to the minister of the day: it contained an account of that province, which made it appear to be one of the finest countries in the world, and proved it a most valuable acquisition. This was just the report which the world might rationally have expected; for certainly a man on such an errand would take care, first to recommend himself to his patrons, which he could do no ways so effectually as by praising the acquisitions they had made to the skies: in this work, indeed, he did not proceed on those principles of integrity which he ought to have done.

done. An American botanist accompanied him in a part of his journey through the province, and kept a journal; this made a part of the above-mentioned publication; but instead of being published fairly, it was mangled, and the man's general opinion of the country, which was by no means favourable to it, suppressed. Such a conduct, at one stroke, was sufficient to convince the reader that little or no dependance could be placed in what was advanced by a man who could prove, in so material an instance, faithless to the public.

On the other hand, direct contrary accounts were published by others, who were so far from agreeing to the merit of the country set forth by its friends, that they strenuously insisted it had no pretensions to any sort of merit: they totally denied all value to it, ridiculed the title of acquisition, considered the country as a heavy burthen, and condemned the peace-makers with the loudest voice, for accepting such a recompense in exchange for glorious and valuable conquests made in the war. Here therefore were two parties in such direct opposition to each other, that a considerable part of what they wrote might fairly be attributed to political prejudice, and this on

both

both fides, the confequence of which was, that the world could form but a very vague guefs of the real truth.

Such is the ftate of public intelligence concerning the Floridas; all the information to be gained concerning them, is that of private people who have refided there: I have been as attentive as poffible in making numerous enquiries, of planters, agents, officers, &c. who have been any time in thofe countries; I have compared their accounts, and from the intelligence I have gained, have drawn up the following defcription, fupplying fome deficiencies by reafoning from analogy of Georgia and Carolina, and others from public accounts, of a date antecedent to our having any connection with Florida, and confequently free from all party prejudice. The account will be incomplete, as the fources from which it is drawn are fo; but it had much better be incomplete than otherwife, if to make it fo, bad intelligence, or fuch as was unfatisfactory, was taken to render it full. In a few particulars (wherein it would anfwer little purpofe in him to vary from the truth), I follow Dr. Stork.

Eaft Florida is fituated between lat. 25 and 32, it extends confequently much to
the

the south of any of our other colonies, which makes the climate hotter; a confiderable part of it forms a peninfula, which projects to the south : this circumstance is both an advantage and a difadvantage; in the firft place, it makes the air cooler by a regular fea and land breeze, than in the maritime part of Georgia; but on the other hand, this benefit is almoft preponderated by the increafed quantiiy of rain which falls; it is the mifchief of all thefe fouthern coafts of America, that they are deluged with rain, which, ftagnating in the fwamps of a flat hot country, poifons the air. The rains that fall in Florida are almoft inceffant. This in a hot climate muft make it very unhealthy, fince thofe are the wholefomeft countries near the troprics, where it feldom rains. Peru is perfectly healthy, and there it never rains at all. Relative to the health and fertility of this country, there is one circumftance that is decifive; all the fouthern colonies I have elfewhere remarked, confift of a maritime and a back country, the latter of which reaches to the Apalachean mountains; now the flat fandy coaft, full of fwamps and marfhes, is alike in them all, being equally fteril and unwholefome; but when this

flat

flat country is paffed, and you arrive at the hilly dry tracts, free from fwamps, you then find a country perfectly healthy, and very fruitful. Florida, Georgia, the Carolinas, Virginia, and Maryland, are all extremely fimilar in the appearance of their coafts; the flat fandy tract is the fame in them all, except that their fmall degree of fertility increafes as you advance northward, as regularly as the arrangement of the colonies. Now this circumftance is abfolutely decifive againft Eaft Florida, for unfortunately, that province confifts of nothing elfe but the flat fandy country; it has no back country, for where you fhould meet with the rifing drier tract, you come to the fwamps and marfhes of Weft Florida; therefore not a hill is to be met with in the whole province: it confifts of marfhes after marfhes, fwamps after fwamps, pine barrens upon pine barrens, but no found good loam like the hiccory lands in the back parts of Georgia, &c. Indeed the general fpontaneous produce of the province fhews us what the foil is. Good lands in this part of America are covered with woods of tall red hiccories as high and ftraight as elms; white, chefnut and fcarlet oaks; tulip trees; black walnuts; locufts, &c.

ut

But single trees of these are rare in East Florida, and not a wood of them is to be found in the whole province.

Now these two circumstances are such as can neither be mistaken nor misunderstood; the flat situation of the country, and the spontaneous produce; the one may be in a small degree remedied by the sea and land breezes; and small patches of tolerable (not good) land may be quoted in answer to the other; but as to the country in general, it must be condemned on comparison with very great tracts in our old colonies. This I must own appears to me to be clearly deducible from the circumstances in question; party on either side cannot alter or deceive one in such points, because they are certainly matters of fact, and not opinion; nor could there well be a greater piece of imposition on the public, than publishing the direct contrary.

Relative to the soil and face of the country, it resembles, as I before observed, the maritime parts of the other southern colonies: it consists chiefly of swamps and marshes, or tracts of sandy white pine ground; the former are covered with the spontaneous growth of the country, live oaks, chinkapins, bays, liquid amber, wa-

ter

ter oaks, and ſtunted cypreſſes. In fertility
for the product of rice, there are ſome of
them which it is imagined will anſwer well;
when the ſwamps more to the north are
exhauſted or turned to meadow, which,
however, is not likely ever to be the caſe;
and therefore the merit of this capability
is not of much conſequence: the ſwamps
we were in poſſeſſion of, before the acquiſition of Florida was made, would, if culti-
cated, produce more rice than half the
world conſumes.

The reſt of the country is in general a
pine barren, with very ſmall ſpots of better
land, which the Indians of Florida formerly
grew their maize on: now the pine barren
is the worſt land of America, but to ſay
that it is abſolutely ſterile, would be aſſert-
ing an untruth; for no ſoil can be ſuch in a
climate that is very wet and very hot, ſince
thoſe two agents will every where make
the worſt of land produce ſomething: this
pine barren will, when cleared, produce
Indigo, Indian corn, and ſome other crops;
but then it is not the proper ſoil for any
one of them, and ſuch as no perſon would
move to, from the worſt of our colonies;
in order to cultivate them. This ſeems to
be the plain fact, when cleared from the

attendants which prejudice has given it. The country will produce rice and indigo, and a few other unimportant articles; but the culture will not by any means be so advantageous as the same articles in Carolina.

Several plantations have been formed, stocked with negroes, and set to work on rice, indigo, Indian corn, sugar, cotton, hemp, and cochineal. Among these the plantations of Mr. Rolle, governor Grant, the earl of Egmont, and Mr. Taylor, are the principal; none of these have been able to bring any dubious article of culture into profit, such as sugar, cotton, cochineal, hemp, &c. on the contrary, had they not depended on rice and indigo, they would have lost their whole capital, and with the assistance of those articles, which in Carolina, are almost uniformly profitable, they have most of them lost such large sums of money, as to break up some of the plantations, and give no slight languor to them all The description published of the province induced many to set about planting; they expected returns of sugar, cotton, cochineal, and hemp, and made little doubt of soon acquiring great fortunes: all they met with was disappointment on

disapdifappointment; this chagrined them, and perhaps they were then little inclined to do even juftice to their own beginnings. But all men who have any ideas of planting in America, whether by going thither themfelves, or under the conduct of agents, fhould confider well the country which they chufe. Had the gentlemen who have laid out large fums in planting Florida confidered what the country probably was, from reafoning by analogy with Georgia, Carolina, &c. they would prefently have perceived that it would have been more advantageous to fettle in the back parts of our old colonies, than in our new acquifitions of the Floridas.

In refpect to Weft Florida, we have a little intelligence which can be depended on, as it is principally of an older date than our acquifition of it. The whole coaft has been well known ever fince the year 1719, and the many accounts the French have given of it, to be nothing but fuch a fandy defart; " the land is nothing but a fine fand, as white and fhining as fnow *." This is the account they give of the country from the Miffiffippi to Mobile; of

* *Du Pratz Hift. de Louif.* l. 52.

which

which laft an officer of twenty years experience in the country gives his opinion in
thefe words : " I never could fee for what
reafon this fort was built, or what could be
the ufe of it ; although it is 120 leagues
from New Orleans, it muft be fupplied
from thence ; the foil is fo bad, being nothing but fand, that it produces nothing
but pine trees, or a little pulfe, which is
but indifferent of the kind *."   They only
fettled there for the fake of a port in Dau-
phin ifle, and which was choaked up by the
fhifting of the fands in a gale of wind, and
leaves the place without any port above the
depth of nine feet.   Their other fettlements on this coaft, they tell us, " only
deferved an oblivion as lafting as their duration was fhort."   They then took Penfacola from the Spaniards, but found it only
fit to difmantle and abandon, on which
they retired to the Miffiffippi, as we muft
do if ever we would hold that country.
The greateft part of Florida was furveyed
in 1708, by Captain Mairn from Carolina,
who gives this account of it for about an
hundred miles fquare round Penfacola.
" All this country is a *pine barren* (fandy

---

* *Du Mont. Mem. de la Louif.* tom. ii. p. 80.

defart),

defart), without any water in it ;" that is, it has neither earth nor water in it, and muft therefore be very unfit for a *plantation*. All the reft appears to be the fame where it is not fwampy and marfhy.   We may fay of the whole, what Father Charlevoix, who travelled all over it, fays of the next poft at St. Jofeph's, which lies in the middle of the country upon the borders of Eaft and Weft Florida, " it is a wretched country *(un pays perdu)*, and a mere barren fand, on a flat and bleak fea-coaft—the laft place on earth where one would expect to meet with any mortal, and above all with chrif-tians * ."   The following account was wrote by an officer from Penfacola, and has been confirmed by other eye-witnefles. " My expectations with regard to this country, and the hopes of every one elfe, are funk to the loweft pitch. Inftead of the fineft country in the world (as Weft Florida was called), we found the moft fandy, barren, and defart land, that eyes could fee or imagination paint ! not capa-ble of producing a fingle vegetable, nor the leaft profpect of improving it ! as the foil for an hundred miles back is every where

----

* *Hift. N. France,* vi. p. 263.

E 3

the

the same as the sea-shore, and consists not of earth but of the whitest sand you ever saw ;" which agrees with the account of Capt. Mairn above. " In summer it is too hot to go abroad in the day time ; the months of July, August, and September, are said to be as hot as at Jamaica. The winter is very cold ; but as it depends on what wind blows, that is very uncertain. You have often contrary extremes in the same day ; a south wind scorches, and a north wind freezes, which must be very disagreeable. There is so much sickness at Mobile, that almost all the officers are ill, and only sixty men of a regiment able to do duty ;" which was afterwards the case at Pensacola.

This is the first part of North America that was ever attempted to be settled, and has been better known than any part of the continent, although it seems now to be almost unknown and forgotten. It was first undertaken to be settled by John Ponce in 1512 ; Vasquez d'Ayllon in 1520, and 1524; Pamphilo Navarez, who had a grant of it in 1528; Fernando Soto from 1539 to 1541 ; a company of missionaries in 1549; Pedro de Melendez, who had a grant of all the southern parts of North America

America in 1562 to 1586; the French under Ribault and Laudonniere from 1562 to 1567; but they all found the country to be so poor and barren, that they abandoned it, insomuch that it has never been settled as a colony to this day   Soto travelled all over the western parts of the peninsula, from the bay of Spirito Santo, where he landed, and tells us from that to the inland parts of Georgia, " that country which is no less than 350 leagues in extent, is a light and soft sand, full of swamps, and very high and thick bushes, which is very poor and barren;" but where lands bear nothing but bushes or underwoods in America, they are good for nothing.   Narvaez again searched all the eastern and inland parts for 280 leagues, " and found it to be all a low flat sand, full of swamps, with a sad and dismal aspect throughout the whole country."   " Solum omne quod hactenus lustraverant (secundum ipsorum calculum 280 leucarum) planum erat atque arenosum multis stagnis riguum—Tristem & squallidam regionis faciem renuntiavit *."

---

* *De Laet.* l. iv. c. 3.   *Herrera,* dec. iv. l. 4. c. 4.

                              From

From all thefe accounts, and from all the authentic documents with which the council of the Indies in Spain could furnifh him, which were numerous, the hiftorian of America again informs us, " Florida is a poor country, without any commodity but a few forry pearls, and all who ever went to it died in mifery *."

The bounds of both the Floridas were fettled by proclamation in the autumn of 1763: they extend northwards, the eaft province to the limits of Georgia, and the weft to the 31ft degree of north latitude: now it is to be remarked, that the barren noxious country juft defcribed on various authorities, extends a very little farther than lat. 31, for when you come to Manchac on the Miffiffippi the high lands begin, and a country in every refpect the reverfe of Weft Florida. Thofe accounts and writings therefore which reprefent this country in a favourable light, muft undoubtedly have reference only to the tract of high country beyond the *new* limits of the province. I fhall hereafter fhew that that country is one of the fineft in the world.

---

* *Prefent State of Great Britain and North America,* p. 197.

* *Herrera,* dec. iii. l. 8. c. 8.

The

The defcription here given of the two Floridas may be fuppofed to carry a ftrong condemnation of that article in the peace of Paris, which gave to Spain an object of vaft value in return for a province, which apparently was not worth the expence of keeping ; but the fame impartiality which was my guide in defcribing the climate and foil, obliges me to declare, that this idea would not be fo juft as it may at firft fight appear : if Florida was accepted with a view only for cultivation and colonizing upon the fame principles as other colonies, I fhould agree that the remark would be undeniably juft, but the matter may reafonably be put in a quite different light. Florida was an acquifition worth making, upon the principles of removing a dangerous neighbour, and acquiring the poffeffion of a coaft equally well fituated for cramping, in cafe of war, the commerce of the Spanifh colonies, or carrying on a clandeftine trade with them. When Georgia was fettled with a view to rendering it a frontier againft the enemy, and when general Oglethorpe executed the expedition againft St. Auguftine, had he fucceeded in it, and conquered the whole of the two Floridas, we fhould then have had pens in plenty to

prove

prove the importance of the country : confidered in this light it is of importance; at St. Augufline the Spaniards were dangerous enemies, and would have continued fo till Georgia became far more populous than it is at prefent; they alfo afforded a retreat to runaway negroes, which was a great inconvenience. The point of carrying on a clandefline trade with the Spanifh colonies is more important; this may be judged of by the fact of the imports from Weft Florida, amounting foon after the peace, and notwithftanding Mr. Grenville's prepofterous regulations, to the annual fum of 63,000 l. in Spanifh dollars, a fum fuperior to what was received from Georgia thirty years after fettling at an immenfe expence, and is an earneft of what may in future be expected, if a more politic conduct is purfued,

That the poffeffion of fo great an extent of coaft, bounding a ftreight, through which the Spanifh galleons have their courfe, may prove, in cafe of war, a very valuable acquifition, cannot be denied; for by means of the ports this coaft yields us, we may be able to cruize for the enemies fhips with much greater probability of fuccefs, than we ever had before in this part of the world,

world. Nor should it be forgotten that the possession of these provinces renders our dominion in North America complete; the whole territory of that continent, east of the Missisippi, is now entirely ours; the course of that river is now open to us to its mouth, a matter perhaps of more consequence in future than all the other points I have mentioned, and which we could not have had securely without the joint cession of Florida, and the eastern Louisiana; there is a roundness now in our continental dominions which will save our posterity, if not ourselves, no slight expences.

That these are circumstances of merit, can be denied by none but men who are determined to judge and condemn compendiously, and without the trouble of discrimination; but such general and concise determinations are seldom founded in that degree of accuracy and truth which a candid enquirer will naturally demand. How far the country is adequate to the reasonable expectations of the kingdom— for the great sacrifices made for it, is another equiry, not fit to be made at present, while the parties who made the peace, and those who opposed it are yet living, and their politics yet the signal for arrange-

ment

ment in party matters; nor is such an enquiry so nearly connected with the subject of this work, as the objects which I have principally treated of. What I have laid before the reader is sufficient to shew that the rational plan of proceeding with relation to these provinces, is to secure the coasts by a few strong and well situated fortresses, that the country may be safe from the attacks of enemies, and that there may be the proper accommodations for shipping, for the views of attack in time of war, and trade in time of peace; as to planting, none should be encouraged but such as was subordinate to the design of supplying the garrisons and shipping. By no encouragement, however, I do not mean restrictions, but avoiding those public means of bringing new settlers, which are often put in execution: such people will be employed to far more national purposes in other parts of our colonies, which exceed Florida equally in health and fertility. As the strength of the Spaniards is now collected at New Orleans, and as the navigation of the Mississippi is much the most important object we have in this part of the world, the government should be particularly attentive to keeping all the

forts,

forts, stations, and fortresses in that part of the province in the best condition, that in case of a rupture with Spain, we might there be secure. When the new colony of the Ohio comes to flourish, in that manner which it certainly will in a few years, the infinite importance of this object will be striking to every one; nor should we forget the noble tract of fertile country we have on the banks of the Mississippi, which will one day or other be among the most important parts of all America, and which will almost entirely depend on the undisturbed enjoyment of the free navigation of that river.

CHAP.

CHAP. XXVII.

EASTERN LOUISIANA.

Territory eaftward of the Miffiffippi—Cli-
mate — Soil—Great fertility — Produc-
tions—Cattle—Face of the country —
Staples produced here by the French—Pro-
pofed colony—Obfervations.

I Give the name of Eaftern Louifiana to
the tract of country on the eaft fide of
the river Miffiffippi, from the boundary of
Weft Florida to the forks of that river,
formed by its junction with the Ohio.
This country reaches from lat. 31 and $\frac{1}{2}$ to
lat. 37 and $\frac{1}{2}$; and from eaft to weft I extend it to the countries of the Chicafaw,
Cherokee, and Creek Indians, which is a-
bout the diftance of from 150 to 300 miles;
this fpace being entirely free from the ha-
bitations, huntings, and claims of the Indians, having been in the undifturbed poffeffion of the French till their ceffion of it
to Great Britain, and fettled and planted at
various places according to the inclinations
of the individuals, who came from France

or

or Canada.   The country weſt of the river
is that part of Louiſiana which they retained, and afterwards ceded to the Spaniards.

This territory was left as hunting ground
for the Indians in the proclamation, which
ſettled the bounds of our colonies, in 1763,
an arrangement which has ſince been juſt-
ly and ſeverely condemned ; ſince it was in
this inſtance, as well as in that of the O-
hio, the giving up the beſt countries acquired by the late war, at the ſame time
that we planted the worſt.   But as I conceive that this territory of the Miſſiſſippi
will come in a few years to be ſettled and
planted, from the ſame cogent reaſons
which have at laſt induced the government
to allow the ſettlement of the Ohio, I
think it will be highly proper to give the
beſt deſcription of it that can be procured,
in thoſe circumſtances which relate to agriculture.   I am the rather induced to do
this, as I have it in my power, from the
information I have received from an ingenious gentleman of South Carolina, and
likewiſe from two officers, all of whom either travelled through, or reſided in the
country, to lay before the reader a few circumſtances not ſufficiently known before.
Their

Their intelligence also enables me to diftin-
guifh, in the accounts that have been publifhed of the country, facts from errors and
miftakes.

Relative to the climate of this country
it refembles that of the back territories of
Carolina, near the mountains, but is at the
fame time generally allowed to be better
and more healthy; particularly in the circumftance of not being fo hot in fummer,
nor fo cold in winter. The whole territory enjoys much fuch a temperature as
the beft parts of Spain : the air is clear,
dry, and pure, perfectly free from all mifts
and fogs. This quality is much owing to
the country being remarkably high and dry,
in general from one to two hundred feet
higher than the river in its greateft floods:
there is not a fwamp or a marfh in the
whole country; no ftinking unhealthy effluvia to thicken and poifon the air, which
in fo confiderable a tract of our colonies is
deftruction to the health of the inhabitants.
The heats here are very feldom oppreffive,
from the drynefs of the air; and inftead of
the inceffant and heavy rains which fur-
prife Europeans in Carolina, Georgia, and
Florida, it on the contrary feldom rains on
the Miffiffippi, north of the bounds of Weft
Florida,

Florida, that is, in the high country. This circumstance is very valuable, not upon account of healthiness only, but for several valuable articles of cultivation, particularly silk and wine. The reader cannot attend too much to the climate of this country, because very essential interests will by and by depend on it; whenever the proposition to settle it is made, objections may perhaps arise on account of climate, and new tales in support of Lords of *Trade*, who oppose *plantations*; but let the world then recollect the accounts which have been long ago given of this province, and which in every circumstance of climate has been uniformly described by every person that has been there. Had the countries which have been of late years colonized (particularly Nova Scotia and the Floridas) been described in a just and true manner, in all the circumstances of climate and soil, errors which have been made might not have happened. But with relation to the tracts of country on the Mississippi, all travellers, residents, writers, &c. agree in one general and uniform voice, all describe the climate as being perfectly wholesome, free from excessive and oppressive heats, from fogs, damps, rains, and such intense colds, as are felt on the coast of Carolina in the same latitude. In all these respects, no country can be more truly desirable.

The soil of this country is not at all inferior to the climate. Du Pratz, who resided sixteen years in Louisiana, and eight of them at the post at Natchez, and who from his profession of a planter must necessarily be a judge of land, speaks of it in terms, that leave one nothing to doubt. From that part of it to the Ohio, which is about 900 miles, the slope of the lands goes off perpendicularly from the Mississippi, being on the banks of that river, from one to two hundred feet high. All these high lands are, besides, surmounted in a good many places, by little eminences or small hills, and rising grounds, running off lengthwise with gentle slopes. It is only when we go a little way from the Mississippi that we find these high-lands are overtopped by little mountains, which appear to be all of earth though steep, without the least gravel or pebble being perceived on them. The soil, continues he, on these high lands is very good. It is a black light mould, about three feet deep, on the hills or rising-grounds: this upper earth

lies

lies upon a reddish clay, very strong and stiff; the lowest places between these hills are of the same nature, but there the black earth is between five and six feet deep. The grass growing in the hollows is of the height of a man, and very slender and fine; whereas the grass of the same meadow on the high lands rises scarce knee deep, as it does on the highest eminences. All these lands are either meadows or forests of tall trees, with grass up to the knee; the timber is oak, hiccory, mulberry, &c. Even reeds and canes grow on the hill sides, tho' they are found in our maritime colonies only in the richest swamps.

All the accounts we have had, both public and private, agree in these circumstances, and nothing can be more decisive of the excellency of the lands in this country. In the southern parts of this continent grass is very scarce every where but on the richest lands; insomuch that it is no unsatisfactory proof of the soil being good to find a plenty of any grass, much more such a luxuriant produce of it as is met with even on the hills of this country. The trees are no less indications of what the nature of the land is, being such as are

only

only found on good foils, and of a fize and ftraitnefs met with alone on the very richeft.

Charlevoix, who from the vaft extent of his travels was no ftranger to thefe appearances of various kinds which denote good land, and in general a fine country, has feveral particulars which it is proper to tranfcribe : fpeaking of his entrance into this country from the north, he fays, " There is not, in my opinion, a place in all Lou-ïfiana more proper for a fettlement than the fork at the junction of the Miffiffippi and the Ohio, nor where it is of greater importance to have one ; the whole country watered by the Ouabache and Ohio, which runs into it, is extremely fertile, confifting of vaft meadows." A later writer, of our own country, makes the fame remark : " the moft important place in this country, and perhaps in all North America, is at the forks of the Miffiffippi, where the Ohio falls into that river, which, like another ocean, is the general receptacle of all the rivers that water the interior parts of that vaft continent. Here thofe large and navigable rivers, the Ohio, the Cherokee river, Illionois, Miffouri, and Miffiffippi, befides many others which fpread over that

whole

whole continent, from the Apalachean mountains to the mountains of New Mexico, upwards of a thoufand miles both north, fouth, eaft, and weft, all meet together at this fpot; and that in the beft climate and one of the moft fruitful countries of any in all that part of the world; in the latitude 37°, the latitude of the capes of Virginia, and of Sante Fé, the capital of New Mexico. By that means there is a convenient navigation to this place from our prefent fettlements to New Mexico, and from all the inland parts of North America, farther than we are acquainted with it; and all the natives of that continent have by that means a free and ready accefs to this place. In fhort, this place is in the center of that vaft continent, and of all the nations in it, and feems to be intended by nature to command them both; for which reafon it ought no longer to be neglected by Britain.

"Upon the neighbourhood of the Chifaw river, Charlevoix remarks, that the country is delightful; the meadows preferve their verdure in the winter, and a confiderable number of well-wooded iflands in the Miffiffippi, fome of which are pretty large, form very beautiful canals, through

which the largeft fhips may fafely pafs ; it
being affirmed that there is fixty fathom
water in the Miffiffippi above 150 leagues
from the fea.   As to the forefts, which almoft entirely cover this immenfe country,
there is nothing perhaps in nature comparable to them, whether we confider the fize
and height of the trees, or their variety and
the advantages which may be drawn from
them ; for excepting dying woods, which
require a warmer foil, and are only to be
met with between the tropics, there is
hardly any fort of trees which can be mentioned that are not to be found here. There
are forefts of cyprefs eight or ten leagues in
extent, all the trees of which are of a thicknefs proportioned to their height, furpaffing
every thing we have of that kind in France.
That fort of ever-green laurel, which we
have called the tulip-tree on account of the
fhape of its flower, is now beginning to be
known in Europe. This grows to a greater
height than the chefnut-tree of India, and
its leaf is much more beautiful.   The can-
ton of Natchez is the fineft, moft fertile,
and beft peopled of all Louifiana ; it lies at
the diftance of about forty leagues from the
Yazows, upon the fame fide of the river.
Several little hills appear above th fort,

which

which is called Rosalie, and when these
are once passed, we see on all sides very
large meadows, separated from one another
by small thickets of wood, which produce
a very fine effect. The trees most common in these woods are the oak, and those
which produce nuts: the soil is every
where excellent. The late Monf. d'Iber-
ville, who first entered the Missisippi by
its mouth, having penetrated so far up as
the Natchez, found the country so delightful and so advantageously situated, that he
concluded the metropolis of the new colony could no where be better placed. If
ever Louisiana becomes a flourishing colony, as it may very well happen, it is my
opinion there cannot be a better situation
for a capital than this. It is not liable to
be overflowed by the river, has a very pure
air, and a great extent of country; the soil
is well watered, and capable of producing
every thing. Nor is it at too great a diftance from the sea, and there is nothing
to prevent shipping from going up to it.
Lastly, it is at a convenient distance from
all those places where there can be any design of making settlements."

Ths reader will remark, that these several accounts are perfectly consistent; it

is

is evident from them that all this country, to the eaft of the Miſſiſſippi, is one of the fineſt in the world in reſpect of climate and foil; the air is pleaſant and healthy, the heats are never oppreſſive, nor the froſts injurious; the atmoſphere is clear and dry, and free from the impurities with which it is loaded in countries abounding with marſhes and ſwamps : the circumſtance of the face of the country being high, and either hilly or ſloping off in gradual aſcents, and the foil at the fame time deep and rich, is uncommon and particularly valuable; for great fertility in ſuch healthy regions is by no means generally found. The ſpontaneous productions are alſo ſuch as give the moſt perfect ſatisfaction, whether taken as mere indications of what the foil is, or for their native value. Some of them have been mentioned, but others are equally deſerving attention.

Among theſe I ſhall firſt mention the vine, which, ſays Du Pratz, is ſo common in Louiſiana, that whatever way you walk from the ſea-coaſt for 500 leagues northwards, you cannot proceed an hundred ſteps without meeting with one ; but unleſs the vine-ſhoots ſhould happen to grow in an expoſed place, it cannot be expected that

their

their fruit fhould ever come to perfect maturity. The trees to which they twine are
fo high, and fo thick of leaves, and the
intervals of underwood are fo filled with
reeds, that the fun cannot warm the earth
or ripen the fruit of this fhrub. On the
edge of the favannahs or meadows we
meet with a grape, the fhoots of which refemble thofe of the Burgundy grape : they
make from this a tolerable good wine, if
they take care to expofe it to the fun in
fummer, and to the cold in winter. I have
made this experiment myfelf, and muft
fay, that I could never turn it into vinegar.
There is another kind of grape which I
make no difficulty of claffing with the
grapes of Corinth, commonly called cur-
rants. If it were planted and cultivated in
an open field, I make not the leaft doubt
but it would equal that grape. Mufcadine
grapes, of an amber colour, of a very good
kind and very fweet, have been found upon
declivities of a good expofure, even fo far
north as the latitude of 31 degrees. There
is the greateft probability that they might
make excellent wine of thefe, as it cannot
be doubted but the grapes might be brought
to great perfection in this country, fince
in the moift foil of New Orleans the cuttings

tings of the grape, which some of the inhabitants of that city brought from France, have succeeded extremely well, and afforded good wine.

Mulberries are found in vaſt plenty in moſt parts of the country. They have great numbers and a variety of kinds of walnuts and hiccories, and large cheſnut-trees, which however do not grow in plenty within 100 leagues of the ſea. Of the common foreſt timber, the red cedar is the moſt valuable; it is found in great plenty. Next to it ranks the cypreſs: it is reckoned incorruptible; one was found twenty feet deep in the earth, near New Orleans, uncorrupted. Now the lands of Lower Louiſiana have been found to be augmented two leagues every century; this tree therefore muſt have been buried at leaſt twelve centuries. Boats called *pettiaugres* are made of ſingle trunks of this tree, that will carry three or four thouſand weight, and ſometimes more. Of one of theſe trees a carpenter made two, one of which carried ſixteen ton, and the other fourteen. The pines are only found on the ſandy tracts on the ſea-coaſt. The ſaſſafras is here a large and tall tree. The myrtle wax tree is found in plenty, and its wax was always

one

one of the principal articles in the exports from New Orleans. The locuſt *(acacia)* is found on all the higher lands, and is a ſtrong ſign of a good ſoil. The mangrove is found in ſome parts of the country. A-mong their oaks they have the ever-green one and the red ; it is well known that the beſt ſhips built in America are thoſe which have their timbers of ever-green oak, and their plank of cedar; and it is aſſerted that the red oak of Louiſiana is as good as the ever-green one. The aſh, elm, beech, lime, hornbeam, aſp willow, alder, &c. are the ſame as in Europe. Sarſaparilla grows naturally in Louiſiana, and it is not inferior in its qualities to that of Mexico. Hops grow naturally in the gullies in the high lands. The canes or reeds grow to vaſt height ; one kind comes in moiſt places to eighteen feet, and the thickneſs of the wriſt. The natives make mats, ſieves, ſmall boxes, and other works of it. Thoſe that grow in dry places, are neither ſo high nor ſo thick, but are ſo hard, that, before the arrival of the French, the na-tives uſed ſplits of theſe canes to cut their victuals with. After a certain number of years the large canes bear a great abundance of grain, which is ſomewhat like oats, but

about

about three times as large. The natives carefully gather thofe grains, and make bread or gruel of them. This flour fwells as much as that of wheat. When the reeds have yielded the grain they die, and none appear for a long time after in the fame place, efpecially if fire has been fet to the old ones. Hemp grows naturally in this country; the ftalks are as thick as one's finger, and about fix feet long: they are quite like ours, both in the wood, the leaf, and the rind. The flax which was fown in this country rofe three feet high.——The reader cannot well have greater fatisfaction relative to the high importance of this country, than the preceding recapitulation of part of its natural produce. The productions of agriculture will not be found to fpeak lefs effectually to the fame purpofe.

Maize was not only cultivated by the Indians in fmall quantities for their fubfiftence during a part of the year, but alfo by the French as an article of confiderable exportation to the fugar iflands: it was here found to thrive better on a black and light earth than on a ftrong one. Such as began plantations of it in the woods, thick fet with cane, found an advantage in the maize which made amends for the labour

of

of clearing the ground; a labour always more fatiguing than cultivating a spot already cleared. The advantage was this; they began with cutting down the canes for a great extent of ground; the trees they peeled two feet high quite round. This operation they performed the beginning of March, as then the sap is in motion in that country: about fifteen days after the canes being dry, were set on fire, and burnt, burning or at least killing the trees with them. The following day they sowed the maize, in squares four feet asunder; the roots of the canes which are not quite dead shoot out fresh canes, which are very tender and brittle, and as no other weeds grow in the field that year, it is easy to be weeded of these canes, and as much corn again used to be made in this manner as in a field already cultivated.

Wheat, rye, barley, oats, pease, and beans of many sorts thrive no where in the world better than on the high lands in this country, in every spot where the French planted them, and yielded a produce much greater without manure than can be gained in common lands in Europe with great manuring: the temperature of the climate suits wheat extraordinarily, and no soil can

be

be better adapted to it. But in Lower Louiſiana upon the coaſt, which is the ſame country as Weſt Florida, the French found that it would not thrive at all.

Indigo was commonly cultivated in this country, than which none more favourable, either in climate or ſoil, is any where to be found: the high lands produce it naturally. In the iſlands from the heat of climate they cut it four times; three good cuttings are had in Louiſiana, of as good a quality at leaſt, and producing as much as their four. In the particulars before given, concerning indigo in Carolina, I ſhewed that this plant required a rich, deep, black, dry loam, which is ſcarcely any where to be found in ſuch perfection and plenty as in the country on the eaſt of the Miſſiſſippi. No where in all North America will this ſtaple be cultivated with ſo much ſucceſs as here: the lands on the Ohio are as rich in many parts, but the climate is not ſo warm, being hardly warm enough for cultivating this plant with great ſucceſs. Indigo is highly profitable both to the planter and the nation; it will therefore be found, whenever this noble country is colonized, that it muſt be one of the chief ſtaples of it, and tho crops

which

2

which will be here raifed will certainly induce the people on the barren unhealthy coafts of our old colonies to quit them, and fettle here, where their profit will prove very different, and they will thereby advance the interefts of Britain as much as of themfelves.

Hemp, I before obferved, grows wild in Louifiana; but upon the eaftern banks of the river, for a long way, there are very few tracts of low, marfhy, ftrong land, fuch as hemp delights in, the lands being in general high and dry; that quantities might be made on the deep black mould, I doubt not, and perhaps if it was tried, it would not be found to require fo much moifture; but, as upon the Ohio, hemp is alfo found fpontaneous; and as the country is more various, having fome tracts of low moift land on a ftrong clay, which would do admirably for this plant, and in which is found great natural crops; for this reafon hemp might be confidered as a ftaple for the Ohio, and the rich dry lands of the Miffiffippi applied to thofe crops which will only thrive in fuch.

Tobacco is another plant indigenous in this part of America; the French colonifts cultivated it with fuch fuccefs that had

they

they received any encouragement from their
government they might soon have rivalled
Virginia and Maryland; but inftead of this
they were taxed heavily for cultivating it,
by duties laid on the trade; what they produced was of fo excellent a quality, as to
fell fome at five fhillings a pound. This
was raifed in the country about Fort Ro-
falie, and to Yafouz. And there is one advantage in this culture here which ought
not to be forgotten: in Louifiana the
French planters, after the tobacco was
cut, weeded and cleaned the ground on
which it grew, the roots pufh forth frefh
fhoots, which are managed in the fame
manner as the firft crop. By this means
a fecond crop is made on the fame ground,
and fometimes a third. Thefe *feconds* indeed, as they are called, do not ufually
grow fo high as the firft plant, but notwithftanding they make very good tobacco.
Whereas in Virginia and Maryland the
planters are prohibited by law from cultivating thefe *feconds*; the fummers are there
too fhort to bring them to maturity, but
in Louifiana the fummers are two or three
months longer, by which means two or
three crops of tobacco may be made in a
year, as eafily as one in Virginia. And a
very

very experienced perſon in the tobacco trade aſſures us, that the freſh lands on the Miſſiſſippi will produce thrice or four times as much per working hand as our old plantations in Virginia and Maryland. This is perfectly conſiſtent with the beſt accounts we have received from thence, which agree in deſcribing the ſoil as very rich and very deep, of a black colour, and light and dry; ſuch a ſoil is of a boundleſs fertility from its depth, where there is only a thin ſtratum, though the richneſs may be great for a time, yet ſucceſſive crops of exhauſting plants will wear it out in no great number of years; but when the ſoil is, like that on the country on the eaſt of the Miſſiſſippi, the ſame for three, four, or five feet deep, the planter has nothing to fear. Every circumſtance that is neceſſary to ſucceſs in tobacco planting is found in this territory: Firſt, the right ſoil is the greateſt plenty. Second, very extenſive tracts of fertile meadow, covered with the moſt luxuriant graſs, for the maintenance of immenſe herds of cattle. Third, a navigation cloſe to the tobacco lands, which admits ſhips of five hundred tons. Fourth, a climate much better for this culture than that of

our tobacco colonies.   If all thefe circumftances are duly confidered, it will be
found, that whenever the tobacco trade
declines, or threatens a decline, the wife
conduct will be to plant it in a country fo
highly favourable to the bufinefs.

Silk may be produced in this country in
any quantities that the population will allow of; for the mulberry is found in great
plenty all over the high lands.   The leaves
of the natural mulberry-trees of Louifiana
are what the filk-worms are very fond of;
I mean the more common mulberries with
a large leaf, but tender, and the fruit of
the colour of Burgundy wine.   The province produces alfo the white mulberry,
which has the fame quality with the red.
Du Pratz has a very juft obfervation on
making filk in this country.   " The culture, fays he, of indigo, tobacco, cotton,
&c. may be carried on without any inter-
ruption to the making of filk, as any one
of thefe is no manner of hindrance to the
other.   In the firft place, the work about
thefe three plants does not come on till
after the worms have fpun their filk: in
the fecond place, the feeding and cleaning
the filk-worm requires no great degree of
ftrength; and thus the care employed
about

about them, interrupts no other sort of work either as to time or as to the persons employed therein. It suffices to have for this operation a person who knows how to feed and clean the worms; young negroes of both sexes might assist this person, little skill sufficing for this purpose; the oldest of the young negroes, when taught, might shift the worms and lay the leaves; the other young negroes gather and fetch them; and all this labour, which takes not up the whole day, lasts only for about six weeks. It appears therefore that the profit made of the silk is an additional benefit, so much the more profitable as it diverts not the workmen from their ordinary tasks. If it be objected, that buildings are requisite to make silk to advantage; I answer, buildings for the purpose cost very little in a country where wood may be had for taking; I add further, that these buildings may be made and daubed with mud by any persons about the family, and besides may serve for hanging tobacco in, two months after the silk-worms are gone."

There is another circumstance in which the high lands of this country are peculiarly adapted to the culture of silk, which is the dryness of the climate. Upon the

mari-

maritime parts of our old colonies, the continual rains are very detrimental to this tender worm, which requires a fine healthy climate, as much as a man of a tender conftitution : in fuch the filk is always made in larger quantities, and of a far better quality.   This is a point which has not been fufficiently attended to, but whenever we come to plant this country, the great advantage of it will be found in making filk.

Cotton is another article which the French cultivated with fuccefs in Louifiana, but which like others never came to be a national objeft for want of more people, and perhaps for want of encouragement, owing to their fear of rivalling their fugar iflands, which alfo produce it in large quantities.   The cotton they cultivated here is a fpecies of the white Siam.   This Eaft India and annual cotton has been found to be much better and whiter than what is cultivated in our colonies, which is of the Turkey kind; both of them keep their colour better in wafhing, and are whiter than the perennial cotton that comes from the iflands, although this laft is of a longer ftaple.   It is not fo long nor fo foft as the filk cotton.   It is produced, not from a

tree

tree as in the East Indies, but from a plant,
and thrives much better in light than in
strong and fat land; in the lower lands of
Louisiana it never was so fine as on the
higher ones. It may be planted on lands
newly cleared, and not yet proper for tobacco, much less for indigo, which requires a ground well worked like a garden.
The seeds are planted three feet asunder,
more or less, according to the quality of
the soil; the field is weeded at the proper
season, in order to clear it of the noxious
weeds, and fresh earth laid to the roots of
the plant to secure it against the winds.
The cotton requires weeding neither so
often nor so carefully as other plants;
and the care of gathering is the employment of young people, incapable of harder
labour: when the pods burst it is gathered, and the most laborious part of the
work is to separate the cotton from the
seeds, though it is much lessened since the
use of mills was introduced. The high,
light, and dry soil in the territory on the
east side of the Mississippi is all admirably
adapted to this production; and in point
of preparation it is not only the fresh that
may for the first year be planted with it;
after the luxuriance of the soil is abated by

G 3

tobacco

tobacco and indigo, it will do exceedingly well for cotton. This article is not mentioned in this or any other cafe as a proper staple for the fole employment of any colony, but joined with others of greater value, it is a good addition to the beft settlements in America; for I have often remarked, what fhould not be forgotten, that no colony fhould ftick to any one ftaple fo much as to neglect others; the inconveniences of fuch a conduct are to this day, and have been long felt in our tobacco colonies, where, for want of other ftaples, fuch as filk and wine, they have gone too much into common hufbandry, which produces nothing wanted in Britain.

The olive tree is common in Louifiana, and very beautiful. The Provençals who were fettled here, affirmed that its olives yielded as good an oil as thofe of their own country. The crop is always very abundant. This is an article which would prove of great advantage to Britain, and of profit to the planters; and no produce would be a ftaple more proper for a colony. In Carolina, on the coaft, the frofts fometimes kill large olive trees, but fuch extremes of weather are never met with in the high dry territories of this country.

Thefe

These are the principal staples which should be attended to when this country is planted; wine, silk, indigo, tobacco, and cotton; they are valuable commodities, come truly within the definition of a colony *staple*; commodities which this nation either consumes herself, or could command a ready market for; and which are of such value as to enable the planters to purchase negroes in great numbers, so as to enter largely and effectually into their culture. I before shewed that the climate, in respect of health and pleasantness, possessed every advantage that could promote the interests of every branch of agriculture, an object which is of great importance, and in which the British colonies upon the coast, through all that part which is flat and sandy, are greatly deficient. In other respects, |the advantages attending this country are equally valuable.

Among these the plenty of wild cattle is not the least, since they not only indicate the fertility of the land, but will afford, for many generations, immense supplies of meat and hides: the principal kinds are deer and buffaloes. All Louisiana contains prodigious tracts, almost boundless they might be called, of rich

G 4

mea-

meadows, covered with a luxuriant growth
of very fine grafs, tracts that have fcarce
any interruptions of foreft, hills, or vallies,
extend from five to ten and twenty leagues :
fuch immenfe paftures of the richeft land,
in a warm and fine climate, where the
winters yield a plenty of food as well as
the fummers, could fcarcely be free from
herds of cattle ; and accordingly they are
found in fuch prodigious numbers, as to
aftonifh all travellers that go through the
country.

This beaft is about the fize of one of our
largeft oxen, but he appears rather bigger on
account of his long curled|wool, which makes
him appear to the eye much larger than
he really is.   This wool is very fine and
very thick.   A pretty large bunch rifes on
his fhoulders, in the place where they join
to the neck.   He is the chief food of the
natives, and was the fame with the French
from the beginning of the colony.   The
quantity of tallow they yield is very great,
and their fkins are an object of no fmall
confideration.   The natives drefs them
with their wool on, as Du Pratz informs
us, to fuch great perfection, as to render
them more pliable than our buff.

The

The plenty of deer in all parts of this country is very great, notwithstanding the numbers that are constantly killed; they are much the same as the deer of Europe: their skins form one of the most valuable articles of commerce in all the southern colonies of America, and in this country the plenty is yet greater from the immense space of uncultivated land which they have to spread over. Nor is it only in these two articles, which are native to the country, that a great plenty is found; for all the the animals which have been brought from France and the English colonies have multiplied exceedingly; horses, cows, hogs, sheep, &c. are, I apprehend, cheaper than in any of our colonies; this is not to be wondered at, for in no part of America are there found such plenty of natural meadows. The fruits of this country are in the same plenty as Carolina, but of a finer relish from the dryness of the climate; they have besides grapes, plums, papaws, peaches, oranges, citrons, figs, apples, &c. The French colonists planted the peach stones about the end of February, and suffer the trees to grow exposed to all weathers. In the third year they will gather from one tree at least two hundred

peaches,

peaches, and double that number for fix or feven years more when the tree dies. As new ones are fo eafily produced, the lofs of the old ones is not in the leaft regretted.

Upon the whole, there is the greateft reafon to conclude, that the territory ou the eaft of the Miffiffippi, which is at prefent in our poffeffion, is one of the moft valuable countries in all America, and one which will pay admirably for colonizing, whenever the meafure is thought proper by government to be embraced. It appears on refpectable authority, not only of able writers, but gentlemen now living who have travelled through it, that the climate is as fine as any in the world, equally favourable to the production of many valuable ftaples, and to the health and pleafure of life. That the foil is as fertile as any in the world, though high and dry, circumftances almoft invaluable. That the country abounds in an immenfe plenty of food for cattle, and is fpread with vaft herds of buffaloes and deer. That fruits, of various kinds, are fuperior in plenty and flavour to thofe of any other part of the continent. That indigo, tobacco, hemp, flax, vines, filk, olives, and

other

other valuable ſtaples, may be cultivated here with much greater ſucceſs than in moſt of the other parts of America. To this if we add the navigation of the Miſſiſſippi, and the rivers which fall into it, we ſhall find the territory to be deficient in no one circumſtance that can contribute to render it a flouriſhing and wealthy colony.

As ſuch, I think there can be no objections rationally made to ſettling it. The eſtabliſhment of a new colony on the Ohio might be thought at firſt ſight to ſuperſede it, but if better conſidered it will not be found ſo. There is one circumſtance in which this territory is much ſuperior to the Ohio, which is that of navigation : the latter has a land carriage acroſs the mountains of forty miles, which will lay a heavy burthen on thoſe commodities that are not very valuable, ſo as to make it neceſſary, perhaps, to ſend them down the Miſſiſſippi, in which caſe the ſame commodities may be ſent to market from this country upon cheaper terms. Nor ſhould we forget to add, that the greater degree of heat on the Miſſiſſippi would prove more favourable to ſeveral of the ſtaples than the climate of the Ohio, which is not ſo hot—

and

and we may in general conclude, that the value of the staples of all colonies that are healthy, will be found to increase in proportion to their proximity to the line. This comparison of the two climates' concerns only certain articles, for instance, indigo, cotton, and olives, which require for a perfect culture a hotter climate than the Ohio, though indigo may be produced there with profit. But in the case of tobacco, hemp, flax, silk, wine, &c. the Ohio is fully equal; and in all the productions of common husbandry, except Indian corn, perhaps superior. But in another case there is found a strong propriety, at least, in settling the Mississippi, which is the forming a chain of settlements along the banks of that river to the junction with the Ohio colony, in order for strengthening the country on one side against the Spaniards, and on the other against the Indians. The Creeks, Chactaws, Cherokees, and Chicasaws, would then be entirely surrounded, and we should never more have any thing to dread from their resentments: the scheme long ago proposed by several gentlemen of America, well versed in Indian affairs, to stop all supplies of gunpowder for them in case of a war,

would

would then be practicable; and without doing them any injury, we should lay the foundation for a perfect security.

In case of such a settlement being made, the whole valuable part of that continent, the southern division of it, would then be in the desirable state of improvement: the population, from being so spread round a great extent of frontier, would increase without giving the least cause of jealousy to Britain, land would not only be plentiful, but plentiful where our people wanted it; whereas at present, the population of our colonies, especially the central ones, is confined; they have spread over all the space between the sea and the mountains, the consequence of which is, that land is become scarce, that which is good having been all planted or patented, the people therefore find themselves too numerous for their agriculture, which is the first step to be manufactures, that step which Britain has so much reason to dread. Nothing therefore can be more political, than to provide a superabundance of colonies to take off all those people that find a want of land in our old settlements; and it may not be one or two tracts of country that will answer this purpose; provision should

be

be made for the convenience of some, the inclinations of others, and every measure taken to inform the people of the colonies that were growing too populous, that land was plentiful in other places, and granted on the easiest terms; and if such inducements were not found sufficient for thinning the country considerably, goverment should by all means be at a part of the expence of transporting them. Notice should be given that sloops should always be ready at Fort Pit, or as much higher on the Ohio as it is navigable, for carrying all families, without expence, to whatever settlements they chuse on the Ohio or the Mississippi. Such measures, or similar ones, would carry off that surplus of population in the central and northern colonies, which has been, and will every day be more and more the foundation of their manufactures. They never could establish such fabrics, while the plenty of good land in a good climate was so great as to afford every man an opportunity of settling; for while that was the case, none would let themselves as workmen in a manufacture. Consistent with these ideas, we see that those colonies where the good land is most plentiful in a good climate, the manufactures

are

are trifling, or none to be found, which is the cafe with the tobacco colonies and with the fouthern ones; but in the northern settlements, where thefe circumftances are different, we there find many fabrics.

Nothing can be more fortunate than the navigation of the Ohio quite to the Apalachean mountains, at the back of the center of all our colonies, fince by that means people may, with only a fmall or a moderate journey, arrive at a navigation that will carry them through all that immenfe tract which we may in future colonize, a part of which we are now about to fettle, and yet more of which I am urging the propriety of likewife fettling.   Were it not for this vaft navigation, to the very fpot almoft that one would wifh to have it, there would be difficulties in the people getting to the countries we wanted them to fettle in; but as we poffefs this great advantage, it would be unpardonable not to make effectual ufe of it, in cafe the eftablifhment of new colonies did not of itfelf draw the whole furplus of population away from thofe provinces, the numbers in which want fo much to be thinned.

Nor is the advantage of drawing off people from the northern colonies confined to the prevention of manufactures; it is further of vaft confequence to take them from countries that produce nothing valuable in a Britifh market, and fix them in others abounding with ftaples of high importance to the commerce and manufactures of the mother-country : this fingle idea ought to be the corner-ftone of all the regulations and meafures adopted by this country in her tranfactions with America ; and if it is well purfued in future, will keep off the dangerous rivalfhip, which there is fo much reafon to fear, from the manufactures and commerce of the northern colonies.

If the country on the eaft bank of the Miffiffippi was fettled, and that to the fouth of the Ohio alfo, there would be fuch a variety of land, climate, and productions, that every new comer, either from Europe or our own colonies, would have it in his power to chufe the culture with which he was beft acquainted, or by which he expected to make the moft confiderable profits : they might fix on the climate moft agreeable to their conftitutions, and in all other refpects have fuch a variety of circumftances to felect from, that the temptation to move would be very great.

I

great. At the same time that they suited themselves, they could not fail, fix where they would, of promoting the interest of the mother-country in a very sensible degree. By not delaying such a measure, there would be a population, and with it a power fixed in the most important part of all this continent, upon this immense inland navigation, which spreads far and near, from the Atlantic Ocean to the South Sea, and from the Gulph of Mexico to Hudson's Bay : the river Mississippi with its branches spread over most of it, and the lakes, with the St. Laurence, whichare nearly connected with the former, go through the rest. It is of prodigious future consequence to be masters of this navigation, and to have early a power fixed on it, in order to over-awe and keep the Spaniards from designs against our colonies. We ought not to forget their jealousy of us in this country, and that they have at present a much greater military force there than ever was possessed by the French. It is a mistake to imagine that the Spaniards have been inattentive to the *security* of their American colonies ; as backward as they have always been in their improvement, they have been far enough from negligence with relation to a military power, I mean since the last peace, for upon the con-

 clusion

clufion of it, their whole army was difpatched from Old to New Spain, and the arrangement of the former left entirely to new levies. This was a very bold and decifive meafure, and which fhewed a refolution to be ftronger in America than ever was experienced before: it is for this reafon that we ought to be particularly attentive to the ftrength of our territories on the Miffiffippi, and to give them it effectually muft be done by peopling them, inftead of keeping the whole country in as defolate a condition as it was a century before the French difcovered it.

General O'Reilly, when he took poffeffion of New Orleans, had a force of five thoufand regular troops, with a good train of artillery, and every requifite for a fmall but well appointed army. This force they have maintained here; it is much fuperior to any thing we have in Weft Florida and upon the Miffiffippi; our government therefore ought certainly to be upon their guard in this part of the world, and not only to have a fufficient military force in the forts and armed floops upon the river, but a chain of populous fettlements to cut off all poffibility of communication between the Spaniards and the Indians to the eaft of the Miffiffippi; a point which may in future prove of very great confequence.

CHAP.

CHAP. XXVIII.

THE ILIONOIS.

*Country of the Ilionois — Climate — Soil—
Productions—Importance of this territory
—Observations.*

BY the country of the Ilionois, I mean
all that territory to the north-west of
the Ohio, extending on both sides the river
Ilionois quite to Lake Michigan and the
river St. Joseph, the settlements made by
the French on the river Myamis; but in
particular the country east of the Mississippi, between the Ohio and Ilionois river, to the distance of about an hundred
miles from the former. This territory
went among the French by the general
name of the country of the Ilionois. It
claims attention in this work, first because
we are in possession of all the settlements
made by the French in it, and notwithstanding its being deficient in all government but that of the commanding officers
of our forts, they have increased considerably by the wandering settlers from our

H 2   colonies :

colonies : and fecondly, becaufe the great richnefs of the foil and fertility of the climate will hereafter attract fo many inhabitants, as to make the eftablifhment of fome civil government highly neceffary. The public accounts given of this country are not numerous, but what there are, are very confiftent with each other, and alfo with the private information I have received from the officers with whom I have converfed, that made a confiderable refidence here.

Charlevoix, who paffed through this country, has given fome flight defcriptions of different parts, which will afford a pretty good idea of it: he entered it by Lake Erie, the country upon which though not included in it, yet is fo near as to deferve our attention here.—Of the tract on the very fouthern point of that lake, he fpeaks as follows. " I coafted along a charming country, hid at times by very difagreeable profpects, which however are of no great extent. Wherever I went afhore, I was quite enchanted by the beauty and variety of a landfcape, which was terminated by the noblest forefts in the whole world. Add to this that every part of it fwarms with water-fowl; I cannot fay

whether

whether the woods afford game in equal profusion; but I well know that there is a prodigious quantity of buffaloes. Were we always to fail, as I then did, with a serene sky, in a most charming climate, and on water as clear as that of the purest fountain; were we sure of finding every where secure and agreeable places to pass the night in, where we might enjoy the pleasure of hunting at a small expence, breathe at our ease the purest air, and enjoy the prospect of the finest countries in the universe, we might possibly be tempted to travel to the end of our days."

Of the country between Lakes Erie and Huron, he says, "It is pretended that this is the finest part of all Canada; and really, if we may judge by appearances, nature seems to have refused it nothing that can contribute to make a country delightful; hills, meadows, fields, lofty forests, rivulets, fountains, rivers, and all of them so excellent in their kind, and so happily blended, as to equal the most romantic wishes; the lands, however, are not all equally proper for every sort of grain, but most are of a wonderful fertility, and I have known some produce good wheat for eighteen years running, without any

manure

manure; and befides, all of them are proper for fome particular ufe.   The iflands
in the channel, between the two lakes,
feemed placed on purpofe for the pleafure
of the profpect; the river and lake abound
in fifh, the air is pure, and the climate
temperate and extremely wholefome.
There grow here citron trees in the open
fields, the fruit of which, in fhape and colour, refemble thofe of Portugal, but they
are fmaller and of a difagreeable flavour.
On both fides of the channel the country
is faid to preferve its beauty for ten leagues
up; after which you meet with a fmaller
number of fruit trees and fewer meadows;
but after travelling five or fix leagues further, inclining to Lake Erie towards the
fouth-weft, you difcover immenfe meadows, extending above a hundred leagues
every where, and which feed an immenfe
quantity of thofe buffaloes, whereof I have
more than once made mention.   Twelve
leagues off this channel, before you come
to Lake Huron, is a village of Miffifaguy
Indians, feated on a fertile foil, at the en-
try of three magnificent meadows, and in
the moft moft charming fituation that can
be, the country for the whole twelve
leagues continuing always moft delightful.
This

This is a noble channel, as ftrait as a line, and bordered with lofty forefts, interfperfed with fine meadows, with many iflands fcattered up and down in it, fome of which are confiderably large."

Of the territory on the river St. Jofeph, he fpeaks as follows. " The river St. Jofeph has more than an hundred leagues of courfe, its fource being at no great diftance from Lake Erie ; it is navigable for fourfcore leagues, and as I was failing up towards the fort, I faw nothing but excellent lands, covered with trees of a prodigious height. Tobacco grows well here, and by making a proper choice of foil, we might raife a moft excellent fort of it."

· Proceeding to the fouth by the river Huakiki, which falls into the Ilionois, he obferves, that " at about fifty leagues from the fource the country becomes beautiful, confifting of unbounded meadows, where buffaloes are to be feen grazing in herds of two or three hundred. Where the Huakiki joins the Ilionois, the latter becomes a fine river ; it does not yield in largenefs to any of our rivers in France, and I can affure you, it is not poffible to behold a finer and a better country than this which it waters. Before we came to Lake Pimi-

teouy

teouy, we croffed a charming country, and at the end of that lake came to a village of the Ilionois; than which nothing can be more delightful than its fituation: oppofite to it is the profpect of a moft beautiful foreft, which was then adorned with all the variety of colours, and behind it is a plain of an immenfe extent, fkirted with woods. The lake and river fwarm with fifh, and the banks of both with game. From the lake to the Miffiffippi the river Ilionois, both in breadth and depth, is e-qual to any of the greateft rivers of Europe. After failing five leagues on the Miffiffippi, we arrived at the mouth of the Miffiouri. Here is the fineft confluence of two rivers that I believe is to be met with in the whole world, each of them being about half a league in breadth; but the Miffouri is by far the moft rapid of the two, and feems to enter the Miffiffippi like a conqueror, carrying its white waters, unmixed, acrofs its channel quite to the oppofite fide; this colour it after-wards communicates to the Miffiffippi, which henceforth it never lofes, but hurls with precipitation to the fea itfelf."

About Fort Chartres the French have feveral fettlements, and live pretty much

at

at their eafe : they fow wheat, which fuc-
ceeds very well ; and they have black cattle and poultry. The banks of the river
are extremely high, fo that though the
waters fometimes rife five and twenty feet,
they feldom overflow their channel. All
this country is open, confifting of vaft
meadows, to the extent of five and twenty
leagues, which are interfperfed with fmall
copfes of very valuable wood. White mulberries efpecially are very common here ;
but I am furprifed that the inhabitants
fhould be fuffered to cut them down for
the building of their houfes, efpecially as
there is a fufficient quantity of other trees
equally proper for that purpofe. The
whole country, from hence to Kafcafquias,
and around the latter, is very fertile ; it is
capable of becoming the grainery of Louifiana, which it is able to furnifh with corn
in abundance, even fhould it be peopled
quite to the fea. The foil is not only extremely proper for wheat, but befides, re-
fufes nothing neceffary or ufeful for human
life. The climate is extremely temperate,
lying in 38 deg. 39 min. north lat. Cattle and fheep would multiply here wonderfully, even the wild buffaloes might be
tamed, and great advantages drawn from

a trade

a trade of their wool and hides, and from their fupplying the inhabitants with food. The air is very wholefome. Frofts are fometimes felt that are very fevere ; the river laft winter was frozen over in fuch a manner, that people croffed it in carriages, notwithftanding it is at that place half a league broad, and more rapid than the Rhone. This is the more furprifing, as for the moft part, excepting a few flight frofts occafioned by the north and north-weft winds, the winter is in this country hardly fenfible ; the leaves fall fooner in this place than in France, and do not begin to bud till about the end of May, notwithftanding that it fnows very feldom here, and although, as I have already obferved, the winters are exceeding temperate. What then can be the reafon of this backwardnefs of the fpring ? for my part I can fee no other than the thicknefs of the forefts, which prevents the earth from being warmed by the fun foon enough to caufe the fap to afcend. At Cape St. Anthony I faw the firft canes."

I have been led to make thefe long extracts from Charlevoix, becaufe his authority has always been juftly efteemed, and he gave this account long before the coun

try

, try became fubject to Britain: although he only touches upon certain circumftances of the foil and climate, as a traveller and not a refident, yet may we gather from it that both are excellent, that the foil is fertile in yielding tobacco and the articles of common hufbandry, particularly wheat; that the forefts are among the fineft in the world; the meadows of an unbounded extent, and full of buffaloes; that the air is pure and healthy, and the climate in every refpect temperate and agreeable; and laftly, that the beauty of many tracts of this country is as great as the fineft affemblage of wood, water, hill, and dale can make it.

Much later accounts confirm thefe particulars. When Charlevoix was there, in 1721, the French had but begun to cultivate it, but fince that period they have made a great progrefs; fo that at the peace of 1762 they had a fine and well fettled colony about Kafcafquias and Fort Chartres, and alfo many fettlements on the river Myamis, principally inhabited by emigrants from Canada: fome of thefe fold their effects, and retired upon the conclufion of the peace, but the major part remained under the Britifh government; nor has the country declined fince, notwithftanding

standing the only government established in it is that of the commanding officers of the garrisoned forts.

Mr. Pownal, in his *Administration of the Colonies*, gives, from very good authority, a few particulars concerning the country of the Ilionois. " This country, says Charlevoix, in 1721 will become the grainery of Louisiana; and in 1746 we find it actually becoming so, for in that year it sent down to New Orleans fifty ton of flour; in 1747 we find it well furnished with provisions, and having fine crops; and in a letter of Monf. Vandreuil's, in 1748, we have an account of its produce and exports—flour, corn, bacon, hams both of bears and hogs, corned pork, and wild beef, myrtle-wax, cotton, tallow, leather, tobacco, lead, copper, some small quantity of buffalo wool, venison, poultry, bear's grease, oil, skins, and some coarse furs; and we find a regular communication settled with New Orleans, by convoys, which come down annually the latter end of December, and return at latest by the middle of February."

The private accounts I have had of this country confirm the preceding articles of intelligence, and give the greatest reason

for

for determining that it ranks among the best and most agreeable of America; especially in every circumstance that concerns the plenty and agreeableness of living, and all the productions of common husbandry, in which I believe it yields to no part of the world.   As to staples in a British market, it will be by no means deficient in them, whenever the advantages of the climate are any ways seconded in these respects by the skill and industry of the planters. Tobacco may undoubtedly be produced here in any quantity, and of a quality equal to any other : the country, most of it, in the same latitude as Virginia and Maryland, with the advantage of a much more regular climate, and winters less severe. Charlevoix expressly says, that in general the winters are exceedingly temperate; whereas in Virginia extreme sharp frosts are common: but through all our southern and central colonies the maritime parts are exposed to greater degrees of heat and cold than the internal country. The navigation of the Mississippi will make the culture of tobacco very profitable. Wine may also be a most beneficial staple to this country, the climate is perfectly agreeable to it, and high, dry, and hilly tracts common through-

out

out the whole territory: the navigation
will be equally favourable to the product
of this country. Silk is another which
will undoubtedly be made in confiderable
quantities whenever the territory is peopled, fince the healthinefs and temperature
of the climate cannot in this latitude but
agree admirably with the worm, and mulberries are plentifully fpread over the whole
of it. In a word, it is deficient in no article that can tend to render it a valuable
colony, and whenever it is fettled will be
found of that importance to this kingdom,
of which we have already experienced
thofe to be that poffefs ftaple productions.

CHAP.

C H A P. XXIX.

J A M A I C A.

Climate — Soil — Productions—The culture of Sugar—Expences — Produce — Profit —Observations —Other staples — Settlements—Remarkable instances of beneficial improvements—Observations.

THE amazing importance which has attended the culture of the sugar cane, is perhaps one of the most extraordinary instances of the effect of agriculture that the world has produced, and it shews clearer than any other circumstance wherein consists the true and beneficial nature of colonies : the profit which this nation reaps from her islands in the West Indies ought above all other things to make her attentive to every particular in the culture of the sugar cane.   As Jamaica is our principal colony for this production, I shall be more minute in my account than in the description of other islands, as they will call only for the circumstances wherein they differ from that island.

Jamaica

Jamaica lies between 17 and 19 deg. north latitude, from whence it is eafy to judge that the climate is extremely hot : indeed the fun paffes directly over their heads, and would, in the height of fummer, render the air too fuffocating to breathe, were it not for the trade wind and land breeze which refrefh and cool the air. Yet with this advantage which Jamaica enjoys in common with the reft of the iflands, the climate is in general pernicious to European conftitutions. The extreme heat is not fo great an enemy as the dampnefs and moifture which attend it : and we may in general remark, that this is the circumftance which in all latitudes, but efpecially hot ones, decides the healthinefs of a country. A dry and pure air, fuch as is found on hilly or mountainous fea-coafts, free from marfhes or fwamps, is always healthy, though under the line ; but when a meridian fun unites with a marfhy rotten foil, in which the heavy rains ftagnate, then it is impoffible for a country to be tolerably healthy. The people of Jamaica lament their thunders and lightnings, their tempefts and hurricanes—the laft are indeed very fatal to their profit ; but if health was only confidered, a low marfhy tract

of

of land, in parts of which the rains ſtagnated, ſhould be conſidered as a much more fatal circumſtance. The great evil of the climate is its moiſture, which, united with heat, brings that numerous liſt of fatal diſtempers which are common in this iſland; which renders caution in diet and living remarkably neceſſary, and which is worſe than fatal in cauſing that extreme languor of the body and oppreſſion of the ſpirits, which make the inhabitants ſuffer worſe than death through half their exiſtence. In a word, the climate of Jamaica is ſuch an one, as nothing but the hope of wealth could induce an Engliſhman to live in. With an exception, however, of the hilly tracts, which, and the mountains, are by no means unhealthy for a hot climate.

The iſland is entirely out of the reach of froſt and ſnow, nor have they ever any weather that can be denominated cold: they have properly neither winter nor ſummer, for the trees never loſe their leaves; the only diſtinction of ſeaſon is that of the rains, which fall in July, Auguſt, and September, but principally in Auguſt. They have alſo heavy ones in May and October, and ſometimes a ſeaſon (that is a rain) happens in January. Their hurricanes are extremely dreadful; in ſome of them the

wind is fo furious, and rifes to fuch a pitch
in a few minutes, that every obftacle flies
before it; trees of an immenfe fize are torn
up by the roots, and blown away like
chaff—whole groves difappear in an inftant
—buildings, however folidly conftructed
of ftone, and the walls, many feet thick,
purpofely conftructed to withftand thefe
terrible blafts, are deftroyed in a moment;
in a word, the furface of the earth is truly
bared, every thing is fwept from it with ir-
refiftible violence: it may eafily be imagined, that, in fuch a fituation, the canes
and other objects of culture are the firft to
be blown away. Thefe ftorms of wind are
not all of equal violence, nor do they fpread
a large tract of country at once; buildings
very ftrongly built fometimes efcape, at o-
thers every thing gives way.

Jamaica is about one hundred and forty
miles long by fixty broad, and contains a-
bout four millions of acres. But much
the greater part is not patented to any
owners, and a very fmall portion of it is
cultivated. The face of the country is extremely various. Along the middle of the
ifland, from eaft to weft, runs a vaft
chain of mountains, called the Blue Mountains: thefe occupy above half the ifland,
for they fpread in various ridges, fome
higher

higher than others, with deep furrowed glens between them ; and in some places flat vales of amazing fertility are found, quite surrounded with rock and precipice. The hills are all either rock or stiff tenacious clay ; every thing else is washed down into the vales by torrents, cascades, and waterfalls, which are numerous, or by the heavy rains in general ; thus all the lower lands are found to be a loose friable mould, prodigiously fertile—as the want of roads and navigation prevent their being cultivated, they are generally covered with fine grass, but some are forest. Most of the hills and even the rocks, though apparently without earth, are covered with large and strait timber trees of various sorts : so that nothing can be seen more romantic or noble to behold than the mountainous scenes, which are usually formed of a great intermixture of rocks, mountains, woods, and waterfalls, with gleams of vale of the finest verdure. The country from the sea-coast to the hills is various, but generally consists of woods, marshes, swamps, savannahs, or meadows, and cultivated plantations ; many tracts are sandy, but there are none but what produce some article or other spontaneously, which adds to the wealth of the owners, except indeed some of the undrained swamps, which are totally useless.

Among the productions of this island we may reckon sugar, cocoa, indigo, pimento, wild cinnamon, coffee, cotton, tobacco, fustic, red wood, logwood, guaiacum, china root, sarsaparilla, cassia, tamarinds, venilloes, cochineal, mahogany, manchineal, &c. Among these articles, what chiefly claims our notice at present, is the culture of sugar.

The sugar cane is a reed, smooth and jointed, of a shining, greenish, yellow colour. Their size varies according to soil, culture, &c. but the height is generally from four to eight feet, but in some soils they do not rise above two or three feet; in others we sometimes see them nine, ten, or more. In the French islands we are told by Labat, that canes have been known four and twenty feet in length, exclusive of the top and lower joint, and each weighed twenty-four pounds. The largest canes are three or four inches thick, but generally not above an inch.

They are propagated by cuttings; pieces from fifteen to eighteen inches long are cut from the tops of the canes, a little be-

low

low the upper leaves: the more knots or eyes there are, the better. The season of planting is principally August, being the height of the rainy season; but it is a work which is done also in September and October, and even quite to January and February, but not later. Before we proceed with the culture, I shall describe the soils usually chosen for a plantation.

In Jamaica the best soil for sugar is the red brick earth, strong, but not clayey; black mould on clay is excellent; all loose friable lands, not very sandy, will do very well, and are of a value proportioned to their moisture; drained swamps, marshes, and bogs, from which the water is carried clean off, frequently do well. But let me in general remark, that a sugar planter's choice of soil is very similar to that of a good English farmer; so that good land is the same in all countries; the mere stiff clay is not good with either; but all loams are excellent; brushy wet gravels are rejected by both; light sands in a hot climate are worse than in England, black mould is every where excellent; and drained bogs and marshes, wherever found, are generally fertile: thus is there not that mystery in judging of soils in different climates that many would persuade us. Poorer lands in Ja-

maica,

maica, as well as in England, require the affiftance of dunging and other manuring, and the beft yield crops proportioned to fuch management. The richeft foils are frefh woodlands, which when cleared from the wood, and much of the rubbifh burnt upon the land, prove for many years an inexhauftible fund of fertility and wealth to the planter; but thofe woodlands in Jamaica, which are near enough to water-carriage, are moftly taken up and cleared, for if this requifite is wanting, the richeft foils will not pay for culture.

Refpecting the preparation of the ground, it is brought into tillage and rendered clear of weeds; the former is effected by hand-hoeing, and is repeated till the weeds are all deftroyed: the worft is the *withe*, which like couch grafs in England has fuch a vegetative property, that the leaft bit left in the ground grows and multiplies very faft; it climbs up and ftrangles the canes. The roots of trees muft alfo be deftroyed if they are of a kind that fends up fuckers or fhoots; this is done by burning or fcorching them: but other roots they are not attentive to deftroy, for as the tillage is given with hoes, it is not neceffary to extract fuch obftructions as would ftop

 the

the plough. If the land to be planted is freſh, or in great heart, they do not manure, but if it has been long under canes, or out of order, ample manuring is neceſſary. In raiſing dung, they rank among the beſt farmers in the world, and this I take to be owing to the difficulty of procuring it; in England, where the winters enable good huſbandmen to raiſe almoſt any quantity they pleaſe, it is much neglected; but in Jamaica, where they have no winter, and where the heat of the ſun is in general a great hindrance to the work, they are forced to be indefatigable in the work, or they would never effect it.

The refuſe of the ſugar canes aſſiſts them as litter and food for the cattle; the cane tops and leaves of Guinea corn are given the cattle plentifully in pens, where they waſte enough to make litter; the pen is firſt ſpread thickly with marle or earth, generally the former, and by feeding many horſes, aſſes, mules, cows, oxen, and ſwine in them, by their dung and urine and waſte of food they add a layer upon the marle; and prodigiouſly enrich the whole compoſt. Then more marle is carted in, and the cattle fed upon that in the ſame manner; and ſo in ſucceſſion till it is

 wanted

wanted for the plantation, when the cattle are moved into other pens, and the compost is turned over and mixed well together, after which it will in a little time be ready for carrying out. This management of cattle lasts through the whole year.

I must observe upon it, that it is a system which deserves universal imitation in all countries, how far feeding fat cattle in pens would do in summer is not clear, but as to all lean stock, such as draught oxen, horses, cows, young cattle, swine, &c. it would beyond all doubt answer extremely well : marle, chalk, clay, turf, or earth, should, as in Jamaica, be carted into the farm yards and spread in an even layer about them ; upon this should be all the foddering which the farmers bestow upon their cattle; and in summer the system should be continued, by feeding them with grafs or clover, &c. mown and given fresh in racks ; upon this plan their food would go infinitely farther than in the common way, and they would make four times the quantity of dung they do at present. Necessity obliges the planters in Jamaica to pursue a method, which, if the farmers of Britain would pursue, they would certainly find the same great advantages from.

When

When the plantations are upon a clay or a ſtiff ſoil, they mix ſand with the compoſt, by carrying it in and forming a layer in the pens in the ſame manner as marle ; and the good effects have been often experienced. Aſhes of all burnt vegetables are uſed with care, and their effects ſaid to be great.

After the field has been ſufficiently prepared it is marked out, and holes made in regular rows to receive the dung, upon which the canes are planted.   This work is called *holing :* the methods uſed are not all the ſame, nor the diſtances.   Some make the holes four or five feet aſunder, or four by five, and put two or three ſets in a hole ; but the moſt common method is to make trenches from four to eight inches deep, according to the weather, in which they lay the canes, and cover them ; theſe trenches are ſometimes laid out by lines, and ought always to be.   The diſtance between the rows and betwixt the plants in each row may in good ground be about three feet and a half ; in poor worn-out grounds two feet are ſufficient.

But let it here be remarked, that this way of regularly diſpoſing the canes is only followed by the beſt planters ; there are more that plant promiſcuouſly, but it is a very

erroneous

erroneous method, which ought to be exploded.   The land planted in either cafe is in fquares, formed by intervals fifteen feet wide, which crofs the field at right angles, and are of great ufe in feveral inftances; they admit carts to be loaded in harveft with the canes, without going over the ploughed ground, which is very mifchievous to the crop; and they prevent the fpreading of fires, made on purpofe to burn trafh, or accidental ones; they give a free path to the planter to view the ftate of the canes, and the negroes when employed in hoeing them; nor is the land occupied by fuch intervals loft, as peafe, beans, potatoes, and other plants may be cultivated in them, that come off before the fugar canes are cut.

When the canes are about eighteen inches high, which will be in a fortnight or three weeks after planting, they are cleared from weeds, and the foil about them loofened by hand-hoeing; and this operation is repeated two or three times, as it happens, till the plants are arrived at fuch a growth and thicknefs as to kill all weeds by their thick fhade.

The canes are cut when in full maturity, which in dry loofe foils is generally at the

end

end of fourteen or fifteen months after being planted; but in cold clay foils not till
fixteen or feventeen months. They are
cut with hand-bills, as clofe to the ground
as poffible, then cleared from their leaves,
&c. and cut into fhorter pieces, from two
feet and a half to four feet in length. The
chief precaution here is, that the cane be
cut off fmooth, without hacking the root,
which in the dry feafon is of great prejudice to it. The top of the cane, to the diftance of three or four inches below the
flag, fhould be cut off along with the
leaves: fome are accuftomed to fave this
part, and endeavour to turn the whole of
the cane to advantage; but this is a piece
of ill-judged frugality: the top of the cane
is always green, and contains only a crude,
unripe juice, which, mingling with the
reft, will greatly debafe it.

On cutting the canes they are immediately carried to the mill, ufually a windmill, in which being ground between iron
cylinders, the juice is preffed out, and flows
through a tube into a vat; thence it is con-
ducted through a pipe into another vat, and
after that to the cauldron in the boiling
houfe; it is then boiled, and as faft as any
fcum arifes it is taken off; it runs from
this

this boiler through four or five more, smaller and smaller, in all which it is likewise boiled till it becomes a thick glutinous confiftence: when boiling can be carried on no farther, a fermentation is raifed by lime water, which is fubfided by a fmall piece of butter, after which it is taken into coolers, where it dries and granulates. In this operation of boiling, the fires are kept in night and day, and the boilers filled in fucceffion, as faft as empty, with frefh juice; the fewel is dried cane trafh ftacked ready for ufe, and faggots cut from copfes planted on purpofe, or from logwood hedges, which are of a very quick growth.

After the fugar is dried and grannulated, it is put into pots of a fugarloaf form, open at the point, through which aperture the dregs of the fugar falls; thefe dregs are melaffes, or treacle, when it has fufficiently purified itfelf, it is called mufcovado fugar, being then in order to be put into the hogfhead and fhipped off. Some planters chufing to refine it yet farther, cover the fugar in the pots with white tobacco-pipe clay kneaded with water, which, finking through the fugar, carries down more of the melaffes than will go off without it, leaving the fugar much whiter than the mufco-

mufcovado: and at the difcretion of the planter the work is repeated once or twice more, the quality each time increafing in value, but the quantity diminifhing. After this operation it is called *clayed* fugar.

From the melaffes rum is diftilled, by means of fermentation in the common method of gaining all other fpirits; they gain in this ifland from a puncheon to 65 hogfheads of rum to every hogfhead of fugar, but much of their melaffes are fold to New England to be diftilled there.

In the continuation of the culture it is to be obferved, that after the canes are cut the land is hoed quite clean, and mifcarriages among the canes replanted: the fhoots that are fent forth by the ftools are called rattoons, which in due time yield a fecond crop nearly as luxuriant as the firft, but not always fo, the management of which is exactly the fame as of the firft crop. The duration of the plants, however, depends upon the foil; in poor or worn out ones they will have only one rattoon crop, but but in very rich and frefh foils they cut feveral. Labat fays, that in fome of the French iflands they will continue yielding for fifteen or twenty years; but no fuch thing happens generally.

Upon

Upon the fyftem of cutting a crop but twice the planters divide their cane land into three parts. One is fallow, prepared either with the plough or the hoe for planting ; the fecond is the crop in its firft year ; the third is the crop in its fecond year. By this means a third is planted new, and two thirds cut in every period of the growth of the crop ; that part which this year (of fifteen or fixteen months) is fallow, next year is the crop of the firft growth ; that part which this year is the crop of the firft growth will next year be the rattoon crop ; and that part which this year is the rattoon crop, will next year be fallow. Cane grounds are in general from ten to twentyfive acres each piece. The whole fyftem is transferred continually from old ground to new, according to circumftances.

The buildings upon a plantation are very confiderable and expenfive ; they confift principally of a manfion-houfe, windmill, boiling-houfe, furnaces, ftore-houfes, fheds, &c. the furniture of which, fuch as cylinders, vats, coppers, pipes, tubes, refervoirs, coolers, &c. are coftly.

Before I give any account of the expences and profit of the culture, I fhall make fome obfervations on the effential faults with

which

which their agriculture in this article a-
bounds.   Firſt, the preparation of the
ground, which is generally fallowed with
hoes; though ploughs are uſed by a few
planters, yet the number is inconſiderable.
In clearing a piece of freſh ground, they
deſtroy the wood in the manner practiſed in
the colonies, that is, ſaw it off and leave
the ſtump to rot in the ground: this effectually precludes the plough.   The hoeing
culture is more trivial than can eaſily be
credited; for in ſtrength and efficacy it is
not comparable to the ſame operation given
by the farmers in England to ſeveral crops.
Three, four, or five hundred negroes have
been ſeen hoeing a piece of forty acres;
they cut about an inch deep, ſometimes if
the ſoil is looſe a little deeper, and at others
not half an inch; if the planter attains any
depth that approaches that of ploughing,
the expence he is at to get it is enormous.
Now it ſhould not be forgotten, that the
cane roots at a depth proportioned to the
looſened mould upon ſoils that have any
tenacity, indeed in very friable ſandy loams,
or looſe hazle mould, the roots ſtrike much
deeper than the hoe has been, or they
would not thrive at all; and to remedy
theſe evils it is that holing is practiſed, in
which

which they dig small holes where the canes
are to be set, to receive the dung and cane
set: but such methods in every article of
husbandry throughout the world are bad:
the roots of all crops should be encouraged
to spread over the whole land, instead of
being confined to spots where the dung is
put, which is always the consequence of
not dunging the whole land. Then comes
the planting, in which the planters exclude
every thing but the hand-hoe, by setting
the canes promiscuously; those that plant
in rows, use no other tool; the consequence
of which is, that the keeping the spaces
between the plants loose, in good order,
and free from weeds, is all performed by
the negroes with their hand-hoes, which is
just such management as to use no other
tool between the rows of a field of cabbages
in England, planted wide enough to admit
of horse-hoeing; which in this country
would be an expence of ten or twelve shillings for very badly performing an operation, which might be very well done for
half a crown.

The two errors I have here disclosed are
very essential ones, and in the conduct of
them render such prodigious flocks of negroes necessary, as eat amazingly into the
profit

profit of the planter.   Hence therefore a-
rifes the neceffity of pointing out methods
whereby they may efcape fuch expences,
and at the fame time execute their work in
a much fuperior manner.

In the preparation of my ground, I would
carry the ideas of the improved hufbandry
of England into that of fugar in Jamaica;
I would, in clearing my frefh land, remove
all obflacles which might ftop the plough,
fuch as roots or large ftones; this expence
would be well repaid by my fucceffive advantages.   I would then plough the fallow
of a depth proportioned to that of the foil;
in rich deep lands I would go a foot, but
in fhallower foils eight inches: before the
laft ploughing I would fpread the dung or
compoft all over the land; and immediately turn it in by the laft ploughing, leaving
the furface, when the work was completed, flat on dry foils, and ridged on wet
ones.

In the next place, my ploughman fhould
draw furrows by the eye, as ftrait as an ar-
row, at the diftance of three, four, or five
feet, according to the diftance of the rows
of canes, which fhould be regulated by
the fertility of the foil: the richer the land
the greater the diftance.   In thefe furrows

I would lay the cane sets, and cover them by drawing mould over them by negroes with hand-hoes : let us suppose the rows equally distant four feet asunder. As soon as the plants were a foot high, I would run a Berkshire shim, the cutting plate three feet wide, through the intervals; it should cut about two inches deep, in order to cut down the weeds, and loosen the surface of the land : at the same time the rows should be hand-weeded. But if the soil was stoney, instead of the Berkshire, the Kentish shim should be used, which has three tri-angular shares instead of one flat one in the other.

These operations should be repeated often enough to keep the soil loose : when the plants were come to that point of growth that made earthing proper, I would run a double-winged plough, the mould-board of which extends or contracts at pleasure, through each interval, the wings so ex-tended as just to throw a surge of mould along the roots of the plants. Such a plough will perform that work better than any hand-hoe ; and by thus earthing once or twice, after other operations of horse-hoeing, the well tilled earth of the inter-vals, after being well mixed and intimately

united

united with the dung, would be thrown to the roots to supply them with nourishment as their growth demanded it.

After a trench was thus opened in the middle of each interval, I should go in with shims that took a narrower cut, in order to keep pulverizing the interval till the growth of the canes shut out the horses. After the crop was cut in the usual manner, another great advantage would arise; by laying them in bundles on the top of every third or fourth ridge, carts constructed so as the wheels should spread eight feet, and go each in a trench with the horses in that between them, the carts would be admitted to every part of the plantation without doing the least injury to the stools or roots of the cane: it is upon this system that farmers in England carry cabbages, &c. from off wet lands in winter without poaching.   Another benefit arising from this mode of culture, would be the following operation.   After the plantation was cleared, I should widen the wings of the double plough, and passing it through every interval, throw a ridge of mould over the cane stools, covering them up, which with such an implement is very easily performed, and very completely in the effect: this

K 2

prac-

practice, performed with hoes at a great expence, has in several of our islands been found excellent; consequently this compendious way would do it in a manner much superior, and at a twentieth of the expence.

If any considerate person reflects upon this system, in comparison of the method of hand-work now in use, which is certainly the most expensive conduct that is known in any part of the world—he will, I am confident, allow that the saving of expence would be prodigious, and the culture at the same time performed in a manner far superior. The objections that will be made to it (for what plan was ever thought of, against which objections could not be started?) I can easily suppose may be numerous. Those which I have heard, that carry any appearance of reason with them, are the following.

First, that the number of mules, &c. which would be necessary, could not be kept without a greater expence than the present number of negroes. I must be allowed to deny this, as a circumstance perfectly incredible: let it be remembered, that most of the planters are obliged to keep very large herds of cattle merely for the

pur-

purpofe of making dung, why not therefore let a larger proportion of them be draught cattle for the purpofe of tillage? A well-fed beaft that works will make as good dung as a beaft that does not work; but granting that a larger ftock of cattle would be neceffary, the quantity of dung raifed would be proportioned, and that advantage, where dung is fo valuable, would go far to pay the extra expence. But why not appropriate a larger part of the eftate to the production of food for cattle? I do not apprehend there is any part of the world in which cattle pays fo well, and the want of food is rather owing to the negligence of the cultivator than denied by the climate. Cane tops at one feafon afford the moft luxuriant fupply in the world —and ftacks of them are made by way of hay, which yield a plenty through fome months: the leaves of Indian corn are alfo made the fame ufe of, and found of high advantage: but the returns made in Jamaica by Scotch grafs, as they commonly call it, the greater panic grafs, is prodigious. The quantity of its produce exceeds that of any other fodder whatfoever, and yields in value a produce to the amount fometimes of fifty or fixty pounds an acre.

K 3 When

When such ample products are to be had, with the assistance in many parts of Jamaica of large savannahs or meadows, and barley, pease, and beans imported from North America at a very moderate price, it must surely be evident enough, that any quantity of cattle might be kept for the advantageous purpose of substituting horse or mule tillage for that of hand-work—and the profit attending the practice would certainly be immense.

But let us suppose the expence attending cattle greater than it really is, are we to be allowed nothing in the saving of negroes, that most expensive mode of labour? Two mules or oxen and one man with a shim will do more work in a day than twenty good negroes; but who will be so hardy as to assert, that the former can possibly cost the planter as much as the latter: in the earthing up the plants three mules or oxen, a double mould-board plough, and two men, will do more work than thirty-five negroes. In the preparation of the field a plough, two, three, or four mules, and one or two men will, supposing the depth of tillage the same, perform more work than an hundred negroes; but they will not be able to go the depth at all, and therefore the superiority

ority is the greater : if a lefs depth is ftirred, the plough, or a wide fhim of four feet, would do a proportionate quantity of land. Now can any perfons be fo fenfelefs or pre-judiced, as to fuppofe that the faving in negroes would not infinitely more than pay for the increafe of expence in cattle?

Secondly, it is objected that the nature of the climate is fuch as will not admit of the tillage and horfe-hoeing I have recom-mended ; that the rains are fo amazingly impetuous, and the fucceffive fun-fhine fo powerful, as to bind many foils into a hard cement, which could not be wrought by the tools I have defcribed : but in anfwer to this, I appeal to the common fenfe of every underftanding perfon, whether horfe-work will not prove more effectual than the weak exertion of the negroes hoes ? The harder the foil is bound, the lefs able are they to make an impreffion on it : if the land was like a baked hard trodden path, the hoes would be ufelefs ; but no turn-pike road in England is too hard to be torn in pieces by horfe-work. But the affertion is not true ; cane grounds fo hard as to be difficultly worked by horfe-hoes, would be in fuch order as none but a floven could bear ; the crop would be nothing ; it is a

K 4

plant

plant that requires as loose friable a soil as any other, and always in that condition: stiff soils must be rendered open with much dung and compost; and a soil that is well manured can never bind in any climate. As to such degrees of baking as really happen, small variations in the horse-hoeing would answer: I would, for instance, be provided with a scarificator or plough of coulters alone to] spread two or three feet of ground, and cut it into stripes, which would destroy all that caking of the surface which the objection supposes, and which would prepare it for the other operations I have proposed. Another tool proper to be provided with is a spiky roller, weighing several tons, about eight feet long, for working the fallow; and also a small globular one to work in the trenches of the intervals between the rows of canes; these three instruments would effectually answer all such objections as this.

Thirdly, it is answered, that the distances of the rows necessary for the admission of the horse-hoes I have described would be too great for the production of a full crop of canes;—I am sensible that the majority of planters set their canes in the promiscuous method, at nearer distances

than

than I have suppofed; but let me obferve, that suppofing fuch practice judicious and neceffary, yet is it no objection to my fyftem, fince I could horfe-hoe wherever the negroes could hand-hoe. Englifh farmers, upon much the fame principles, affert, that four or five bufhels of beans fhould be fown broad caft over an acre, and the men afterwards to hoe amongft them as well as they can; this affertion, in oppofition to the Kentifh culture of that vegetable, is like quoting the ideas of the common Jamaica planters in anfwer to my argument. The moment the growth of a vegetable is known, every perfon, the leaft converfant in the different modes of hufbandry, muft be able to decide at once whether the horfe-hoeing mode is well calculated for its culture; and when the fugar-cane is defcribed, that is a ftrong reed, an inch diameter, and from four to eight feet high, will they not laugh at promifcuous planting and hand-hoeing which, comparatively fpeaking, is like hand-hoeing a grove of oaks. The article of culture known in England which moft refembles fugar, is beans, and all our farmers who cultivate that crop to confiderable profit agree, that the drill and

horfe-

horfe-hoe is the only mode which can be attended with great fuccefs.

And here I fhall make a few remarks on the conduct of the Jamaica planters in the management of their negroes, which may very juftly be ranked among the errors of their hufbandry.

In the account I gave of the culture of tobacco and rice by negroes, I had occafion to obferve, that the ftock of Blacks was there kept up by natural increafe; and that the planters were all in the method of tafking their flaves; that is, they allotted them a portion of work every day, which the overfeers attended to fee well done, but never exacted a larger portion of labour. The management of Jamaica is very different: no tafk is there fet, confequently the men know no end of their labour; they are followed throughout their work by the lower overfeers with whips, exactly in the fame manner as horfes are in England, or if there is a diffe-ence, it is that the negroes are more hardly ufed. The confequence of this fyftem is feen in the decreafe of the ftock; fo that a plantation in Jamaica, which employs one hundred flaves, requires an annual fupply of feven to keep up the number. This deftruction

cannot

cannot be owing to climate, becaufe the coaft of Guinea is very fimilar, and the heat is never oppreffive to them ; it is owing merely to exceffive work and bad ufage.   Nothing can be clearer to common fenfe than the evidence of this fact.

The expences, profit and lofs of the fugar culture in this ifland have never been laid before the public with the leaft degree of accuracy ; I have, by making repeated enquiries among Jamaica planters and agents, gained many particulars, which will enable me to give a very fatisfactory eftimate, and fuch as, I am clear, will yield more information than has by any other perfon been publifhed.

Calculation of a confiderable plantation in Jamaica.

		£.
600 acres of land purchafed at 11l. per acre,		6600
Two windmills,	1000	
Refervoir, &c.	260	
Boiling-houfe, coppers, &c.	1350	
Curing-houfe,	460	
The ftove, &c.	180	
The ftill-houfe, &c.	180	
Sheds,	90	
Stab'es, cattle-pens, &c.	230	
Manfion and three other houfes,	1600	
	————	5350
Implements of all forts exclufive of fixtures,		500
10 negroes at an average of 120l.		1200

Carried over, £. 13,650

	Brought forward £. 13,650
167 negroes at 50l.	8,350
100 head of cattle, 15l.	1,500
100 ditto at 10l.	1,000
30 mules at 25l.	750
100 swine, 15s.	75
	£. 25,325

One year's expence.

Overseer, managers, drivers, clerks, agent, farrier, &c.	650
9 negroes,	450
Expences on 177 ditto at 3l.	531
Repairs of buildings,	200
Wear and tear,	100
Cattle,	150
Lumber,	200
Taxes,	100
Sundries,	119
	2,500
	£. 27,825
Interest at 5 per cent.	1,391
	£. 29,216

If borrowed in Jamaica, the interest will be 8 per cent.

Product.

400 hogsheads of sugar of various sizes, but at an average of 15l.	6,000
Rum, 270 hhds.	2,434
	£. 8,434

Expence.

Sundries as above,	2,500
Profit,	5,934

which is 20l. 6s. per cent. on 29,216l.

This

This upon a very moderate average : the intereſt per cent. will vibrate from 15 to 30 ; and the planter, if he is very ſkilful, will carry this 20 to 25 at leaſt ; but he muſt in either caſe reſide on the ſpot. And here it is neceſſary to remark, that leſs intereſt for a capital cannot be ſuppoſed in a climate highly inſalubrious to European conſtitutions, and which is expoſed to the moſt dreadful accidents of earthquakes and hurricanes : ſome allowance, indeed, is made for theſe in the preceding calculations, but ſuch cannot be adequate, and excludes articles of entire deſtruction : that the intereſt is not leſs, we may alſo judge from the planters reſiding in England, leaving their eſtates to the management of agents, &c. and yet making from four to ten per cent. of their capital, according to their conduct and ſagacity, which, all things conſidered, is a great proof that the culture muſt be very profitable. And I ſhould further obſerve, that if more enlightened ideas were introduced into the modes of cultivating the cane, the profit would be far more conſiderable ; I have no doubt but 40 per cent. on the capital might be made with as much or more eaſe than 25 at preſent. And the reader ſhould note in this caſe of the ſugar culture in Jamaica, as

well

well as in all the branches of hufbandry on
the continent, that the part of the capital
employed in the purchafe of the eftate pays
as great intereft as the reft of it, which is
employed in the cultivation ; an advantage
no where to be met with in Europe.   If
a perfon engages in hufbandry in England
he may make a good profit on his farming, but as to the purchafe of his eftate he
will not make above 2½ or 3 per cent. by
it.   Upon the whole I am inclined to believe, that the agriculture of fugar might
be, of all other branches, the moft profitable ; and fo it ought, for men who facri-
fice themfelves with fuch fortunes, in fuch
a climate, ought furely to make a larger
intereft of their money than if they were
employed in their native, or fome wholefome climate *.

Befides fugar, this ifland produces fome
other ftaples which are or might be of very
great importance.   Among thefe cotton is
a confiderable article, the export amount-

---

* Since this was written a New Hiftory of Jamaica
has appeared, which makes the intereft 10 per cent.
that is, 6 for intereft paid, and 4 for the planter ; but
that this is very inadequate, every perfon, on reflection,
muft allow, for the planter muft very foon be in gaol : if
the circumftance of planters refiding in England, and
making 6 per cent. be confidered, it will certainly be allowed, that on the fpot it ought to be 20.

ing

ing to about 2000 bags; coffee, but nothing like what the French make in their
iflands; pimento; mahogany; cocoa was
once a very great article, but it has much
declined; indigo was once the ftaple of the
ifland, but the attention now given to fugar has rendered all other articles of but
fmall comparative account.

The following is an account of their exports.

		£.
48,515 hogfheads of fugar at 15l.	-	727,825
Rum and melaffes,	- -	433,591
Cotton 1626 bags at 10l. 15s.	-	17,479
Coffee 220 cafks,	- -	2,342
Pimento 438,000 lb.	- - -	15,632
Mahogany,	- - - -	17,858
Sundries, as logwood nicarago, fuftic, lig- um vi·æ, cocoa, ginger, canella, or win- ter's bark, peruvian bark, balfams, indigo, aloes, bides, ftaves, dry goods, bullion, &c.	}	32,140
Total, *		1,246,868

This is a prodigious fum for an ifland to
produce, the cultivated part of which does
not exceed three or four hundred thoufand
acres; but as the whole contains four
millions, it ought to be a fpur to our government to remedy the monftrous evil of
fuch a proportion of it remaining wafte:
much is certainly incapable of culture, but
the tracts of fine foil which would yield

---

* *Political Effays,* p. 286.

fugar

fugar, and the yet greater tracts which might be most profitably applied to the culture of other staples, are so many nuisances to the public, which deserve the most serious consideration: the monopolies of wastes are infinitely detrimental, and ought not only to be guarded against in future, but even remedied in past.

Settlements might be made most advantageously upon the lands in this island not yet granted away, if not for the culture of fugar, at least for those of other staples, such as cotton, indigo, cocoa, &c. which require small capitals, and would prove very profitable. A little management in government would bring such culture into more repute, and spread it through those waste tracts which are such a reproach to the nation.

There have of late years been a few very important improvements made in particular spots; but these, though reflecting great honour on individuals, are not of such extent as to remedy the evil of so large a portion of the island remaining uncultivated. Among these one deserves particular attention; it is the improvement Mr. K— wrought.

That gentleman purchased a swamp for a thousand pounds, which was at the time

of

of his purchaſe reckoned a very large price for it: his firſt work was to ſurvey it carefully in order to mark out the drains that would be neceſſary to lay it dry. Having performed this with as much accuracy as poſſible, he cut a main drain, through the center of the ſwamp, into a navigable river, wide enough for canoes to paſs and repaſs; by properly directing this drain, he found ſo much immediate ſervice from it as to give him the greateſt hope of ſucceſs; this was a very heavy and expenſive work to him, for at the time that he firſt planned the deſign of a drain, he had his eye on the convenience of a navigation in the future cultivation of the land.

When this main cut was finiſhed, he began croſs cuts, through the ſwamp on each ſide the main drain and communicating with it; theſe were of a ſomething leſs dimenſion, but yet ſufficient for navigating, and as faſt as they were finiſhed the ſwamp became nearly dry, and to appearance ſound land: but this was rather deceitful, for upon the ſubſidence of the ſurface of the ſwamp he found it neceſſary to ſink all his drains, which was a work of much trouble and expence.

Having completed a conſiderable part of the draining, he erected ſugar works, with

all the neceſſary buildings, upon the moſt
convenient ſpot for that part of the ſwamp.
which was firſt dry, purchaſed negroes,
and all things neceſſary, among which,
however, cattle made but a ſmall article.
In this reſpect he made a wonderful uſe of
his navigable croſs cuts; by multiplying
them from croſs to croſs he made them fully
anſwer all the purpoſes of roads, and intervals between the diviſions of the cane
grounds: thus every article of *carriage* in
the plantation was by this means transferred from negroes and mules to boats, even
to that of the bundles of canes to the
mills, &c. This contrivance rendered very.
few cattle neceſſary: reſpecting the object
of raiſing manure, for which ſo many
planters are obliged to ſacrifice many other
intereſts, this gentleman, from examining
the ſoil of the ſwamp accurately, found it
of ſo fertile and promiſing an appearance,
that none would be neceſſary for many
years, as the land looked as if the canes
would rather be too luxuriant in their
growth than not enough ſo; but as he alſo
knew that ſuch a quality is continually on
the decreaſe after the land becomes cultivated, he made an ample proviſion for cattle, by bringing into tillage with the plough
ſome of the larger diviſions, and ſowing
them

them with Scotch grafs (panic), and other plants, fo that the profitable part of cattle-keeping might at any time be practifed, without the expence of fupporting them merely for their work and dung; there is no part of the world in which cattle for provifions anfwer better than in Jamaica: this fyftem therefore was anfwering every beneficial purpofe that could be wifhed. It was executed by degrees as the other works went on.

When drained, the foil of the fwamp was found to be a light hazel mould inclining to a peat, about eighteen inches deep, on a bed of ftiff loam five feet deep, and under that a white clay: nothing could fhew greater figns of inexhauftible fertility than the experiments made with feveral plants on the firft divifion that was completely drained.

The firft eftablifhment for the purpofe of planting was that of 100 negroes, with all the buildings requifite, and which was began before the firft work of draining was in all parts finifhed. Nothing could exceed the crop which was reaped, and contrary to expectation the fugars proved of a very fine grain. Every working hand made three hogfheads, which was a produce that

is

is but rarely met with. Every year, for six succeſſive ones, Mr. K—— increaſed his ſtock of negroes conſiderably, and the produce did not fail him in any one of them ; ſo that the immenſe receipts from his plantation repaid him part of the ex- pence of his drainage : when it was finiſh- ed, three hundred negroes more were thrown to planting, and the ſugars they made were ſuppoſed to exceed in quantity per head thoſe of any other plantation in the iſland.

Upon this great ſucceſs attending the undertaking, many perſons were deſirous of purchaſing parts of the ſwamp in order to convert them in like manner into ſugar plantations ; but Mr. K—— was deſirous of having only one trouble with the whole, and offered it to ſale to any perſon or per- ſons that would bargain for the whole pur- chaſe. The event of the affair is perhaps the moſt extraordinary inſtance of improve- ment that was ever known : the whole, that is land, buildings, negroes, &c. were ſold for ONE HUNDRED THOUSAND POUNDS.

This vaſt ſum was to be paid by inſtall- ments, bearing intereſt 8 per cent. till paid. In the valuation the land was reckoned at 6ol. an acre, and the negroes at 6ol. each, one with another. The following account

is

is not absolutely accurate, but the particulars are not far from the truth.

		£.
Produce of the sale, - - -		100,000
Profit on the planting, after the improvement, during seven years, - - -	}	32,000
	Total receipt, £.	132,000

Purchase, - - £.	1000	
Drainage, expence in negroes, &c.	27500	
Buildings, - -	13000	
Negroes, - - -	14700	
Implements, - -	2080	
Cattle and fundries, - -	7500	
		65,780
Clear profit, - - -		66,220

It is very much to the honour of this sensible gentleman that he had sagacity enough to understand the advantages which might be made by draining such a swamp: his plan, before the execution, was treated as a visionary scheme by all the old planters, who laughed at the project, and foretold the ruin of the undertaker. The work turning out so successfully will have most beneficial consequences: there are other swamps in the island equally accessible, of the same soil, and as easily to be drained; all which circumstances are clear from the almost immediate rise in the price of such lands upon the success of Mr. K——; and some other undertakings of the same

L 3   kind

kind have been begun, from which there is reafon to expect a fimilar fuccefs.

Improvements of this and other kinds are more wanting in Jamaica than in any of our other iflands, for here we have the largeft territory we poffefs in the Weft Indies. Not above a fourth of this ifland being patented, and not a fourth of that fourth under any fort of culture, ought to inftigate men to more activity, and a more acute examination of the diftricts in this ifland, which have been hitherto rejected or neglected. Doubtlefs there are many extenfive tracts among them, which might be applied to fugar, if planters would, like the gentleman who executed the above improvement, apply to raifing that commodity in new methods, varied and adapted to circumftances in the foil and fituation not ufual in the old plantations.

CHAP.

CHAP. XXX.

BARBADOES.

*Climate — Soil — Productions — Exports —
Observations on the culture of sugar in
Barbadoes.*

THIS little island, deservedly one of
the most famous in the world, is
situated in 13 degrees north latitude:
it is about twenty-five miles in length,
and in breadth fourteen, containing one
hundred and forty square miles, and by
supposition 100,000 acres. The climate is
in some respects preferable to that of Jamaica, and in others inferior: the face of
the country on the coast is higher and more
free from low grounds and swamps, much
of it being quite walled with rocks; this
makes the air drier, and consequently
healthier; but the nights are hotter from
the want of the land breeze, which in Jamaica is owing to the mountains, and Barbadoes having none cannot possess this advantage; but upon the whole, the climate

L 4

is

is reckoned superior to that of the other island.

The soil is generally a light hazel loam, of a dark or reddish colour, with exceptions for stiffer tracts; it is in every spot of the island capable of bearing some valuable product or other; contrary to Jamaica, every inch being under cultivation. Of their products, sugar is the grand article; indigo they still cultivate; ginger is a very good article; they have some cotton and pimento. Among their other products they reckon oranges lemons, citrons, pomegranates, pine apples, guavas, plantains, cocoa nuts, Indian figs, prickly pears, melons, &c. In general, the produce of the island is as rich as any other in the West Indies.

The great value of it to this country will appear clearly from the progress of its trade and export. In 1650, which was only twenty years after its first settlement, it contained between 30 and 40,000 white inhabitants, and a yet larger number of blacks. Upon the Restoration the colony granted 4½ per cent. duty on its exports towards maintaining the forts and fortifications, but which has been shamefully misapplied to other purposes.

It

It is very remarkable, that the people of this island spent forty years in raising indigo, ginger, cotton, and tobacco ; and then learnt of the Portugueze at Brazil the art of planting the sugar cane, and this acquisition in no longer space than ten years totally changed the face of affairs in the island : the planters who were before in but low circumstances, became remarkably wealthy.

In 1676 the island was at its meridian ; by a calculation that was made with great exactness there were then found in it 50,000 white people of all sorts, and 80,000 negroes : this was a degree of population truly amazing. The author of the *European Settlements in America* justly observes, that Holland itself, or perhaps even the best inhabited parts of China, were never peopled to the same proportion ; and Dr. Campbell remarks, with equal truth, that never any colony of ours, or any other nation, was so populous as this : and to make this still clearer to an English reader, we shall observe, that Barbadoes is rather less than the county of Rutland, the smallest county in England, and that according to the highest computation, the number of people in that county in 1676 did not exceed 20,000.

But

But this may be made ftill clearer by comparing that whole ifland with this in point of extent; for if England and Wales taken together confift of near forty millions of acres, then if they were as populous as Barbadoes, they ought to contain fifty millions of people—whereas Sir William Petty, who was a very able man in computation, and is thought not to have undervalued this country, but rather the contrary, never reckoned the people higher than eight millions, which fhews what a vaft difproportion there is between the peopling of the two countries. But to proceed farther ftill; the fame great man afferts, that in Holland and Zealand, which are looked upon to be the beft peopled countries in Europe, there are a million of fouls inhabiting about as many acres; and confequently it appears from hence, that even this country was not fo well peopled as Barbadoes.

At prefent the number of whites are computed to be near 30,000, but the flaves amount to about 100,000. About the fame time that the population was at its height, fo alfo was its wealth. In the year 1661 King Charles II. created on the fame day thirteen baronets in Barbadoes, none of

them

them having lefs than one thoufand pounds, and fome of them ten thoufand pounds a year. At this time their trade actually maintained four hundred fail of fhips, one with another of 150 tons; their annual exported produce in fugar, indigo, ginger, cotton, &c. amounted to upwards of 350,000l. and their circulation cafh at home was 200,000l. Thefe are facts that may be depended upon, that deferve in every refpect the greateft confideration, and that plainly demonftrate at once the great value of this ifland, and the prodigious confequence of our plantations in general *.

Let us exclude all that accrued from Barbadoes to the people of England before the Reftoration, and eftimate its produce from 1660 to 1760 at 16,000 hogfheads of fugar, which make 12,000 ton annually, and omitting entirely the rum or fpirits, melaffes, cotton, ginger, aloes, and all the other commodities of the ifland, eftimating this at 20l. a ton, it will amount to 240,000 l. per ann. or 24,000,000 l. in the courfe of the century either gained or faved to this nation, which, confidering

----

* *Harris's Voyages*, vol. ii. p. 256.

that

that Barbadoes is not bigger than the *Isle of Wight*, must appear a most amazing sum; and yet in proof of the modesty of this computation it would be easy to name a very intelligent author, who before the close of the last century affirmed, that no less than thirty millions had been gained by our possession of Barbadoes at the time he wrote. But though his zeal might possibly carry him a little too far then, there is not now the least room to question that the very best judges, by which is to be understood those who are best versed in these kind of things, and who also best understand this trade, would more readily concur in fixing the amount of our profits during the period before assigned, at thirty than at twenty-four millions *.

As to the present produce of this island, the following is the best account we have had.

		£.
Sugar, 20,266 hogsheads, at 15l.	-	303,990
Rum and melasses,	-	203,992
Sundry articles, such as ginger, cotton, indigo, sweetmeats, aloes, cassia,	}	30,000
		£. 537,982

---

* *Considerations on the Sugar Trade*, p. 27.

But

But in this account is included all the rum that can be made from the total of melaffes : I think that article too high : if 100,000l. is allowed for rum, the total will amount to above 400,000l. a year. The cuftom-houfe books for 1763 make the Britifh imports from this ifland above 300,000 l. if to this North America is added, the total, probably, would be as large as above mentioned.

Confidering that the export of only 400,000l. a year amounts to 4l. annually for every acre in the whole ifland, and as towns, roads, water, rocks, &c. which yield no produce muft neceffarily reduce the 100,000 acres confiderably, it would amount probably to 4l. 10s. upon the cultivated part of the foil : and confidering further that a large portion of the food of the people, both whites and blacks, is raifed upon the ifland, and alfo that the planters are obliged to keep many cattle, the principal part of whofe fubfiftence grows there, it will be evident that a large part of it is applied to other ufes befides yielding the exported produce : further confidering that a third part of all the cane grounds is fallow every year, and it will then appear that the part of the ifland actu-

6 ally

ally yielding exportable produce is small in comparison of the whole, I should not imagine that more than 25,000 acres in that situation, consequently the produce per acre is 15l. But whatever produce is taken, most certainly agriculture never flourished in any country in the world equally with what it has done here : for many years it has been on the decline, not in the value of its produce, for that is as great as ever, but in the *quantity* of it : in the last century they made, it has been asserted, more sugar than at present, consequently the real product of the island was once greater even than the above account : it is the rise in the prices of their commodities that has kept up the total value of their products. But let me slightly remark, that I recollect no particular accounts of the exports in the last century, which shews any decline at present even in the quantity.

Relative to the culture of the sugar-cane in this island, there is no material difference between their method and that described under the last article. But the Barbadoes planter labours under greater difficulties and larger expences. The soil of the island has been so long employed in yielding crops,

crops, that it requires more dung than the fresh grounds in Jamaica; it is not worn out, as many superficial writers have asserted, for a good soil never wears out; bad management in the culture of sugar, as well as in any other branch of culture, will exhaust the soil, and it will be inferior till good management restores it. But as long as the planters conduct themselves upon rational principles they will find the produce of their island great as ever. As to the fertility of fresh lands, it is exhausted much sooner than commonly imagined: planters are too apt to take liberties with such land, and pour in a succession of crops in haste to reap the benefit of the goodness of the land, without giving it sufficient rest, or changing their system: when this is the case, the fertility of new lands is gone in ten or dozen years, and they will be even inferior to neighbouring tracts that have been in culture a century, but managed upon good principles.

In these there is nothing of greater importance than manuring; this they understand very well in Barbadoes, where every planter keeps considerable stocks of cattle merely with a view to the dung they raise him. They confine them to pens, in which

they

they are fed, that all their dung, urine, and wafte of food may be retained in a bed of marle, which they fpread in each pen ; at certain feafons they mix the heap well together, and find it a mafs of manure admirably calculated for the improvement of their land ; fuperior even to what a fimilar quantity of dung alone would be. This I attribute to the marle retaining the juices of the dung, and parting with them gradually to the roots of the fucceffive crops. Nor has the fun (which in this hot climate is a material point) near fuch power to exhale the beneficial parts of the manure when united with an abforbent earth, as it has upon dung alone.

The great difficulty of the planters is in fupporting cattle fufficient for the purpofe of raifing the requifite body of manure : the fmallnefs of the ifland, which is fo crammed with people, denies them the extenfive favannahs or meadows which they poffefs in Jamaica ; their crops of Scotch grafs are not near fo great, nor have they the land to fpare for it of the right fort ; their dependance therefore is principally on cane-tops and the leaves of Indian corn, both which they feed with green, and alfo make into large ricks in hay. But if they

would

would be perfuaded to cultivate lucerne,
they would furely reap great benefit from
it in the fupport of their cattle, than which
they have no object more effential.   The
length of the root would fecure the plant
from the fun, probably when its beams
were moft violent, and afford, through the
heats of fummer, frefh crops of green food
every month regularly for the cattle : this
is what they moft want, for at that feafon
all their grafs is burnt up, and, contrary
to the practice of colder climates, the fummer is the feafon for feeding with dry fodder, and the winter that for green.   Lucerne therefore would prove of the higheft
advantage to them.

Another article in their management,
which might be much improved, is the arrangement of their grounds for crops : the
cane grounds they keep under canes for
ever, with only the affiftance of fallow and
dung.   But on the contrary, the canes
fhould be planted by turns on all the lands
of a plantation : fometimes a field fhould
be under grafs ; fometimes yams, plantains, garden plants, cotton, indigo, &c.
&c. at others fallow ; and at others under
canes, &c.   This change of crop would
be of great fervice, the canes would in the

VOL. II.   M   fuccef-

ſucceſſion have the advantage of what may,
to them, be called freſh land ; and leſs
dung would do than when they are planted
always in the ſame ſpot.

Nothing hardly is more profitable to a
planter than yams, potatoes, and plantains ; and theſe three crops have the ſame
effect in meliorating the ſoil and preparing
it by their ſhade, for exhauſting crops, as
potatoes, clover, peaſe, &c. have in England : nothing therefore can be better management than to make a change of product the foundation for ſugar.   Let graſs
lands, when of a proper age, be broken up
for thoſe roots, &c. and let the roots be
ſucceeded by canes ; after canes, other ſtaples, corn, &c. then fallow, and upon that
canes again, then graſſes, &c.   By means
of ſuch a ſyſtem the food for cattle would
be much increaſed, all the lands of an eſtate
kept in good order, the graſſes ſuperior to
the common ones, and the canes from ſuch
a change would yield more plentifully.

CHAP.

CHAP. XXXI.

LEEWARD ISLANDS.

*Antigua—St. Chriſtopher's—Nevis—Mont-
ſerrat — Barbuda —Anguilla — Climate
—Soil—Products — Exports —Agriculture—Obſervations.*

ANTIGUA, or Antego, as it is ſometimes written, lies in 16 degrees 11
minutes north latitude. It is circular in
its form, being about twenty miles in diameter and ſixty in circumference, containing about 70,000 acres of land. The climate is inferior to that of Barbadoes, being hotter, and is reckoned more ſubject to
hurricanes. Only a part of it is yet cleared, being in many places covered with its
original woods ; a circumſtance to the benefit of the preſent planters in many reſpects. The face of the country in one reſpect is very ſingular ; there is neither a
brook, rivulet, or ſpring in the whole
iſland, which obliges the inhabitants to depend on artificial ponds, ciſterns, and re-
ſervoirs of water for all their uſes. Threaten-

ing

ing as this was originally, experience has removed the difficulties which flowed from it, and they have been able to fupply themfelves very regularly with this neceffary of life.

The foil of the ifland is generally fandy, but not therefore infertile; on the contrary, there are nowhere more flourifhing fugar plantations to be met with than in this ifland; for there is a loamy mixture in the fand which keeps it from burning; and the reddifh earths, though fandy, are found excellent cane lands.   The produce of the ifland has been thus ftated :

	£.
15,500 hhds. fugar at 15l. -	232,500
Rum, - - -	63,933
Sundry articles, - -	10,000
	£. 306,433

Thefe fundry articles are ginger, a little indigo and tobacco, fruits and other things, common in all the iflands; but the quantities are but fmall, and I fhould rather think 10,000 l. too great an allowance for them.   We have no ifland in the Weft Indies, Jamaica and the ceded ones excepted, that is capable of fuch improvement as Antigua: indeed the induftry of its

owners

owners has carried their agriculture to a much greater height than it was ever expected they would attain; for the time was when Antigua sugars could find no market in Britain, but were sold at low prices to Hamburgh and the North. A very great change has been made since, for at present we do not often see finer muscovado sugar than comes from this island. The improvements to be made are principally those of bringing into culture the lands yet waste or underwood; most of which, it is not doubted, but will produce good sugar, perhaps from freshness superior to the old plantations; if this measure was well effected, we should annually receive from Antigua 20,000 hogsheads of sugar, and a much greater quantity of rum would be made than is at present, proportionably to the quantity of sugar.

St. Christopher's is situated in 17 deg. 25 min. north latitude; it is about seventy-five miles in circuit, yet are there not in it above 24,000 acres of land that can ever be brought to yield sugar, for part of it is covered with very high mountains. The soil is remarkable for producing the finest sugars in the West Indies; it is a light, ha-

zel

zel mould on brick earth, of a surprising fertility, which soil is justly supposed to be of all others the best for producing sugar. The climate is as agreeable and temperate as any other island in that hot latitude. The products are,

	£.
10,000 hhds. of sugar at 15l. a hhd.	150,000
Rum, - - -	41,250
Sundries, - -	7,000

Total, £.	198,250

I have had an account of a small plantation in this island given me, which it is proper to introduce here. It is as follows. One hundred and ten acres of land, only part of which is fit for sugar, with a small mansion, one mill, and a proportioned sett of buildings, coppers, &c. were purchased about five years ago for the sum of

	£.
	3200
Paid for the implements, &c. at the same time,	113
For 47 seasoned negroes at 62l. a head, -	2914
For cattle, &c. - - -	640

£.	6867

The gentleman who made the purchase left it to the management of an agent, who also had the care of some other plantations.

He

He has generally shipped him 60 hogfheads of sugar a year, and 26 hogsheads of
rum.   l. s. d.

				l.	s.	d.
60 hdds. sugar at 15l.	-	-		900	0	0
26 rum at 9l.	-	-	-	234	0	0
Total receipt,	-	-	-	1134	0	0

Deduct.

		l.	s.	d.
Interest of 6867l. at 5 per cent.	343	0	0	
Agent's bill of charges,	-	655	10	0
		998	10	0
Neat proceeds,	-	-	-	135	10	0

Hence it appears that the planter in Eng-
gland gains only 2 per cent. for his money
more than he may be supposed to pay for
it, or 7 per cent. which for a security any
ways hazardous, and that of every plantation is much so, must be reckoned miser-
able interest for his money. This, however, is not owing to the fault of sugar, but
of agency: plantations that are left to the
conduct of agents and overseers, generally
turn out so. There is reason to believe from
this instance, as well as many others, that
greater extortioners are hardly to be met
with than West India agents, attornies,
and overseers, who generally take such advantage of the distant residence of their employers as to make those estates carry the

M 4   worst

worſt aſpect, which ought in fact to be highly valued. But it is farther curious to ſee the profit they allow their maſters, which is juſt calculated to prevent their ſelling their eſtates, when themſelves ſhall borrow money in the iſlands at 8 and even 9 per cent. to throw into a buſineſs, from which they remit the owners no more than 7 ! The truth is, planting ſugar upon the fine ſoil of St. Chriſtopher's will, with proper management, pay from 25 to 35 per cent. for the money employed; but then reſidence is neceſſary; for as to living in London by agriculture in the Weſt Indies, it is an impracticable ſcheme to unite ſuch contraries with profit.

St. Chriſtopher's was many years ago in a very thriving condition; as may be gathered from the ſale of the French lands in the iſland, after the ceſſion of their part of it at the peace of Utrecht, produced ſo large a ſum, that the princeſs of Orange's marriage portion of eighty thouſand pounds was paid out of it.

Nevis is ſituated ſo near St. Chriſtopher's as to be ſeparated from it only by a narrow channel; it is about ſix miles a-croſs, and near twenty in circumference;

for

for want of the high lands of St. Kitt's, the climate is not so good, nor is the soil reckoned quite equal to it; yet is this small island inhabited by 5000 whites and 12,000 blacks; a great number for so little a spot, and shews how completely cultivated most of it must be. Its produce is,

	£.
6000 hogsheads of sugar at 15l.	90,000
2000 hogsheads rum at 9l. -	18,000
Sundries, - -	3,000
Total, £.	111,000

The island of MONTSERRAT lies in 17° north lat.; it is about nine miles long, and nearly of the same breadth. There is no part of the West Indies that is more healthy or agreeable than this little island. There are some high mountains in it which cool and refresh the air by a land-breeze; and these being at the same time well covered with tall cedar and other.wood, the shade afforded is delicious, as well as the prospect it yields lovely. The vallies are extremely fertile, yielding all the West Indian productions in perfection; and they are at the same time well watered. The number of white inhabitants in the island is about 4500,

4500, and the flaves 12,000. The product is about 3500 hogfheads of fugar; but it is on the improving hand both in population and product.

			£.
3500 hogfheads at 15l.	-		52,500
1110 hogfheads rum at 9l.	-		9,900
Sundries,	. -	-	1,500
		Total, £.	63,900

BARBUDA lies in 17 deg. 30 min. north latitude; it is about fifteen miles long. The climate is not equal to that of Montferrat, from the lownefs of the lands. The foil is very fertile, yet the inhabitants have not gone upon fugar; this has not been from any defect in the foil, climate, or fituation, but has been owing to that degree of cuftom and habit which are fo apt to govern mankind. Long after our firft fettling this ifland the native Caribbees remained in it, and more than once burnt and plundered the new fettlements; this deterred every body from erecting and eftablifhing fuch expenfive and hazardous works as thofe for fugar; but after the natives were carried off the ifland, this motive ceafed, and the conduct fhould have ceafed like-

likewife; but the people being got into the courfe of common hufbandry, they knew not how to quit it: the beft part of the ifland was in hands who, from their eafe and comfort of their life, would not part with their farms, which excluded new comers from introducing fugar; and thus has the ifland continued to the prefent time applied almoft entirely to raifing corn and provifions, principally the breeding of cattle. The neighbourhood of the fugar iflands, with whom alone they have any connection, affords them a certain and good market for every thing they have to fell. The number of people in the ifland is about 1500, among whom are very few negroes. The property of the ifland is in the Codrington family, the head of which puts in a governor at Barbuda, having the fame prerogatives the other lords proprietors in their feveral jurifdictions in America. Their anceftor, colonel Chriftopher Codrington, governor of Barbadoes, who dying in 1710, gave two plantations in Barbadoes, and part of this ifland, valued in the whole at 2000l. per ann. to the fociety for the propagation of the Gof-pel, for the inftruction of the negroes in Barbadoes, and the reft of the Carribbee iflands iſlands in the Chriſtian religion, and for erecting and endowing a college in Barbadoes. This great man was a native of Barbadoes, and, as has been well obſerved, for a great number of amiable and uſeful qualities both in public and private life, for his courage and his zeal for the good of his country, his humanity, his knowledge, and love of literature, was far the richeſt production and moſt ſhining ornament Barbadoes ever had.

I before obſerved, that the people of Barbuda addicted themſelves to breeding and feeding cattle, and raiſing corn. Their meadows are ſome of them very fine ones, abounding plentifully with thoſe graſſes which in the Weſt Indies are found moſt profitable: their herds are not large, from the diviſion of property, but very numerous: having many cows and young cattle, horſes and aſſes, for breeding mules, ſome ſheep, and particularly ſwine; the products of America are peculiarly adapted for rearing and feeding hogs; moſt of the trees yield plenty of maſt; the leaves of many of their ſucculent vegetables do well for them, and the products of roots much exceed any thing in Europe. An acre of potatoes and yams in Barbuda will yield as

much

much as three or four acres of potatoes in England. Their method of planting them in this ifland is thus: they plough the land three times, and then carrying on fuch manure as they have, mark the field by line into ftripes of five feet broad; on each fide the line, at the diftance of eight inches from it, they lay a row of potatoe fetts, and as they proceed cover them with earth, taken with fhovels from the fpaces between the lines. Planters lefs attentive will do the fame work without lines, but then their land is far from having any neat appearance. As the crop grows they keep earthing it up in the fame manner, quite through the fummer; and when they take up their roots, they do it with fpades or forks: as to the produce, I have been affured they fometimes get from one acre of land up to fifty-three or fifty-four tons, and that from thirty-five to forty are common crops. It is eafy to conceive what a fource of profit fuch products muft be, where potatoes bear a conftant price, as they do all over the Weft Indies; and to what advantage the people of this ifland may breed fwine upon the very offal of fuch crops.

The

The way of life among the farmers of Barbuda refembles that of the little freeholders in New England; thefe alfo having the property of their farms, feldom renting them from others. Each man has his comfortable dwelling, and his well inclofed fields around it, a fine grove of trees for fhelter, his orchard and garden filled with delicious fruits, his meadows for his herds, fome lands for Indian, called here Guinea Corn, and others for roots, &c. Confidering the vaft plenty which hufbandry in fuch a climate yields of almoft every thing, it may truly be faid thefe little farmers lead a life very much fuperior to that of their little brethren in Europe.

ANGUILLA is fituated in 18 deg. 12 min. north latitude; it is thirty miles long by ten broad, and is in every refpect too fine an ifland to be left in the condition we fee it. There are not above 800 people in it, who are to be divided into two claffes; one a fet of induftrious farmers (like thofe of Barbuda), among whom there was a few years ago one or two fugar works, and the other a fet of lazy people who live like Indians, purfuing no other occupation than that of tending a few herds, and living on

them

them and the spontaneous fruits of the island. It is very remarkable, and indeed is a circumstance of curiosity, that there is no government in this island, every head of a family being truly a sovereign, and yet the settled part of the inhabitants live in peace and security, notwithstanding the wandering class, who know neither law nor gospel. This seems a great contradiction; but so it is.

The farmers in this island principally follow the planting Indian corn, in which they have good success, and sell considerable quantities of it to the sugar islands: their crops are reckoned very good: they also plant some tobacco, which, after neglecting for many years, they have lately taken up again, but the quantity is not considerable. Great improvements might be made, if a deputy governor was fixed here with a regular civil government; which it has been apprehended would draw people of property to make purchases in the island, with a view to plant sugar; for there are large tracts of land in it of a fine sandy loam, of a reddish colour, which resembles the brick earth of Jamaica, and which in its fertility in

the

the production of such crops as the people plant, shews how excellently it would do for sugar. The scarcity and dearness of land in our islands make it the more surprising that this has never been done.

CHAP.

C H A P. XXXII.

CEDED ISLANDS.

Dominica—St. Vincent—Granada—Tobago —Importance of these islands—Their produce—Improvements—Observations.

BY the peace of Paris we procured the cession, or rather the confirmation, of our right to these islands; the degree of merit that treaty possesses on this account does not turn on the value of these acquisitions, but on our degree of right to them before; and as that enquiry is not connected with the subject of this work, I shall dismiss the idea of it; but proceed to describe them, as well as the imperfect accounts we have had will allow, with the assistance of such private information as I have been able to gain, some of which has been valuable.

DOMINICA lies in 15° 30′ north lat. between Martinico and Guadalupe; it is twenty-eight miles long by thirteen broad, and in circumference about ninety: it is supposed to be about twice as large as Barbadoes. The air, except in some places

 that

that are marſhy and overgrown with wood, is generally reputed wholeſome. There is no doubt but when the iſland is cleared it will, like the reſt, become ſtill more healthy, or at leaſt more agreeable to European conſtitutions. The face of the country is rough and mountainous, more eſpecially towards the ſea ſide, but within land, there are many rich and fine vallies, and ſome large and fair plains. The declivities of the hills are commonly gentle, ſo as to facilitate their cultivation, and the ſoil almoſt every where a deep black mould, and thence highly commended for its fertility by the Spaniſh, Engliſh, and French. It is excellently well watered by at leaſt thirty rivers, ſome, and particularly one of them is very large and navigable for ſeveral miles, and the reſt very commodious for all the purpoſes of planting. Hogs, both wild and tame, are here in great abundance, as well as all ſorts of fowls, and ground proviſions, ſuch as bananas, potatoes, manioc; none of the iſlands produce better. Their fruits alſo are excellent, and the ſettlements, which however were not numerous, which the French made upon the iſland, flouriſhed very much, and produced ſugar, cotton, coffee, cocoa, and

moſt

moft of the articles common in the Weft Indies *.

Since it has come into our poffeffion, a confiderable progrefs has been made in cultivating it : many tracts of lands have been purchafed, and fugar-works erected on them. Infomuch that in 1763, only a year after the peace, the export from the ifland to Great Britain amounted to 46,211l. 17 s. 9 d. a very confiderable fum for fo fhort a time after the poffeffion. Since that time the products have increafed confiderably, fo that at prefent it is one of the moft beneficial iflands we have; infomuch that laft year its exports amounted to above two hundred thoufand pounds.

St. Vincent lies in the fame atitude as Barbadoes, at the diftance of only thirty leagues. It is from north to fouth twenty miles long, and in breadth about twelve; the circumference being about fixty miles. It is fomething larger than Antigua. The warmth of the climate is fo tempered with the fea-breezes, that it is looked upon as very healthy and agreeable, and on the eminences, which are numerous, the air is rather cool. The foil is wonderfully fertile,

---

* *Confiderations on the Nature of the Svgar Trade.*

 though

though the country is hilly, and in some places mountainous. But amongst the former, there are some pleasant vallies, and at the bottom of the latter, some spacious and luxuriant plains. No island of the same extent is better watered with rivers and streams, yet are there no marshes nor stagnant waters. There are here great quantities of fine timber, and excellent fruit trees, some peculiar to this island. It abounds with wild sugar-canes, corn, rice, and all sorts of ground provisions. In the south part of the island, where the French have raised some spacious and flourishing settlements, they have coffee, indigo, cocoa, anatto, and some very fine tobacco. They have likewise abundance of cattle and poultry, and send from thence *lignum vitæ* and other kinds of timber to Martinico, where they were employed in building houses and in their fortifications. We may collect, that if this country was thoroughly and regularly cultivated, it would, in respect of its produce, be very little, if at all inferior to any of the islands that we already possess.

But there is one circumstance very capitally in disfavour of this otherwise excellent island, which must not be overlooked;

it

it is the number of native Indians and free negroes that are in poffeffion of it.   In the year 1735 it appeared, by an authentic report that was then made to the government of Barbadoes, that according to the beft information, which could be at that juncture obtained, there were about fix hundred French, four thoufand Indians, and fix thoufand negroes in St. Vincent's : it is, however, faid, that the numbers have fince been much decreafed, owing to a cruel war breaking out between the Indians and negroes, which lafted for many years *.

Several reafons have been brought to fhew, that fo far from efteeming thefe prior inhabitants a difadvantage, we ought to reckon them a valuable acquifition.   But fuch arguments are far enough from being founded in fact or experience.   The author of the *Confiderations* fays as much on this head as can be faid ; but in fpite of all that can be advanced, practical men know well enough, that till an ifland is clear of Indians and free negroes, no fugar can be planted to advantage.   The inftance of the Jamaica negroes proves this, rather than contradicts it, as may be feen by any perfon, who reflects on the immenfe loffes,

---

* *Confiderations, &c.*

                    expences,

expences, and trouble it cost that island
not to extirpate, but make a peace with a
handful of men; and the example of the
French proves the same thing, for though
no island can be more favourable in soil and
climate to sugar, than St. Vincent's, yet
did they not, though at peace with both
Indians and negroes, venture upon that
culture; confining themselves to provisions
and other articles that required little expence.   But if this reasoning should not be
satisfactory, what are we to think of the
transactions now going on in this island,
which in the violation of the natural rights
of mankind are of such a hue, as to have
brought on the enquiry now before parliament* ?   It shews plainly enough, that the
island was of no worth while possessed even
in part by the natives, and that in order to
render it valuable, means had been taken
which it is to be feared will make but a bad
appearance in the face of day.

The island of GRANADA lies in 11 deg.
30 min. north latitude, the farthest to the
south of any of the Antilles.   It is upwards
of thirty miles long, and about half as many
broad, being seventy-five in circumference.
It is twice as large as Barbadoes, and con-

* This was written at the time of the enquiry into
the affair of St. Vincent's.

tains

tains one third as much land fit for culture as is to be found in Martinico. The climate, as may be supposed from the latitude, is very hot, yet is it refreshed by the sea-breeze; it is well known to be as wholesome as any other island in these parts; notwithstanding the fever which has gone under the name of this island, but which is owing to the thickness of the woods, and of course declines every day. The seasons, as they are styled in the West Indies, are remarkably regular; the blast is not hitherto known; the inhabitants are not liable to many diseases that are epidemic in Martinico and Guadaloupe; and, which is the happiest circumstance of all, it lies out of the tract of the hurricanes, which, with respect to the safety of the settlements on shore, and the security of navigation, is almost an inestimable benefit.

There are in Grenada some very high mountains, but the number is small, and the eminences scattered through it are in general rather hills, gentle in their ascent, of no great height, fertile, and very capable of cultivation. But exclusive of these, there are on both sides the island large tracts of level ground, very fit for improvement,

N 4

the

the foil being almoſt every where deep, rich, mellow, and fertile in the higheſt degree, ſo as to be equal in all reſpects, if not ſuperior, to that of any of the iſlands in the Weſt Indies, if the concurrent teſtimonies both of French and Britiſh planters may be relied upon. The former indeed have conſtantly, in their applications to the French miniſtry, inſiſted, that this might be very eaſily made one of the moſt valuable, though hitherto it has remained the weakeſt and the worſt ſettled of all their colonies.   It is perfectly well watered by many ſtreams of different ſizes ; there are alſo ſmaller brooks running from moſt of the hills.   The great produce of the country before our cultivation in it, and indeed partly ſince, is a prodigious variety of all the different ſorts of timber that are to be met with in any of the Weſt India iſlands, and all theſe excellent in their reſpective kinds ; ſo that whenever it comes to be tolerably cleared, vaſt profits will ariſe from the timber that may be cut down, and for which markets will not be wanting. Cattle, fowls, and proviſions, are in the utmoſt plenty.   But the diſtinguiſhing excellency of Grenada does not lie ſimply in its great fertility, or in its fitneſs for a vaſt variety of valuable commodities, but in the peculiar quality of its foil, which gives a furprifing and inconteflible perfection to all its feveral productions. The fugar of Grenada is of a fine grain, and of courfe more valuable than that either of Martinico or Guadaloupe. The indigo is the fineft in all the Weft Indies. While tobacco remained the ftaple commodity, as once it was of thefe iflands, one pound of Granada tobacco was worth two or three that grew in any of the reft. The cocoa and cotton have an equal degree of pre-eminence. For fome years before it came into our hands, the French planters in this ifland fent home twelve thoufand hogfheads of fugar annually, befides coffee, cocoa, and a large quantity of excellent cotton. Yet it is generally allowed, that never one half of the country was properly fettled that might have been obtained, if the inhabitants had been better planters, and had been alfo better fupplied with flaves. An Englifh gentleman, who has had great opportunities of knowing, thinks as much fugar is raifed here as in Barbadoes, which is not at all impoffible, though it did not find a regular paffage to France. The Grenadines run from the foutbern extremity of the ifle of Grenada;

nada; they are twenty-three ſmall iſlands, capable of cultivation, the ſoil being remarkably rich, the climate pleaſant, and all the neceſſaries of life, as faſt as they are ſettled, eaſily obtained. According to the ſentiments of the beſt judges, large quantities of indigo, coffee, and cotton may be raiſed upon them, nor are they at all unfit for ſugar. Beſides theſe, there are five larger iſlands, generally comprehended under the title of the Grenadines, *Carioua-cou*, *Union*, *Cannouan*, *Moſkito* iſland, and *Bequia*, called by the French Little Martinico. The firſt is of a circular figure, ſix or ſeven leagues in compaſs; it has been repreſented, by thoſe who have viſited it, as one of the fineſt and moſt fruitful ſpots in America; the ſoil remarkably fertile, and from its being pervaded by the ſea-breeze, the climate equally wholeſome and pleaſant. It is covered with valuable timber, interſperſed with rich fruit trees, and when ſettled and cultivated is capable of all kinds of improvement; and it has alſo the advantage of as deep, capacious, and commodious an harbour as any in the Weſt Indies. *Union* is three leagues long. *Cannouan* is three leagues long, and one and an half broad. *Moſkito* is three long and one
broad.

broad. All of them very pleafant and fertile iflands. *Bequia* is the largeft, being thirty-fix miles in circumference, confequently larger than Montferrat : the foil is equal, if not fuperior to any of the reft, but it has little frefh water, and abounds with venomous reptiles *.

As a ftrong proof that thefe reprefentations were well founded, I fhall remark, that Grenada and its dependencies fent home in 1763, to the Britifh market, only fugar and other commodities, to the amount of 206,889l. which tallies extremely well with the above mentioned product of 12,000 hogfheads of fugar. St. Kitt's produces 10,000, and its total export 198,250 l. confequently 12,000 muft at leaft be equal to 206,889 l. Since that time our people have made a wonderful progrefs in planting this ifland : many very capital plantations have been eftablifhed by gentlemen in England of the largeft property, and the fuccefs which has attended, and is daily attending, fuch as refide on their eftates in this ifland, and at the fame time underftand the bufinefs of planting, fhews clearly that in a few years this will

---

* *Confiderations, &c.*

be

be one of the most valuable settlements we
have in the West Indies. I have been fa-
voured with an account of one plantation,
which I shall lay before the reader, as in
several points it is very satisfactory.

		£.
Purchase of 350 acres of land for canes (200 cleared) and 95 of woodland in the hills for raising provisions, &c.	}	2,560
Mansion and one set of buildings,	-	2,600
Utensils,	-	480
200 negroes at 56l. on an average,	-	11,200
Cattle,	-	320
	£.	17,160

One year's expence.

Expences on 200 negroes, including overseers, 4l. a head. }	800	
Repairs of buildings,	90	
Wear and tear,	100	
Cattle,	40	
Taxes,	32	
Extra charges,	86	
Supply of negroes,	460	
		1,608
	£.	18,768

Product.

	£.
89 hogsheads sugar, at 19l.	1,691
70 at 18l.	1,260
276 at 15l.	4,140
	7,091
200 hhds. of rum,	1,800
Carried over, £.	8,891

Brought forward,			£.	8,891
Timber and sundry articles,		-	-	75
				——
Total,	-	-	-	£. 8,966
Annual expence,	-	-	-	1,608
				——
Annual profit,	-	-	-	7,358

This is near 39 per cent. interest of the capital, but it was drawn up from the particulars of an extraordinary year: while the poſſeſſor was on the plantation himſelf, he made near 27 per cent. ſince he has been in England, his neat produce is only 9 per cent. a freſh inſtance of the loſs attending any perſon poſſeſſing eſtates in the Weſt India iſlands without living upon them.

There is a very great error in the culture of the new lands in this iſland, which is the clearing them of wood in ſuch a manner as to exclude the uſe of the plough: this has been the caſe with all our iſlands, but the new ſettlers in Granada have, through an eagerneſs for profit, left the ſtumps ſo thick that no plough can be uſed; and even for hoes, by the accounts I have received, the inconvenience muſt be great.   It is much to be regretted that they will not beſtow a little extra expence upon this article in their firſt undertaking, and at the ſame time determine upon introducing

ducing horfe-culture in every branch of their agriculture where it is practicable. Another circumftance of confequence, and which demands equal attention, is their making free with the fertility of the frefh lands fo much as our planters are too apt to do; the confequence of which will be, exhaufting them in a few years, and then they will be in a worfe ftate than if the foil under good management had not been of a comparable richnefs.

TOBAGO lies a little to the fouth-eaft of Granada; it is thirty-two miles long, and about nine broad, being feventy miles in circumference; it is rather larger than Barbadoes. The climate, though it lies only eleven degrees and ten minutes north from the equator, is not near fo hot as might be expected, the force of the fun's rays being tempered by the coolnefs of the fea-breeze. When it was firft inhabited, it was thought unhealthy, but as foon as it was a little cleared and cultivated, it was found to be equally pleafant and wholefome, which the Dutch afcribed, in a great meafure, to the odoriferous fmell exhaled from the fpice and rich gum trees, a notion borrowed from their countrymen in the Eaft Indies,

who

who are perfuaded that cutting down the clove trees in the Moluccas has rendered thofe iflands very unhealthy. Another circumftance which may recommend the climate, is the ifland's lying out of the track of the hurricanes. There are many rifing grounds over all the ifland, but it cannot be properly ftyled mountainous. The foil is very finely diverfified, being in fome places light and fandy, in others mixed with gravel and fmall flints, but in general it is a deep, rich, black mould. Hardly any country can be better watered than Tobago, for befides fprings that are found in plenty all over the ifland, there are not fewer than eighteen rivulets that run from the hills into the fea; but there are very few or no moraffes or marfhes, or any lakes, pools, or collections of ftanding waters, which of courfe muft render it more healthy. It is covered with all that vaft variety of timber that is to be found in moft countries in the Weft Indies, and many of thefe as extraordinary in fize as excellent in their nature. The fame may be faid with refpect to fruit trees, and amongft thefe there are fome that are peculiar to Tobago; fuch, for inftance, as the true nutmeg tree, which the Dutch, who

of

of all nations could not in that refpect be deceived, affirm to have found here. It is true, they fay, it is a wild nutmeg, that the mace is lefs florid, and the tafte of the nut itfelf more pungent, though larger and fairer to the eye than the fpice of the fame kind brought by them from the Eaft In-dies. The cinnamon tree grows likewife in this ifland, though the bark is faid to have a tafte of cloves as well as cinnamon. Here likewife grows the tree that produces the true *gum copal*, refembling that brought from the continent of America, and very different from what goes by the fame name in the reft of the Weft India iflands. All ground provifions are produced here in the utmoft abundance, as well as in the higheft perfection. There is likewife plenty of wild hogs and other animals, together with great quantities of fowl, and an amazing variety both of fea and river fifh. In the time the Dutch were in poffeffion of this ifland, which was not many years, they exported large quantities of tobacco, fugar, caffia, ginger, cinnamon, faffafras, gum copal, cocoa, rocou, indigo, and cotton; befides rich woods, materials for dying, drugs of different kinds, and feveral forts of delicious fweetmeats. We fhall here

take

take the liberty of obferving, that there is
at leaſt the higheſt probability of our being
able to produce all the valuable ſpices of
the Eaſt Indies in this iſland.   Cinnamoh
is ſaid to grow in ſome of the other Weſt
India iſlands, and general Codrington had
once an intention to try how much it might
be improved by a regular cultivation in his
iſland of Barbuda.   It is univerſally allowed, that the bark of what is called the wild
cinnamon tree in Tobago is beyond compariſon the beſt in all the Weſt Indies, and
even in its preſent ſtate may be made an article of great value.   The bark when cured
with care differs from that in the Eaſt Indies, by being ſtronger and more acrid
while it is freſh ; and when it has been
kept for ſome time it loſes that pungency,
and acquires the flavour of cloves.   This is
preciſely the ſpice for which there is a very
conſiderable ſale at Liſbon, Paris, and over
all Italy. This kind of ſpice is drawn principally from Brazil, and the Portugueze believe that their cinnamon trees were originally brought from Ceylon, while it was
in their poſſeſſion, but that through the al-
teration of ſoil and climate they are dege-
nerated into this kind of ſpice, and this
may very probably be true : however, from

their size and number it seems to admit of
no doubt, that the common trees actually
growing in Tobago are the natural production of that island, and the point with us
is to know what improvement may be made
with respect to these.   The nutmeg tree,
as well as the cinnamon, is a native of this
island: we cannot doubt of the fact, that
is, of the nutmeg's growing here; because
we find it asserted in a book addressed to
M. de Beveren, then governor of Tobago.
A man who had invented a falsehood would
hardly have had the boldness to repeat it,
not only to a respectable person, but to the
person in the world who must have the
clearest knowledge of its being a falsehood.
The nutmeg tree that naturally grows in
Tobago, is in all probability as true, and
may, by due care and pains, be rendered as
valuable a nutmeg as those that grow any
where else; for the fact really is, that
wherever there are nutmegs, there are wild
nutmegs, or, as some style them, mountain
nutmegs, which are longer and larger, but
much inferior in the flavour to the true nutmeg, and are very liable to be worm-eaten;
the point is to know how these defects may
be remedied, or, in other words, wherein
the difference consists between the wild,

taste-

taftelefs, and ufelefs nutmeg, and that which is true, aromatic, and of courfe a valuable fpice *.

This idea, with other arguments to inforce it, too cogent to be overturned, are to be met with in the fame work, which it muft be confeffed by every one is very well reflected, and drawn up with much candour and judgment : but unfortunately for the interefts of this country, they have met with no more attention than if the author had wrote concerning raifing fpices in the moon : it is near ten years fince he compofed his treatife, yet has not there been the leaft ftep taken towards making the experiment, though nothing can be more obvious than the defign, nor more eafy than the execution, of taking plants wild from the foreft, and trying what change a regular cultivation will make in their flavour and nature. Our minifters have attended enough to *felling* the lands in thefe ceded iflands, but as to the national improvement of them, they have neither thought nor cared about it. Very much is it to be regretted, that fomething at the public expence has not been done towards afcertain-

---

ing the degree of improvement which the native productions of thefe iſlands are capable of receiving. A very ſmall public plantation for this purpoſe, under the conduct of an able botaniſt, would be ſufficient for the experiment; nor can I ſee any good objections to ſuch a ſcheme, upon the ſcore of an expence which could hardly amount to more than a few hundred pounds a year.

Dropping the idea of improvements, which we may be certain will, for want of public virtue, never be executed, it remains for us to remark, that the ceded iſlands of St. Vincent, Dominica, Granada, and Tobago, are among the few principal acquiſitions made by the late glorious war. Before the ſucceſſes of that war took place, it was a common complaint in our iſlands that good ſugar-land was ſo ſcarce, that the product of that commodity was entirely at a ſtand, while our rivals, the French, were making an amazing progreſs, owing to the great plenty of excellent land at their command: but the acquiſition of theſe iſlands has at leaſt lifted us from that ſtagnant ſituation, in which nothing but a decline could be expected; the purchaſe of land in theſe territories, and their cultivation, has animated our people ſince the laſt peace, and

given

given them some of that activity which ever attends advance: in commerce and politics no enemy is more to be dreaded than standing still. Had we not secured these islands, our ruin in the West Indies must soon have followed, without the greatest dexterity of management, for France has made a much greater acquisition by gaining the Spanish half of Hispaniola in exchange for Louisiana; which is such an acquisition of valuable territory in the West Indies, as we can never hope again to make.

But while our rivals have such an advantage of territory, be it our aim to gain the ascendancy in industry; and that is principally to be done in the quick and thorough cultivation of these islands. Public arrangements ought to co-operate with private endeavours; encouragement should be given to settlers to plant those parts of the island which do not sell, which will of course be all the parts that do not possess every requisite for cane-grounds; but the climate is highly propitious to commodities as valuable as sugar: encouragement should be given to such settlers to go upon coffee, indigo, cocoa, cotton, cochineal, and other articles, so that every part of the islands, except those which it would be proper to

leave

leave in wood from ruggedness of situation, might be brought into some kind or other of profitable culture. With respect to spices, which certainly our India company might long ago have secured in some of their settlements, small plantations, of the native growths, should be made, in spots selected for that purpose, to see what perfection culture would bring them to; we should probably, by this means, gain at least some articles that would be useful and profitable in certain branches of our commerce. The expence would be small, the benefit might be great.

CHAP.

CHAP. XXXIII.

BAHAMA ISLANDS.

PROVIDENCE.

Climate — Soil—Productions—Observations on their neglected state—Proposals for their improvement.

THE Lucayos, or Bahama iſlands, are ſome hundreds in number, ſome of them many miles in length, and others little better than rocks or knoles riſing above the water, which render navigation among them remarkably dangerous. They are ſeated in the fineſt climate of the world, between 21 and 27 deg. north latitude, which, though very hot on the continent, is in theſe iſlands but another word for an almoſt perpetual ſpring. The iſle of Bahama is in lat. 26 deg. 30 min. being about 50 miles long, but very narrow. Providence is in 25 deg. it is 28 miles long, and 11 broad. Some of them are of much larger ſizes than theſe, but not above three or four inhabited : Providence is the ſeat

of

of government. In 1763, the imports to Great Britain were above four thousand pounds from Providence.

I before remarked, that the climate is excellent in most of them ; of this I have been assured by a gentleman who spent some time among them during the late war: he added, that the heats were temperated in the very hottest months by the sea breezes, and the number of the islands surrounding, gave them more than an equivalent to the land-breeze, by generally fanning them with eddies and gales of wind.   Nothing of that suffocating heat which renders the West Indies so pernicious to European constitutions; and which strictly confines the inhabitants to their houses during the best part of the day ; on the contrary, in July and August you may be out about any kind of rural sports or business without the least inconvenience.   The healthiness of the islands is owing greatly to the dryness of their soil : there is not a swamp, a marsh, or a bog in any one that has been examined ; they are high, dry, hilly, or rocky spots admirably watered with streams, being in the exemption from bad water, and in the possession of good, equal to any country in the known world.

While

While the heats in summer are so little oppreſſive, the ſpring is a ſeaſon too delicious to admit deſcription, and the winter is entirely free from ſnow or froſt; the tendereſt fruits of the Weſt Indies flouriſh throughout them, and are of flavour equal to what is taſted in much hotter climates. The uncommon healthineſs of the few inhabitants, proves how juſt this repreſentation of the climate is.

Reſpecting the ſoil, it is in moſt of the larger iſlands various, but every where excellent. It conſiſts generally of a loamy ſand, in ſome places mixed with flints, and in others free from them : very conſiderable tracts are of a black rich mould, light, but of a putrid appearance, and of a good depth; this is not found only in the vallies, but along the ſlopes of the hills to a great tract of country through many of the iſlands. The extraordinary growth to which all vegetables, cultivated and ſpontaneous, arrive, is proof ſufficient of the great fertility of this land. Among its productions are to be reckoned ſugar, cotton, indigo of a remarkable fine quality, cocoa, ginger, pimento, wild cinnamon, pine apples, guavas, bananas, plantains, oranges, lemons, citrons, &c. theſe valuable articles

are

are either wild, or cultivated in gardens; for the quantity in regular culture by way of plantation is very fmall, as may be judged by the whole product of all the iflands at the Britifh market being under five thoufand pounds, and in that fmall fum their cedar and other valuable timber make a confiderable portion.

If the finenefs of the climate, and the richnefs of the foil be confidered, it will appear felf-evident, that every article ufually cultivated in our Weft India ifles, might with a certainty of fuccefs be raifed here. Is it not therefore aftonifhing that they fhould be left in fo neglected a ftate? That fo few enterprifing minds fhould be found to undertake plantations in them: tracts of land might here be chofen and had for no other expence than paying the ufual fees of office; whereas 60l. per acre for land not better, is a common price in our fugar iflands. That commodity might beyond all doubt be cultivated to no fmall advantage, for it thrives luxuriantly in much more northerly climates; and if the advantage of plenty of land, with all forts of lumber on the fpot, with a profufion of provifions of all kinds, both for the flaves and cattle of a plantation; if thefe circumftances

stances are confidered, with the difference of having the land almoft for nothing, or paying 6ol. an acre for it—if thefe points are confidered, it will be fufficiently plain, that confiderable eftates might be made by fugar-planting in thefe iflands, as it is moft certain that lefs crops than the produce of Jamaica and Barbadoes would pay better intereft for a capital here, than large ones there, all expences carried to account.

But fuppofing that equal profit by fugar could not be made, which is much more than there is any neceffity to grant, why fhould they not be applied to indigo, cotton, vines, tobacco, &c.   In thefe articles there has never been a doubt of the climate being hot enough—nor can any perfon doubt but they would yield larger crops than are gained of them on the continent.   And a beneficial culture of thefe commodities, in fuch of the iflands as are capable of cultivation, would bring into this nation an annual profit of one or two hundred thoufand pounds a year, without reckoning anything for fugar: but if the moft was made of them that they are capable of, knowing people well acquaintied with them, have thought they would be worth half a million

lion

lion a year to Britain; inftead of producing not five thoufand pounds.

The navigation, I am fenfible, of thefe iflands has always been reckoned very hazardous; but this notion muft not be adopted in general; when fhips have been driven in ftorms among their rocks and fhoals, feveral have been wrecked, but as to thofe that have fteered regularly thither as their courfe, the navigation has never proved dangerous: there is a regular communication open by fhips often paffing to and fro between Providence and Charles Town in Carolina, Philadelphia, &c. and alfo to the Leeward Iflands, not to fpeak of thofe which pafs between England and that ifland. And if the navigation is frequented for the fmall concerns of thefe iflands at prefent, and the few commodities of value they export, furely by a parity of reafoning we may fuppofe, that if more valuable products were raifed, and in much greater abundance, the navigation would not then be objected to: if it is fufficiently fafe to induce fhipping now to frequent it, moft certainly they would then. Nor fhould I omit to remark, that the inhabitants on the few iflands that are at all peopled, are the moft dextrous feamen in all

America;

America ; one principal branch of their employment is building floops and other fmall veffels, with which they carry on a traffic between the northern colonies and the fugar iflands, and export their own provifions in tolerable quantities to thofe iflands ; this makes them able navigators, and gives plenty of pilots for moft of the paffages and channels of their own Archipelago.

But there is another view in which thefe iflands may be confidered, which though not effential, yet deferves mention : it is that of affording perhaps the moft agreeable and eligible retreat for men whofe active or variegated lives have taken off that relifh for the world which once actuated them ; and to whom nothing appears with fuch charms as a profpect of a fafe, eafy, and agreeable retreat.   Or to men who from failures, loffes, difappointments, or a general want of income for living agreeably in a wealthy, luxurious, and expenfive country, are defirous of fpending, at leaft, fome years of their life in a retirement, where their little fortunes may be fufficient for providing them with fuch enjoyments as their own country denies them : to any fuch, thefe iflands could hardly

appear

appear in any other light but that of a paradise upon earth, which will plainly appear, from considering them with this view.

In the first place, here is an air and climate perfectly unexceptionable, as healthy to an European constitution as almost any other part of America; where the heats are never excessive, and where severe cold was never known: a clear serene sky, and an atmosphere free from every species of damps and fogs; a soil as fertile as any in the world in the production of all the articles that form the necessaries and superfluities of life, from bread to pine-apples, and that in a profusion which scarcely any other country experiences. In addition to these circumstances, here is further to be met with a plenty as remarkable of both sea and river fish, with various sorts of wild fowl and game: timber in every island for all the purposes of building whether houses, or sloops and boats. And in point of agreeableness, many of the islands abound in situations which are equally pleasing and romantic. There are in Mogane and some others of them the finest slopes of country that can be imagined. A wave of gentle but varied declivities from the

tops

tops of very high hills, shelving down to a bold sea-shore; in some places spread with open lawn, in others scattered with open groves of tall trees, rivers winding in slopes, and in other places falling down the hills in cascades, the whole bounded generally by thick woods: some of these scenes take in the space of three, four, or six hundred acres, and have from the shipping the noblest effect imaginable.

Where now can such persons as I have mentioned, find a more eligible retreat than in such scenes as these! Much more so than the Bermudas Islands, where there is a confined society, which in the nature of things must be full of all the jars and bickerings of the world; and where the people are in too low a sphere of life to afford conversation pleasing or satisfactory to a man of any ideas. But the Bahamas are so circumstanced, that a man may live in just that degree of retirement he likes—that is, he may live entirely to himself, and come again into the world whenever he wishes for it.

IMPOR-

IMPORTANCE

OF THE

AMERICAN COLONIES

TO

BRITAIN.

C H A P.   XXXIV.

Principles upon which colonies are established —How far answered by those of Britain— Wherein their importance consists—Depends on climate—Observations.

IN conducting the reader the tour of all our colonies, I have laid before him every circumstance that was necessary for giving a complete idea of their agriculture; little has been said of their commerce or of their manufactures, because it was conceived, that it is upon the culture of their lands that the interest of this country in America chiefly depends; and because the channels through which my intelligence

came,

came, principally afforded communications relative to agriculture. Upon the general importance of the colonies there has been much wrote, and by able pens; but from the extravagance to which certain arguments have been carried of late, we may reasonably conclude, that clear ideas are not yet entertained, not so much upon the importance in general, as the points upon which that importance principally depends. A very little discrimination is sufficient to convince us, that however well our best writers agree in that general circumstance, they are far from attributing effects to the same causes. What I shall chiefly attend to therefore in this chapter, will be to point out in what manner Britain reaps such great advantages by her colonies—in what degree it depends on their agriculture—what variations there are in husbandry, which are attended with corresponding variations in the interest of the mother-country. In making this enquiry, I shall be naturally led to clear up some apparent difficulties, which the reader might remark in his progress through the preceding pages.

There are three grand reasons for a country's planting colonies. *First*, affording

ing

ing a *national* retreat to fuch perfons as will emigrate. *Secondly*, affording a retreat to the emigrants of foreign countries. *Third-ly*, raifing the productions of climates different from their own, and thereby faving the purchafe of fuch productions.

As to the firft reafon, every one muft know that there is a certain degree of emigration at all times going on from all nations; neceffity or private inclination will carry many people from one country to another, and very many of the number are indifferent where they go, provided it is from home—or to a country in which they can maintain themfelves better than at home; if they go from Britain to France or Spain, thofe countries are proportionably ftrengthened, and we are weakened; it is therefore of particular importance to provide a colony for fuch perfons, that they may not, by their emigration, add to the population of an enemy's country, or that of a rival. For the fame reafon that makes this rule of conduct advifeable, it is alfo to be wifhed, that the emigrants from our enemies and rivals may make choice of our colonies, by which means, at the fame time that they weaken them, they ftrengthen us. From the many favours nature has

fhowered

showered down upon some of our American settlements, we see them resorted to by numbers of French, Dutch, Germans, Danes, Swedes, and Switzers, adding thereby greatly to the populousness of the country, and enriching Britain by their labour. The third reason for forming colonies is no less cogent; countries in a northern latitude, like Britain, cannot raise either sugar, tea, coffee, wine, silk, tobacco, indigo, cochineal, and many other articles; nor can their own territories yield a sufficiency of hemp, flax, iron, timber, &c. all such commodities must therefore be purchased in the way of trade from other nations; but if the import is large, the country is under a necessity of exporting other commodities or manufactures in great quantities, or a considerable balance must be paid in bullion, to the impoverishment of the country: and in proportion to the import of such commodities, is the industry and wealth of other nations increased at the expence of Britain. Hence the value of colonies that will provide us with such commodities, which spares our taking them from foreign nations, which sell them to us not for bullion but for manufactures; and whose increase in people and wealth is

P 2

so

so much added to the scale of Britain, instead of that material deduction which the
increase of some of our neighbours makes
from us. This is so evident, that it can
scarcely be contradicted with propriety.

Here therefore we deduce, that the population of the colonies is an increasing
weight in the scale of Britain, and that their
producing those commodities which the
climate of Britain refuses, or which we
cannot raise in sufficient quantity, is an advantage of the first magnitude. The ex-
cess to which the first may be carried in
time, will be more properly examined,
when I come to consider the probability of
their independance.

In the production of such staples as Britain cannot produce herself, there are some
circumstances which demand distinctions;
for the policy of colonization is one of the
most curious speculations that can be made
in general politics. When the products
are raised, should they be brought to Britain in British or American vessels? Should
the same products be sold to other nations,
and in what manner? Should the colonies
pursue other employments, such as commerce, manufactures, or fisheries? How are
they to be restrained? And in these que-

ries

ries it is not to be supposed merely what a mother-country would wish for—but what she would command, from the nature of her superiority.

A wide field for discussion here opens itself, but having been so much discussed by others, the less will suffice from me.

Two circumstances require equal attention ; first, preserving the natural and political rights of the Americans ; and secondly, the interest of Britain : it is not necessary that either should be sacrificed to the other, but then a sensible and attentive conduct is essential : things must not be left to their own progress, but thrown by artificial means into that train which is necessary for both. Colonies may naturally think themselves entitled to the common privileges of raising what commodities they please—selling them to whom they please —navigating their vessels how and where they please—and, in a word, acting to all purposes as a mother-country. But on the other hand, if all this is indulged, instead of being colonies they are independant states, and a country can never have any interest in planting and supporting such.

That a strong distinction must be made here is evidently necessary : the mother-country discovers, founds, peoples, and

sup-

supports the people for some ages; does not this lay them under an obligation different from what is experienced by any original and independant people? Does it not, upon the very face of it, imply a dependance, or an agreement to certain conditions? Is it to be supposed, that any people would plant colonies with any other idea? And is it not clear that the people who go to them do in that action, and in accepting the protection of the mother-country, tacitly acknowledge and agree to a submission to those reciprocal terms of agreement which are supposed to bind them? These *supposed* terms (for no absolute expression can be given to so uncertain an idea) are a general obedience to the acts of the British legislature, when legally, and according to the laws of nations, exerted. In the establishment and progress of all our colonies they invariably obeyed the authority of the British parliament, and in many instances even that of the crown; and what is of consequence, they received perpetual accessions of new settlers during the whole period of their submission to such authority. All this proves sufficiently, that the mother-country has an undoubted right so to regulate

the

he purfuits of the colonies, as to render them confiftent with her own intereft.

It has been found, for inftance, necef-fary to prevent the colonies from trading immediately with foreign nations; a point of policy neceffary in the management of all the colonies which the European nations have fettled in America; for if this was al-lowed, they would to all ufeful purpofes be the colonies of other powers as much as of our own. It has alfo been enacted, that no law paffed in the American affem-blies fhall have force till affented to by king and council in England. Various other in-ftances might be given, but thefe are fuf-ficient to fhew a reftraining and fuperior power. And in the exertions of this power we fee nothing to fhock the political li-berty and freedom of the colonifts, any more than in diftant countries of England being governed by laws paffed at Weftmin-fter, and to which perhaps not a five hun-dredth part of the inhabitants ever gave a direct or virtual affent.

Having premifed thefe circumftances, which prove that the mother country had a right, and muft always enjoy it, of regu-lating the purfuits of the colonies, fo as to turn them to their own advantage, it re-

mains

mains to be confidered how far this conduct
has been purfued by Britain, in which enquiry will be feen thofe errors which have
brought on the differences that have lately
happened between her and her American
plantations.

I before obferved, that one great benefit
refulting from colonies was the production of fuch commodities as the climate
of the mother-country will not yield ; this
advantage Britain has experienced in an
high degree.   Her iflands in the Weft Indies produce that great modern luxury,
fugar, in larger quantities than fhe can
confume ;   fo that after fatisfying her own
confumption, there remains a furplus which
is re-exported to other nations of Europe
that have not fugar iflands.   We have
fhewn in the preceding pages what a confiderable fum this total amount of fugar,
&c. is, which, being in this age a neceffary of life, muft have been bought of
France, had we not poffeffed our Weft India iflands.   The amount of thefe commodities is between two and three millions
fterling, a fum fufficient to drain any na-
tioh, and would at this day, while the
trade of the kingdom is in a moft flourifhing fituation, give fuch a balance againft
                                              her,

her, as to bring on every evil that can accrue from the impoverishment of a people.

If it be said that the West Indies and England are not the same country, and that these commodities, at least as much of them as are consumed, cost the nation as much as if bought of foreigners, I reply, that supposing this was true, which is not the case, still there is this essential difference, that in the transaction with our own islands we pay in manufactures, but in our transaction with a foreign country, we must pay in whatever the balance of the commerce between the two nations is paid in, which, with such a vast import added, would certainly be bullion. We already pay a considerable annual balance to France; but what would that balance be if our import of West India commodities was added to it? Importation of any thing, and in almost any quantity, is harmless, or perhaps beneficial, as long as paid for with manufactures; for such importation is then the means of feeding our poor, and supporting our population. But this is not the only advantage resulting from our islands: in the cultivation and sale of the commodity, there is a great profit made by the planter, as we every day

see

see by the large estates made in that part of the world : all these estates come at last to Britain—every great fortune made enables the possessor to come over and live here, and he leaves his plantation to over-seers. The overseers in their turn make fortunes, and do the same ; and fresh over-seers are left for the same purpose : but the end of the whole is the same, all the money that is made in considerable sums is sure to send its owners to England. What the amount of such incomes spent by absentees is, cannot be discovered, but every one's knowledge must tell him that it must be very considerable. This circumstance is clear profit, from having sugar colonies of our own, instead of buying our sugar, &c. from France or other countries.

Nor is the employment of shipping and seamen to be forgotten, which are of the very first importance to a maritime and commercial power : the navigation to the West Indies breeds and employs many sea-men, all of which would be lost to the nation, if she was to lose her sugar colonies ; or, what would be worse than lost, they might be added to the navigation of France and other countries, than which nothing could be more highly detrimental. The
freight

freight alone of our Weſt India ſtaples a-
mounts to above half a million ſterling,
whereas the ſhare we ſhould have in the
freight of the ſame commodities from European countries would be very inſignifi-
cant in its amount.

I have entered particularly into this enquiry concerning the ſugar colonies, becauſe they are more immediately applicable
to every circumſtance of the argument than
moſt of our other ſettlements: and the inſtance is ſtrong to ſhew us the great importance of planting colonies in ſuch climates as produce commodities totally different from thoſe of the mother-country;
in a luxurious age the products of one zone
are neceſſaries of life in another; in order therefore to have as many commodities as poſſible, without purchaſing them
of foreign nations, the mother-country
ſhould be in one zone and the colonies in
another, which is the caſe with Britain and
her Weſt India iſlands. It is theſe principles which have proved ſo fortunate in the
colonization we have carried on in this
part of the world; and whether we con-
ſider wealth, employment of our poor, of
our ſeamen, ſhipping, and all the attendants of navigation, we muſt decide that

our

our West India islands are in every respect as valuable settlements as any the world can boast. France possesses others in the same region, which are superior only in proportion as they are superior in numbers and quantity; the qualities of one are equal to those of the other.

While we reap such immense advantages from these islands, it is necessary to observe two circumstances, first, that they are gained without laying any violence or constraint upon them, which is contrary to the common principles of all colonies, or the natural liberties and rights of mankind; and secondly, that the benefits we receive from them are greatly owing to their attending to agriculture alone. The first shews, that the national advantage made by colonies does not result from opppression, but from a fair communication of reciprocal benefits. On the second I must observe, that it is the case to a very extraordinary degree: the West India islands are, I apprehend, more free from manufactures than any other territories in the world. In all our continental plantations there are either manufactories or numerous families who spin, weave, and do other works of *manufacture* for the cloathing or answering other

wants

wants of themfelves or a part of themfelves.   But in the iflands there is hardly
to be found a man, woman, or child, that
has a fingle article of drefs, furniture, or
implement of bufinefs, but what is imported : this fhews that hufbandry is the moft
profitable employment they can follow.
While a man was taken up in weaving a
piece of cloth, or making hofe or any other
manufacture which brought him in five
pounds for his labour, he would, in working upon the land, or at thofe trades dependant on the land, earn three times that
fum ; from whence it follows, that manufactures can never be introduced into fuch
a country, fince, in order to make them,
fuch wages muft be given as would render
the fabric vaftly dearer than the fame made
in England, with all the additional charges
of fending it to the Weft Indies, which
would bring ruin to all fuch undertakings.
Neither do the inhabitants of thefe iflands
apply themfelves to commerce, except it
be to the illicit trade with the Spaniards,
in which very great profits are made ; and
even in this many more North American
veffels are found than Weft Indian, for it
much deferves attention, that thefe iflands
poffefs very few fhips, or, more properly
                                         fpeak-

fpeaking, fcarcely any ; their trade is carried on in North American or Britifh veffels—even when the planters turn merchants, as moft of them do, in fhipping their own products, ftill they do it all in veffels belonging to other people. All this is owing to the profit of their bufinefs; when their hufbandry is fo beneficial, as to pay, we will fuppofe, 25, 30, or 35 per cent. it would ill anfwer to have money in fhipping at 8 or 10 per cent.

Here therefore is an example of colonies going of themfelves into the purfuit which the mother-country has the greateft reafon to approve and promote : every circumftance attending colonization in the Weft Indies is precifely in the train beft calculated for the intereft of Britain, and at the fame time for the profit of the planters. This is not the cafe with all our colonies; to what therefore is it owing here ? The anfwer to this is ready enough ; it is owing to *the profit of their hufbandry.* Every people will give their application to that branch of induftry which they find moft advantageous ; if the foil and climate of a colony are fuch as will produce *valuable* commodities, it is to the production of fuch commodities they will apply. Why is not Barbadoes filled with

mer-

merchants, fishermen, manufactures, and farmers, like New England? Because planting sugar is there a more profitable employment. Why is not New England filled with planters? Because trade, fishing, manufacturing, and farming, are more profitable employments. This distinction is that of climate, and it gives a lesson of all others the most important in the politics of colonization, which is to plant them in climates the reverse of the mother-country. This is the principle upon which depends the immense consequence of our West Indian possessions. Britain and those islands are similar in none of their products: the latter wants every thing produced by the former; the former wants every thing produced by the latter; thus it is impossible the one should ever rival the other, as the communication between them consists of a regular exchange of good offices, the one yields upon the balance profit to the other; protection and a ready market are dispensed in return.

If from the West Indies we proceed northward to the southern continental colonies, we shall find as we go continued reasons to shew the great importance of colonies to Britain: by that title I mean the

fettlements to the fouth of the tobacco colonies ; thefe produce rice, indigo, cotton, filk, wine, and other commodities which are of great value in a Britifh market, and which Britain cannot produce herfelf : the fame reafons that make the fugar colonies of fo much value to us, render thefe the fame ; and though fome writers have calculated that thefe fettlements are not fo valuable as the iflands proportioned to the numbers of their people, yet we are to remember, that this is not owing to a want of value in their products, (fome of which, filk and indigo, are far more coftly than fugar), but to the country being more agreeable and healthy to live in, which induces many perfons to refide in their back parts, and cultivate common provifions to fupply the reft with—and alfo to the eafe with which any man who has five or ten pounds, may get a grant of land, build a hut, buy a cow or two, and turn farmer ; fuch people, though they reckon in the numbers of the province, produce perhaps none of the ftaples of it : whereas, if only thofe were reckoned who are employed on the ftaples and the trades dependant, they would be found to raife as great an amount per head as the planters of the fugar colonies.

nies. This circumſtance does not act in
the iſlands from two cauſes, firſt the want
of land, which is ſo far from being given
to whoever will have it, that it is ſold at
conſiderable prices;—ſecondly, the un-
wholeſomeneſs of the climate, which is in
general ſuch, that no perſon would chuſe
to make it their reſidence for ſmall profits,
or with any other view than to make money enough to be able to live elſewhere.
Theſe circumſtances cannot but have the
effect of fixing far more people in the continental colonies, proportioned to the
production of ſtaples, than in the Weſt
Indies.

This kingdom enjoys a very conſiderable
trade by means of theſe colonies; out of
above an hundred thouſand barrels of rice
which they export, we do not conſume
ourſelves above four or five thouſand ; the
reſt goes to Spain, Portugal, Germany,
Holland, and the North. Indigo is an article of the firſt conſequence to our manufactures, ſilk is the ſame, raw hides the
ſame ; ſo that theſe commodities are in
fact equally valuable to us with ſugar :
they are not bought with money, but with
manufactures ; the navigation occaſioned
by them is all our own, ſo that they add to

our strength and wealth in the same manner as sugar, cocoa, coffee, ginger, &c. The southern colonies have no manufactures among them, they are without fisheries, and their commerce consists in nothing but sending lumber to the West Indies, and shipping their staples for a British market in British bottoms.

Objections indeed would have been raised against the production of rice, upon the principle of its being a grain, which in the European markets rivals the exportation of British corn. This has an appearance of truth, and in some years in a small degree may be so: but it is not to be supposed, that if we had sold no rice, we should have added a proportional quantity to the export of corn : nothing can be farther from truth. Rice is purchased by very many people, who would not lay the money out in corn if they could not get the rice : it is used for soup and other different purposes from corn; and if consumed to save wheat by some, it may be a matter of choice rather than œconomy. Nor should we forget that our corn exportation is quite another thing from the export of rice from Carolina, it is uncertain, depends upon the crop; prohibitions have of late been common

mon and continual; and in several years we have imported instead of exported: now it would certainly have been very absurd to have restrained or wished to have restrained the culture of rice, because it is possible that it may rival us to the amount of two or three thousand pounds in four or five hundred thousand pounds worth that is sold. Besides, the export of rice is regular; it is a grain that depends very little on the seasons, and being made not for the consumption of the country where grown, but in order all to be exported, the money gained by the trade comes as regularly as the year; and is, in a word, the very contrary of our corn trade for some years past. For these reasons we may determine rice to be a very proper staple for a colony, and may look on its increase of culture with satisfaction, instead of being jealous of it. If it increases in future, as it has done of late years, it will soon bring more money into the kingdom than any other commodity.

If we advance yet farther northward, and take in the tobacco colonies, those of Virginia and Maryland, we shall find the same reasons to congratulate ourselves upon the great value they are of. Tobacco is the

Q 2

grand

grand ſtaple of theſe ſettlements, a ſtaple as proper as poſſible for a colony, and than which none is more valuable to this kingdom. Out of 96,000 hogſheads made, only 13,500 are conſumed in Britain, and the duty alone of theſe is 26 l. 1 s. per hogſhead, or 351,675 l. The reſt is re-exported to the other parts of Europe, paying alſo a duty, though not ſo heavy, and bringing a flood of wealth into this kingdom.

Every circumſtance that can concur to render a colony valuable to a mother-country, unites in this product, tobacco. Much the larger part of it is conſumed by foreign nations—it could not be profitably raiſed in Britain—it is a bulky commodity, which employs many ſhips and ſeamen—thoſe ſhips are all our own, and the ſeamen belonging to the ports of Britain—it is ſo profitable an article of huſbandry, as to preclude all other employments like ſugar, as long as good land is to be had to plant. All theſe circumſtances are of vaſt importance, and ſhould make us as ſolicitous to increaſe and improve the tobacco culture, as any other article of our American produce.

The

The excellency of this staple is seen in its enabling the planter to buy every necefftry of life except food, and without his attending to any other object. These colonies, so far from rivalling us in fisheries, manufactories, or commerce, have none of the three among them, infomuch that people have found so little profit in herding together, that there has never yet arose a single town of any consequence in either Maryland or Virginia; a strong proof of the advantage they find in spreading over the country as planters, rather than fixing in towns as merchants and manufacturers. These colonies, from the health and fertility of the climate and soil, are grown very populous, and in proportion as their numbers have increased, there has not been an increase of fresh land for their tobacco planting: this has been owing, first, to the confinement which the war gave their settlements, and afterwards to the extreme ill-judged proclamation of 1763, which forbid all settlements beyond the rivers which fall into the Atlantic ocean: this has driven many of their people to common husbandry, to which the soil and climate are equally well adapted. The consequence of this was, that when the export

of

of tobacco is divided among the population of the provinces, the people seem to earn by it but a small sum, compared to those of the islands and the southern colonies. But we are not from thence to conclude that the staple is deficient in value; on the contrary, I am of opinion, that if the amount of it was divided only among the people actually employed by it, and depending on it, it would then be found more valuable even than sugar, or at least as valuable. A part of the population applying, for want of fresh land, to the culture of wheat and provisions, is no fault in tobacco.

But of as great importance as this plant is, yet we are to remember, that it is not the only staple of this colony; it has some other very promising ones.

				£.
Hemp, 1000 tons, 21l.		-		21,000
30 sail of ships,	-		-	30,000
Masts, planks, &c.		-		55,000
Iron,	-	-	-	35,000
Skins,	-	-	-	25,000
Flax-seed,	-	-	-	14,000
Ginseng and drugs,		-	-	7,000

£. 187,000

Besides

Besides 4000 tons more of hemp worked into the uses of their ships, &c. all
these articles are true staples, being such
as Britain either buys of foreign countries,
or can sell to them in any quantities : they
are articles also which promise a considerable increase, and which may be carried to
a height as the population of these provinces increase, which, with the help of
silk and wine, may bye-and-bye be as valuable as tobacco.

It may not be improper here to review
the staples of these colonies, the southern
ones, and the islands, as they all unite in
the circumstance of having such valuable
staples as render them in every respect
highly valuable to Great Britain, and more
so than other settlements more to the north
can prove. The commodities chiefly produced in all our settlements, from Maryland to Grenada, are such as we cannot
have at home, of which we consume great
quantities, which must be purchased of
foreigners, and perhaps of enemies, if we
had not colonies that produced them. This
advantage renders the consumption of those
commodities, not to speak of the re-ex-
portation of many, a benefit to the kingdom rather than an evil ; for as the pur-

chase

chafe is made with our manufactures, the
wealthy part of the nation, in proportion
as they confume American luxuries, find
employment for their poor neighbours; inftead of which, if we had no colonies, the
rental of their eftates would go for the employment of poor Frenchmen and Germans; the immenfe difference of which
is obvious at firft fight. A late writer, from
whom however I have had reafon in the
preceding pages to differ in certain articles,
gives the following table of the tobacco
and fouthern colonies.

	Ships.	Seamen.
Virginia and Maryland, -	330	3,960
North Carolina, - -	34	408
South Carolina, - -	140	1,680
Georgia, - -	24	240
St. Auguftine, - -	2	24
Penfacola, - - -	10	120
	540	6,432
Sugar iflands, † - - -	-	3,600
		10,032

	Exports from Britain.	Exports from Colonies.
Virginia and Maryland,	865,000	1,040,000
North Carolina, -	18,000	68,350
Carried over,	883,000	1,108,350

* *American Traveller.*
† *Editor of Du Pratz.*

Brought forward,	883,0000	1,108,350
South Carolina, -	365,000	395,666
Georgia, - -	49,000	74,200
St. Augustine, - -	7,000	
Pensacola, - -	97,000	63,000
	* 1,401,000	1,641,216
West Indies, † - - -		2,702,060
		4,343,276

These accounts are not the newest, and I have corrected some of the particulars from whence they are drawn, elsewhere, as I observed before; the real totals at present, could they be all known, probably would not be found less than 13,000 seamen, 650 ships, and colony exports of 5,000,000 l. but whether something more, or something less, the conclusions to be drawn are the same: the possession of colonies that produce staples which cause such a prodigious commerce of the most advantageous sort in the world; which is entirely carried on in our own products and manufactures, the balance of which is ours—the profit of which, on both sides, is ours—the ships ours—the seamen ours —the freight ours—a flourishing revenue

* *American Traveller.*
† *Political Essays.*

raised

raifed on them, ours—the population of the countries which fupport this trade, of our brethren and fubjects of the fame crown: when all thefe circumftances are confidered, they will be found to involve a magnitude of interefts which have long fupported the greatnefs of Britain; which now is the moft firm fupport of it; and which, by a prudent and political conduct in future, can hardly fail of being an increafing and improving fupport.

Thefe therefore are colonies that it much behoves this country to give every degree of encouragement to that it is poffible they fhould receive; for by encouraging them, fhe in fact encourages herfelf. I fhall hereafter endeavour to fhew, wherein fuch encouragement ought to confift: but I fhall at prefent obferve, that we ought to be very tender of increafing one branch of their value to us, that of *duties*, for therein we cramp inftead of extending their products. Upon tobacco the duties are near three times the value, which is carrying that taxation to a degree which hardly any other commodity knows. Cafes may happen which may make it very advifeable to lower fuch burthens, though I believe not unlefs our government is very ill advifed

in

in American affairs : but if (which however is hardly to be expected) the governments of those countries which produce
either at home or in colonies the same commodities should take political steps for
greatly encouraging such products, such a
rivalship would render counter operations
neceffary , in which that of lowering duties would be found effential.

As to the northern colonies, all to the
north of the tobacco ones may with propriety be claffed together, fince neither
Penfylvania, New Jerfey, New England,
Nova Scotia, nor Canada, have any ftaple
product of agriculture ; the confequence of
which is their flying to all other employments; the culture of the foil is common
hufbandry, like that of Britain herfelf ; the
employment of their towns, which are
numerous and large, is manufactures, commerce, and fifheries. It is impoffible they
should be fo employed, and at the fame
time be the occafion of Britain's profperity,
like the colonies to the fouth. But fome
writers have carried this deficiency of the
northern colonies too far, in allowing under 100,000 l. for all their ftaples : that
this matter may be fet in a clear light, I
shall tranfcribe here the totals of feveral
arti_

articles before inserted in the tables of their exports, by extracting those articles which may be called staples.

		£.	
Skins,	Hudson's Bay,	29,340	
	Canada,	76,000	
	New York,	35,000	
	Penfylvania,	50,000	
			190,340
Ginfeng and drugs,	Canada,		3,000
Timber,	Canada,	11,000	
	Nova Scotia,	4,000	
	New England,	75,000	
	New York,	25,000	
	Penfylvania,	35,000	
			150,000
Ships,	New England 70	49,000	
	New York 20	14,000	
	Penfylvania 25	17,500	
			80,500
Pitch, &c.	New England,	·	600
Pot-afh,	New England,	35,000	
	New York,	14,000	
			49,000
Flax feed,	New York,	14,000	
	Penfylvania,	30,000	
			44,000
Copper and iron,	New York,	20,000	
	Penfylvania,	35,000	
			55,000
	Total,	£.	572,440

The tobacco of Virginia alone amounts to more money than all thefe ftaples, of all thefe colonies which contain thrice the people of thofe to the fouth: but at the

fame

same time we must acknowledge these to be staples, to every intent and purpose, doubts have been conceived about timber and ship-building ; but when it is considered that there is scarcely any commodity that Britain wants more, witness her imports from the Baltic, and building even men of war with fir, there will not be found any reasons for rejecting them.

The reader will at once recollect that the exports of these colonies amount to far greater sums in fish, oil, wheat, &c. but these are certainly to be rejected, because in proportion as they increase the interest of Britain declines. The most capital article is that of fish, both cod and whale, and therefore I shall give it the first examination ; as it includes more particularly their great navigation—commerce with foreign nations—and the employment of seamen ; all which being of the greatest importance to Britain, we ought to enquire whether they are the same in the hands of the colonies. And this I shall do in the words of a late author, who has attended much to this subject.

We are told by Dr. Mitchel, that the British plantations maintain 45,000 seamen, and employ near 2000 sail of ships. Now

as we have found the number which Britain *poſſeſſes* to be about 12,000, conſequently their own amounts to about 33,000.
A North American writer likewiſe calcu-
lates the ſhips at 2000. That theſe accounts are not exaggerated, there is ſome
reaſon to believe from an aſſertion of another writer, who, ſpeaking of the conſe-
quences of the regulations of the colonies
in 1763, ſays that 20,000 ſeamen and fiſh-
ermen were turned out of employment
there. Now if 20,000 were at once *out*
of employment, the total *in* as well as
out cannot be leſs than 33,000, eſpecially
as the fiſheries were not affected. And if
we come to remark the ſentiments of various writers upon *particular branches* of
their trade, there will be more reaſons e-
qually ſtrong for ſuppoſing this total not
far from the reality. Gee, who wrote a-
bout 40 years ago, ſays, the veſſels belonging to New England alone, employed in
the fiſhery and coaſting trade (without including that to Europe) amounted to 800.
So prodigiouſly as they have increaſed ſince,
the reader will eaſily believe them to be
much more numerous of late years ; and
yet that number, at 22 men each, employed
17,600 ſeamen. To double the number,

would

would bring it much nearer the truth at present. The fishery of the colonies, says Dr. Mitchel, is already much greater than that of Britain : the fishery of New England alone amounts to 255,000 l. a year, which is equal to the amount of the British fishery. And yet New York and Philadelphia, with many other places to the northward, have large shares of this fishery; so that the whole must make a very great amount.

Without turning to more authorities, (although a multitude might be produced) for proving a point which seems so strongly to prove itself, there will not be any danger, according to these several accounts, in determining the navigation *of the colonies* to employ 33,000 seamen; but left any objections unseen should arise, I shall call the number only 30,000. It may possibly be expected that I should enlarge upon the vast consequences of such a number of seamen to a maritime power, and especially after what one of the best of the North American writers has observed with a degree of rapture. " In another century the greatest number of Englishmen will be on this side the water. What an accession of power to the British empire, by *sea* as well as by
land !

land! What increase of trade and navigation! What numbers of ships and seamen! We have been here but little more than 100 years, and yet the force of our privateers in the late war (1750) united, was greater both in men and guns than that of the whole British navy in queen Elizabeth's time." What therefore must they have been in the last war? But notwithstanding all this, I am very far from placing to the account of Britain one jot of all these fine doings. And very clear I am, that the employment of the 12,000 seamen first mentioned, is of twenty times the consequence to this country of all the 30,000 kept by the colonies themselves. The more this subject is enquired into, the more evidently and clearly will it appear, that the production of staple commodities is the *only* business proper for colonies : whatever else they go upon, it is absolutely impossible that they should by any employment whatever make up for the want of the one really necessary. For want of this capital foundation of a colony, our northern settlements, we have found, are full of farmers, manufacturers, merchants, fishermen, seamen ;—but no planters. This is precisely the case with Britain herself; consequently

a rival-a rivalry between them muſt inevitably take place. This in the article of the fiſheries we find fully taken place; for the northern colonies have nearly beaten us out of the Newfoundland fiſheries, that great nurſery of ſeamen! infomuch that the ſhare of New England alone exceeds that of Bri-tain. Can any one think from hence, that the *trade* and *navigation* of our colonies are worth one groat to this nation?

There is not one branch of commerce carried on by theſe trading ſettlements but might juſt as well be in the hands of the inhabitants of this kingdom, the ſupply-ing the ſugar iſlands with lumber alone ex-cepted, and that we have already ſeen is a trifle. Thus the trading part of the colo-nies rob this nation of the invaluable trea-fure of 30,000 ſeamen, and all the profits of their employment; or in other words, the northern colonies, who contribute no-thing either to our riches or our power, de-prive us of more than twice the amount of all the navigation we enjoy in conſequence of the ſugar iſlands, the ſouthern, continen-tal, and tobacco ſettlements! The freight of the ſtaples of thoſe ſetts of colonies bring us in upwards of a million ſterling; that is, the navigation of 12,000 ſeamen: according to which proportion we lose by the rivalry of the northern colonies in this single article TWO MILLIONS AND AN HALF sterling! The hackneyed argument which has been copied from writer to writer, that let the colonies get what they will, it all centers in Britain, will doubtless here be extended; and they will say, if the northern colonies get so much money, that money to them is the same as staples to the southern ones, and equally laid out in merchandize with Britain. But facts prove the very contrary: the consumption of British commodities in them I have shewed cannot be more than to the amount of 108,000 l. They export thither in staples to the amount of 98,000 l. now one of the warmest advocates above quoted asserts the fisheries of New England *alone* to be 255,000 l. according to this reasoning, they would purchase of us only for these two articles to the amount of 353,000, which being more than three times over false, sufficiently proves that they may acquire riches without expending them with Britain.

No one, who has enquired the least into the state of the colonies, can be ignorant that these northern commercial ones carry on a very considerable illicit trade. A late writer

writer fays it amounted to a third of their actual imports.   Now under the title of their imports is included *all* they receive from Britain and the Weft Indies, or in value to upwards of 917,000 l. a vaft fum ! and muft in the nature of things be nearly fo much taken out of the pockets of their mother country.   Another writer lets us fomewhat more into their illicit trade.—— " The colonies to the northward (of the tobacco ones) have very little direct trade with Great Britain ; I mean they have nothing with which they can repay us for the commodities they draw from hence: they only trade with England circuitoufly ; either through the Weft Indies, which is to us the moft advantageous part of their trade, or through foreign European countries, which, however neceffary, is a dangerous and fufpicious channel.   Our Englifh fhips meet others with the fame commodities at the fame markets ; and if thefe markets happen to be overflocked, we interfere with and confequently hurt each other.   But what is ftill more material, there is much reafon to fufpect that no fmall part of the benefit of our North American trade is by this means *left to the mother-country, and paffes to foreigners, and fome-*

times

times to enemies. Thefe northern provinces are in effect not fubject to the act of navigation; becaufe they do not trade in any of the commodities enumerated in that act. They are therefore neither obliged directly to bring their goods to England, nor when they have carried them to other countries, are they neceffitated to take England in their way home. Whereas all the colonies which produce any of the enumerated commodities, under whatever relaxations, are always fubject to one or other of thefe regulations. For inftance, fhips from Bofton may carry fifh, corn, and provifions to France and Italy, and return again directly to Bofton, loaden with foreign commodities, fubject to no other check, than what muft be confidered as none, that of a cuftom-houfe officer in their own colony *. Thefe fhips, however, carry out fomething elfe befides corn and fifh; for the governor of Maffachufet's Bay, in 1733, writes word to the Lords of Trade, that *vaft quantities* of hats are exported from thence to Spain and Portugal: thus they carry out their own to

---

* *Examination of the Commercial Principles of the late Negociation.*

cramp

cramp our market, and bring home French goods to *enlarge* that of *our enemies* *. The general turn of reasoning through this passage is certainly just, though some particular sums are probably erroneous. The consumption of British manufactures in the northern colonies probably much exceeds 108,000l. but that they consume all they import, is most certainly contrary to every article of good intelligence that can be gained in the whole affair.

That fisheries and navigation are improper employments for colonies, and detrimental to the interests of the mother-country, appears clearly enough from hence; and I may add to these reasons, that the practice of the French, whose fishery employs 20,000 seamen, while ours maintains only 4000, proves strongly that *planted* settlements are by no means necessary for success in fishing. When they had Louisbourg, it was only a place of arms; a security to their fishery, and by no means a *colony*; and their fishery is now carried on in full perfection, without so much as that: thus no argument can be more false than that which pretends that our colonies have

---

* *Political Essays.*

not

not robbed Britain, but only created a new fishery from the advantageousness of their situation. We see the fishery of Britain is declined greatly, which, with the increase of that of New England, proves the fact sufficiently. We are told that of New England alone is greater than Britain's; suppose the seamen 5000; can any one imagine the employment of those men, with all the trades they set to work, not to be of the highest value to this kingdom, and the country that has gained them so far rivals and enemies? What advantage do we reap from New England equal to this single lofs?

The second article which I was to consider, is that of corn and provisions, which are exported from all these northern colonies to the West Indies and to Europe. How far these are to be considered as staples, a short enquiry will shew. As to all that are sent to Europe, we may safely determine it to be as pernicious a trade as any the colonies can go into, since it is directly rivalling, and even destroying one of the most advantageous branches of the exports of Britain. American corn cannot come to an European market without doing mischief to the corn trade of England.

This

This trade is not like that of moſt other commodities, which are uſually exported in certain quantities, and to certain markets: on the contrary, it is extremely uncertain in its deſtination, the quantity in demand depends on the accidents of crops, ſometimes it is to one country, ſometimes to another, and the circulation of the trade greatly depending on the ſurplus quantity which certain countries poſſeſs. Poland, England, and Barbary may be called the exporting countries; the latter from the uncertainty of its governments rarely makes the moſt of the fertility of its ſoil, proving but a weak rival to England: this leaves all the ſouth of Europe open to the export of that country, and very advantageous the circumſtance has been, as we have more than once experienced, both to Portugal, Spain, the ſouth of France, and Naples. Let therefore any perſon judge of the propriety of introducing another rival into this trade, which is far more likely to drive us out of it, than all the others we can have in Europe. Wheat, for many years, ſold at 20s. a quarter in America, which was their exporting price, the freight to Marſeilles or Naples is 12s. more, the price therefore delivered has been 32s. a

quar-

quarter; a price at which we have never yet fold in thofe markets, even with the affiftance of the bounty. If this does not fhew the great impropriety, not to ufe a harfher expreffion, of planting colonies in climates that will not produce ftaple commodities, furely nothing can. It may be faid, perhaps, that importation from thefe colonies, even to Britain herfelf, may be an advantageous meafure in dear years; but I cannot but confider fuch an idea as very fatal: it implies a dependence on America, which may grow into a neglect of our agriculture at home; than which a more fatal event can never happen. Britain fhould never look forward to fcarcities of corn; if fhe does, fhe will be fure to find them. Let her, on the contrary, have no other idea but that of exporting, which will be the means of always keeping it cheap, as we have found for near a century.

There is another evil attending this exportation of American corn to Europe; it is the largenefs of the market; while the North Americans were confined to the demand of the Weft Indies, they could look no farther, and raife no more wheat than fufficient for that demand; but having the

European

European market to go to, increases this culture among them prodigiously : the confequence of which is, to draw them off from the culture of ftaples, and from thofe other profeffions which are more beneficial to the mother-country. If the demand for wheat was not large—and the farmers raifing little more than fufficient for their families, they have no encouragement to extend their culture—and the profit on the hufbandry is fmall, in this fituation many farmers had great inducements to move to the fouthward, and turn planters; as many did. But when exportation finds a regular market for all they grow, in a country where land is fo plentiful, it makes the common hufbandry as profitable as planting, and inftead of farmers turning planters, planters turn farmers, than which nothing can be more fatal to the interefts of Britain.

In the fecond place, as to the fupply of the Weft Indies, the fame objections do not lie; for as the iflands find planting too profitable to allow them to attend to common hufbandry, there certainly can be no objection to the northern colonies anfwering the demand—any more than to their fupplying them with lumber; but

let

let me here make a remark, that I do not recollect ever hearing from any quarter, or reading in any of the numerous works that have been published on this subject. It is that Britain in good policy ought to have kept this supply entirely to herself, instead of the uncertain corn trade she has had with Europe; for this, I think, many reasons are to be given; the demand which there has been in Europe for British corn has never been regular; it has been on the contrary very uncertain; and even in years, when exportation has run very high, it has not been answerable to the surplus of our crop, as we may judge from the price at home continuing so low that the farmers could in several countries scarcely live. Now the supply of the West Indies is the most beneficial market that is known in the world; for it is perfectly regular, and absolutely to be depended upon. No where else are such considerable bodies of people as the inhabitants of those islands, to be found, that depend for their daily bread on importation, that attempt to raise scarce any thing that they eat: Britain therefore might have depended absolutely on this market; and the supply of it would have been more beneficial than the corn trade

the

she has at fits and starts carried on in Europe: but the encouragement her agriculture would have received by this *regular* demand would have so animated it, that larger quantities of corn than ever would have been produced, and she would have found no difficulty in supplying the European demand also. This might have been done with great ease, by only laying a duty in the islands upon the import of all corn, except from Britain and Ireland: I do not think this would have been a severity to the islands, because there are many ports for exporting corn from Britain, and many corn merchants in every port; so that there would never have been any reason to fear a plentiful supply, and at a fair price—and if the rate at which the corn came to them was judged too high, the same bounty on the export, or even a larger, if necessary, than what is given at present, would have remedied the inconvenience. As to the distance and freight, we are certain they would have been no material objection, from what we know to be the case at present, which is the supply the islands at present receive from England of beans, and from Ireland of beef. If beans will answer

fwer fuch a freight, moft certainly wheat
would.

Such a meafure as this at prefent would
be perhaps a dangerous one, becaufe all
fudden changes in matters of commerce
are ever hazardous: but nothing would
have been eafier than to have eftablifhed it
before the exports from the northern colonies were fo large, while the trade was low,
and the fupply not confiderable; the meafure might have been brought about by degrees, and nothing is clearer to me than
its proving infinitely advantageous to Britain. It would have given an annual certain export to her; it would have rendered
common hufbandry fo little profitable in
North America, that the northern colonies, from whom we have fo much to apprehend, would not probably have been
one fourth fo populous; inftead of which
we fhould have had many more people
than we have to the fouth of Penfylvania,
and confequently larger products of true
ftaple commodities. It fhould not be forgotten, that one man employed upon tobacco, is of far more worth to Britain than
forty New England farmers. It appears
therefore fufficiently clear, that we may
deter-

determine corn and provisions to be very improper commodities for a colony to deal in, and by no means to be ranked with staples.

Thus does it plainly appear, that a very strong distinction is always to be made between the colonies north of Maryland, and those to the south, in their importance to the mother-country; a distinction which should never be forgotten, as it will remain a lesson to all succeeding ages in what climates to plant colonies. The writer I before quoted, justly remarks on this subject—"That the staple productions of our colonies decrease in value, in proportion to their distance from the sun. In the West Indies, which are the hottest of all, they make to the amount of 8l. 12s. 1d. per head. In the southern continental ones to the amount of 5l. 10s. In the central ones to the amount of 9s. 6d.¼ In the northern settlements to that of 2s. 6d. This scale surely suggests a most important lesson—to avoid colonizing in northern latitudes! Eighteen pounds the export of Nova Scotia after several years settlement, after the utmost attention from the government, after a million sterling of the public money being expended upon it, is an

exam-

example one would think fufficient to deter
the boldeft projector! But if our colonies
to the north produce fuch trifling ftaples,
thofe to the fouth, on the contrary, are im-
menfely valuable ;—indeed of fuch infinite
importance to this nation, that *general ex-
preffions* of the benefit of our fettlements,
fhould never be indulged; let provifoes.
ever come of—*thofe to the fouth.* We have
found in the preceding enquiries, that thofe
colonies which moft abound with manufactures have the feweft ftaples ; and this
is a neceffary confequence, for nothing but
fuch products as bear a large price in Europe will yield a return from thence of the
neceffary manufactures, and much lefs of
fuperfluous ones. But if a colony is fituated in a climate which denies fuch productions, or from a want of due attention
in the mother-country, they are not improved or fuffered to decline, does it therefore follow that the inhabitants of fuch
province are to go without cloaths, furni-
niture, and tools ? By no means; where-
ever there are people, they will moft af-
furedly enjoy thofe neceffaries ; if they raife
nothing from their foil which will purchafe
them in exchange, they will certainly
make

make them themfelves. And if they are a populous flourifhing people, they will find very little difficulty in the attempt. Indeed it is not, properly fpeaking, an *attempt*, but the regular courfe of things; a concatenation of caufes and effects, which take place imperceptibly. And in proportion as they grow more and more populous, their manufactures will increafe beyond the proportion of the people, until they come to work for exportation. It is ever to be remarked, that a people *cannot* FULLY fupply themfelves with any commodity without more than doing it—fome exportation muft take place, or the home confumption will not be regularly fatisfied. It likewife appears, contrary to the ideas of feveral modern writers, that it is very poffible for cultivation alone to fupply a people with *all* the neceffaries of life without any affiftance from *trade* or *manufactures*; and that under the difadvantage of exporting the raw material, and importing the manufacture, by a long and expenfive voyage, under the fubjection of duties, and confequently under complicated charges. The inhabitants of the Weft India iflands and the fouthern continental colonies wear not

a rag

a rag of their own manufacturing; drive not a nail of their own forging; eat not out of a platter or a cup of their own making; nay, the former produce not even bread to eat; and if that was the cafe with all the reft, provided Britain could regularly fupply the deficiency (which under a certain fyftem of policy fhe undoubtedly might), it would be fo much the better for her;—fo entirely do thefe colonies depend on the mother-country for all manufactures! and all from poffeffing beneficial ftaples. Of fuch vaft confequence is it to the country to plant new colonies, or extend our old ones, only in climates which will allow of fuch capital advantages."

In this enquiry I have endeavoured to fhew not only the importance of the American colonies to Britain, but at the fame time to explain wherein that importance confifts; we find it lies in the climate of the colony being different from that of the mother-country, as therein confifts the only probability of the people going upon ftaple commodities. The northern fettlements might be made of much more advantage than they are at prefent; but it

would

would be anticipating the subject to consider that point here, as I shall in another
essay endeavour more particularly to explain it.

CHAP. XXXV.

MANUFACTURES.

*State of the colony manufactures—Difficulties
under which they lie—Means of putting
them down—Buy up the raw materials—
Bounties —Finding other employments—
New colonies—Observations.*

MUCH has been written concerning
the bad effects of the American colonists going into manufactures, but no satisfactory account has been given of the
amount of such fabrics, which has been
owing to Parliament's never having or-
dered a return of them to be laid before
them. Some late writers have urged strongly the magnitude to which these manufactures have arisen, but it has been from calculations founded on dubious authority.
In this case the general idea of the necessity of *making* that we cannot *buy* would

be fatisfactory, did we know the amount of their confumption, and that of their means of fatisfying it.

In confidering this point, we are to drop the idea explained in the preceding chapter, of the ill confequences to Britain which refulted from their trade and fifheries, and here merely take them as means of acquiring wealth, wherewith to purchafe manufactures,

By manufactures are not to be underftood the fabrics of private families, who work only for their own ufe, but thofe only that are wrought for fale, and which are the only or principal livelihood of the perfons concerned and employed in them. This is a diftinction which our writers have not attended to fufficiently; for tho' the population of a fettlement that entirely fupports itfelf is of little or no value to Britain, yet as it is paffive, and no more than fupports itfelf, it is much to be preferred to another branch of population, which is employed in cloathing, &c. itfelf and others too—that is, manufacturing for fale. As to the firft evil, no remedy in the world can be applied to it that will be effectual; nor is it an object which can

ever

ever claim the attention of the mother-country.

It is from hence clear, that the object of enquiry is not the probable total confumption of all the people in the colonies, but of thofe only who do not work up their own manufactures: when the northern fettlements are compared with the fouthern ones—it is of confequence to fhew the great fuperiority of the latter; but as that fuperiority was fully fhewn in the laft chapter, it is not to the purpofe here. The only confumption to be confidered is that of the ranks which *buy* in order to confume. Their making the purchafe, fhews that they have wherewith to pay; and then comes in properly the pretenfions of the mother country, *if you buy, I expect you buy of me*.

Nothing is more difficult than to difcover the amount of their manufactures for fale: we are to confider that there are other articles in their imports befides manufactures, wine, rum, fugar, India commodities, &c. all which amount to confiderable fums. The means by which they can purchafe thofe and manufactures are their exports, the produce of their lands—the produce of their fifheries, and the pro-

fits

fits of their commerce; the two firſt are pretty well known, but the latter, open and clandeſtine, is very great, and no guefs can be given of its amount.

That the manufaĉtures for ſale are not ſo great as ſome have imagined, may be conceived from the vaſt number of inhabitants, who in all probability work entirely for themſelves; in a country where the minute diviſion of landed property is ſo great as in the moſt populous of the northern colonies, and in a climate that will yield little valuable, it is impoſſible that the people ſhould be able to *purchaſe* manufaĉtures: poor countrymen in England do it becauſe all their income is paid them in money, whatever may be their work; but in America day-labourers are rarely to be found, except in the neighbourhood of great towns; on the contrary, the man who in England would be a labourer, would there be a little freeholder, who probably raiſing for many years but little for ſale, is forced to work up his wool in his family, his leather, and his flax, after which, the reſt of his conſumption is ſcarce worth mentioning. The number of people in the northern colonies who come under this denomination is very

great,

great, and confequently the deductions to be made from the total confumption very confiderable : it is not a difficult matter to calculate how much a head would fupply the total of a people with manufactures ; this has been calculated ; but it is extremely difficult to guefs the amount of *purchafed* manufactures, which is the only important point.

In this enquiry we fhould not confine ourfelves to the northern colonies, but take into the account that part of the population of the tobacco ones which is not employed on tobacco ; a confiderable proportion of the total : as any perfon may judge who recollects that foon after the peace the number of people in Virginia and Maryland was calculated at 800,000, the export of tobacco therefore is not much above 20s. a head ; inftead of which, thofe who are employed by that ftaple are able, in all probability, to confume 5, 6, or 8l. a head in imported commodities, and the reft of the people fcarcely any thing, as they muft, like their brethren to the north, manufacture almoft every thing they ufe. If the imported commodities in thefe colonies are affigned to 200,000 people, there will remain 600,000, whofe purchafed

con-

confumption is fmall; and if the common calculation is taken, of their being at the peace 1,000,000 of people in the northern colonies, we then find 1,600,000 fouls, among whom the imports are in fome proportion or other to be divided. The exports from Great Baitain are as follow:

				£.
Canada,	-	-	-	105,000
Nova Scotia,	-	-	-	26,500
New England,	-	-	-	407,000
New York,	-	-	-	531,000
Penfylvania,	-	-	-	611,000
				1,680,500

If the population of thefe was 1,000,000, they imported about 32s. 6d. a head: if we allow 5l. a head for all that *purchafed* their confumption, the number this importation fupplied is 336,000, at which rate (to fpeak nothing of Weft Indian and foreign imports) 664,000 perfons manufactured for themfelves, befides the proportion of the tobacco fettlements. Hence if thefe data are juft, we may fuppofe one third of the people to confume purchafed commodities, and two thirds to manufacture for themfelves; but this fuppofes their

own

own fabrics for fale to be inconfiderable, and that 5l. a head is for only a partial confumption.

There is yet another light in which this point is to be viewed, which is a different claffing of the people; for the fake of explaining the clearer what I mean, I will fuppofe a divifion of the million of people in the northern colonies.

200,000 who confume of foreign manufactures, &c. only 2s. 6d. a head.
500,000 who confume a head 40s.
300,000 who confume 5l.

The firft,	-	-	-	25,000
The fecond,	-	-	-	1,000,000
The third,	-	-	-	1,500,000

	2,525,000
Import from Britain,	-	1,680,500

According to this account, they muft buy of foreigners, or work among themfelves for fale, to the amount of } 844,500

For in this idea the fabrics worked in private families have no place; if they were taken in, the pooreft would confume far more than 2s. 6d. There is nothing extravagant in this account; nor can it be fuppofed that the manufactures of the northern colonies amount to lefs than 844,500 l. In cafe the confumption of the claffes here ftated is greater, then this a-

mount

mount will of courfe be proportionably larger.

Suppofing this fum to be the fact, or near it—or if we call their manufactures for fale a million, I do not think it an a-mount that ought greatly to alarm the mo-ther-country, provided fhe took proper meafures to obviate their ill effects, which meafures would be very eafily planned and executed. It is to be remembered, that a very confiderable portion of this fum muft be expended in fabrics, the whole of which Britain cannot expect to furnifh—and which in fact fhe does not furnifh to any colony, for the laft hand, to a variety of articles, cannot be put at London, but muft neceffarily be executed in America, and the labours of thofe workmen and ar-tizans is there blended with the price of the manufacture.

All that this kingdom can expect from the northern colonies, is to keep down public manufactories, which take the wool from the fheeps back, and convert it into cloth; the flax from the ground, and make it into linen and lace; the fkin off the beaft, and turn it to finifhed fa-brics of leather; the iron from the ore, and convert it into the variety of utenfils
which

which Sheffield and Birmingham exhibit;
and the fame in other inftances: but this
reafoning muft not be carried too far in
any of thefe articles; there are objects
which when completed from wool, leather, and iron, will ftill be of fuch fmall
value, that the very freight from Britain
and carriage to the confumer would be
twice the worth, fuch we may be fure will
be wrought in the colony. But when we
fee them making cloth of 12 s. a yard,
linen of 5 s. hats of 16 s. each, locks,
keys, and curious articles of hard-ware,
which is the cafe, we may then be certain
that the policy of this kingdom is deficient; and that without violence, fuch
manufactures might be put down.

We are to remember, that the colonifts
are under great difficulties in their attempts
to raife manufactories for fale. The mother-country has the power of introducing
her own fabrics as cheap as fhe pleafes, and
under whatever advantages of bounties or
premiums fhe likes to grant; which fhe
can do in her exportation of them to no
other market. Every where elfe they meet
with duties on importation, and perhaps
prohibitions; but in America the manufactories of Britain are openly in every
market

market without duty or clog. In the next place the price of labour is very great, greater take the year through than in Britain, which is a material article ; this muſt neceſſarily be the caſe where land can be had for nothing ; workmen may be gained for high wages, but thoſe high wages will preſently enable them to ſet up for planters in a country where twenty pounds is a fortune ſufficient to begin with ; thus the maſter manufacturers can never keep the men after they have got them, which muſt lay them under almoſt inſuperable difficulties, or ſubject them to expences which will make their manufactures much dearer than thoſe of Britain.

The long winters and ſevere ſeaſon which ſtops moſt employments, have been urged as reaſons why they may manufacture largely for ſale : but I am not of this opinion ; thoſe who are converſant in our fabrics well know, that in very ſharp froſts many of our manufactures are at a ſtand ; what therefore would be at Boſton or New York, where the froſts are in common 20 degrees ſharper than the moſt ſevere we feel in England ; and where the whole winter is froſt and ſnow : people can ſcarce keep their extremities from freezing

who

who attend to nothing elfe, how therefore could the finer forts of manufactures be carried on? What fort of work would a weaver make, whofe fingers were numbed with cold; or a workman in fteel, whofe flefh froze to his manufacture? In fuch a climate manufactures muft be carried on in mild or warm weather, and then the workmen may have what they will afk in the field, and all the advantages here ftated are at once given up. Under fuch circumftances no fabrics can be made cheap enough to under-fell Britain, but fuch as come extravagantly dear from her, and can be made reafonable in America; or others fo inferior in kind, that freight and carriage make a large proportion of the whole value.

But fuppofing the manufactures of thefe provinces, notwithftanding thefe inconveniences, did not get to any height, which in fome articles is the cafe, then Britain might, without having recourfe to what governor Pownal hints at, excifes, take meafures that would bring them down. The eafieft and moft advifeable way would be to raife the price of their raw materials, by buying it up for the Britifh market : the obvious way to bring about any fuch tranf-
action

action as that, is by giving bounties upon the import into Great Britain, and if they are large enough, they certainly will effect any thing. But the objection is, that, in order to create a new trade, the expence, by way of bounty, may be greater than if done by other methods : I would propose to force the import of wool from the colonies into Great Britain to such a point, as would be sufficient to burthen the woollen manufactures of America, by raising the price of their raw materials : at the same time that this laid a tax on the American fabrics, it would give a bounty on the British ones, by lowering the price of their raw materials by the import from the colonies.

The employment of factors, agents, or contractors would be less adviseable far than giving a bounty, provided the latter would have the effect ; but as the wool-dealers in the colonies must be thrown into a different channel, and as the merchants there must open new correspondences, a bounty, in order to force such a new business, must probably be a greater expence than if government did the business, at least for a time, through the merchants ; but when once the business was brought

near

near a regular train, a small bounty would have a greater effect than a large one at first.

Such a transaction would be very heavy upon the manufactures of the Americans; for under the disadvantages which I before stated the colonists to lie, a rise of price in their wool would have the same effect as laying an excise upon their manufactures, but which would be brought about without the heartburnings and disputes inevitable with a new tax. The idea of importing wool from America is not a new one; Dr. Mitchel some years ago remarked—" The wool of the colonies is better than that of the English; it is of the same kind with the Spanish wool, or curled and frizzled like that, and might be rendered as fine by the same management. By the step which the colonies have lately taken to raise all the sheep they can, they will have plenty of wool. With this they have already made cloth worth 12 s. a yard, which is as good as any that is made of English wool. Some of their wool has been sent to England, where it sold for the price of the best. This may perhaps be looked upon as a loss to England; but if she would study to make a right and pro-

per

per ufe of her colonies, this might be of more fervice to her than any one thing they are capable of producing. If the Spaniards fucceed in their attempts to manufacture their wool, England may want it from the colonies more than any other commodity, as it is well known there is not a fingle piece of fine cloth made in England without Spanifh wool." This obfervation came from a perfon perfectly well verfed in American affairs from a long refidence there, and fhews how expedient the conduct would be, with a view to the goodnefs of the wool, as well as the defign with which I propofe it to be done.

The fame conduct might be purfued with fome other raw materials, fuch as fkins, hemp, and flax, all which are valuable articles to be imported into Great Britain ; fome of them are fo already, and if our demand was a little quickened, it would certainly be laying a difficulty upon the American manufacturers that work them. It is true, that in both thefe cafes the price would rife upon ourfelves as well as them, but this I do not apprehend would be of a bad confequence equal to the advantages on the other fide of the queftion ; fince there is no object in the policy of Britain

tain which is of near fuch importance as putting down, or at leaft preventing all increafe in the manufactures of the colonies.

There is another method of effecting this great purpofe, which in fome refpects would anfwer better, though worfe in others: it would be giving a bounty on the export of fuch Britifh manufactures *to America* as the colonifts have made the greateft progrefs in erecting—and this bounty fhould be fufficient to enable the merchant importer inAmerica to under-fell the manufacturer there: this would be a very fimple operation, and might be made perfectly effectual; but it would have this needlefs expence, it would fupply the Weft Indies and the fouthern continental colonies with the fame fabrics as cheap as the northern colonies, which, though an effect of no ill confequence in itfelf, would add to the expence without making an equal return for it: not however that it would be without any return, for thofe Britifh goods being fo much cheaper in thofe markets would extend the confumption of them, and certainly increafe the trade in them which is carried on in the Weft Indies.

Whether

Whether this method or the firſt was choſen, would not be materiel, provided the thing was done: but that ſome method ſhould be taken to effect it cannot be doubted, ſince the grand intereſt of Britain in her colonies is defeated and perverted by their ſetting up manufactories for ſale, a ſtep which, in the natural courſe of it, if left to itſelf, muſt inevitably bring on their independence.

But here it will naturally be remarked, that to put down the manufactures of the colonies, and thereby throw people out of employment, would be a very iniquitous ſcheme, unleſs ſome proviſion was at the ſame time made in an increaſe of other employments; and certainly no perſon can diſpute the truth of this; but this part of the work would be very eaſy: among the true ſtaples of the northern colonies have been mentioned ſkins, drugs, ſhips, pitch, pot-aſh, timber, flax-ſeed, copper, and iron, all which articles, particularly timber, ſhips, pitch, and iron, may be had in any quantities, provided due encouragement was given to procure them. At the ſame time that meaſures were taken to leſſen their manufactures, we ought alſo to

increaſe

Increafe the quantity of thefe ftaples, not only to give employment to the people inftead of manufacturing, but alfo to fupply the country in general with as much or more wealth than they made by that employment. Among thefe articles none have oftener exercifed the pens of ingenious men than that of naval ftores, which we import from the Baltic at fo large an expence, and pay for almoft entirely with bullion: our northern fettlements produce all forts of timber in as great or greater perfection and plenty than the eaft country; this is a point acknowledged by all; mafts, boltfprits, plank, deals of all kinds, and fome articles of timber much more valuable than what we import. Great objections ufed formerly to be made, for want of faw-mills being erected; but that is no longer the cafe, for there are many of them now upon almoft all the rivers of America; fo that every thing is done that could facilitate the fupply, was the article of freight got over. *Gee*, in his *Navigation of Great Britain confidered*, fays, " Our plantations in America abound with vaft quantities of timber, and the navigation from New England, Nova Scotia, or Newfoundland, is not more tedious, nor at a greater diſtance from us, than the bottom of the Bothnic gulph, or Peterſburgh. But thoſe places having been long in trade, and having a conſtant demand from us for that commodity, they always have great ſtocks of timber ready ſquared, and boards lying ready to load a ſhip of five or ſix hundred tons in ten or twelve days ; but hitherto we have never had ſtocks lying ready in our plantations, nor any encouragement for building large bulky ſhips, ſuch as are uſed by the Danes and Swedes, who ſail with a few hands and at a ſmall charge. What timber we have had hitherto come directly to England, has been rather put on board to fill up, when tobacco or other merchandize has not been to be had, and therefore no care has hitherto been taken to make it a regular trade." But this is not at preſent the caſe ; for I am well informed that there are large ſtocks of timber lying in many of our plantations ready for the Weſt Indies, and proportioned to that demand, conſequently the quantity would of courſe increaſe, with any increaſe of demand, and no difficulties of that ſort would be found. But Mr. Gee is miſtaken in his aſſertion of the length of navigation ; for this is ſeen in the freight :

that

that from Riga to England is not above
25s. calculated at the rate per load at
which it is paid for; whereas the freight
from Nova Scotia is 40 s. to 50 s. This
difference will, I believe, generally be
found; and another circumstance in favour
of the Baltic, is the price of labour, which
is not half what it is in our colonies; these
are the only superiorities of the east country. But on the other hand, our American timber comes duty free, and even with
a small bounty, though an insufficient one;
the only object therefore to get over is the
freight; and this can only be done by giving a bounty per ton on all ships belonging
to Great Britain that bring timber or naval
stores from the colonies. Let us suppose
the freight per ton from the Baltic 1l. 5s.
and that from Nova Scotia 3l. which we
may venture to state as an average, though
2 l. 10 s. or even 2 l. may be sometimes
taken; in this case, a bounty of 2l. per
ton would turn the scale of freight by 5s.
which, with the duties on the Baltic timber, would at once change the course of all
the timber and iron trade. By various accounts it has been found, that our import
in iron is 27,500 tons at 12l. is 314,000l.
and timber 200,000 l. these two articles

amount

amount therefore to more than half a million sterling, not to speak of increase in the other branches of their staples. I before shewed, that the manufactures for sale in the northern colonies probably amounted to more than 800,000l. a year; now we find that in these two articles of iron and timber they might earn of Britain alone above 500,000 l. which would enable her to take proper measures to sink their manufactures to that amount, and at the same time leave them with as much wealth as they had before—no hardships would be found from it in the colonies, but the interest of this country would be prodigiously advanced; instead of paying half a million to the Baltic in cash, we should send to the same amount in manufactures to America, the difference of which is very great; and at the same time we should effectually prevent the increase of manufacturing in America, which in future would prove of much more consequence than can at first be imagined.

The expence to the public at which these beneficial effects might be brought about, would not be large. One hundred thousand pounds a year would pay the bounty on 50,000 tons of shipping, that is, 100 fail at 500 tons each. We may venture to affert, that this navigation would anfwer the purpofe, if confined to that a-lone; and the expence of fuch a fum would bear no proportion to the immenfe advantages that muft inevitably accrue from it to this country.

By the export of naval ftores the colonies would find employment for that furplus of their population which has driven them to manufactures—by the import of Britifh manufactures in confequence, and the buying up of their raw materials, their own fabrics would be put down—the manufacturing intereft of Britain would. be moft highly advanced, and the export of bullion to the Baltic would be ftopped; all thefe advantages would furely be well worth the fum they would coft the public in the bounties, which would not be loft to the nation or paid to foreigners, but diftributed among her own people at home, to the invigoration of their induftry. A late writer, after ftarting fome propofals fimilar to this, remarks, " Thefe fentiments are founded in reafon, and tend to render Great Britain independent of the effects of that prodigious commercial manufacturing fpirit, which is now arofe in all Europe.

T 3

There

There are many peculiar motives for importing wool from thefe colonies with the other articles already fpecified. It would be a great affiftance to our own woollen manufactures, and at the fame time have the beft effect we could wifh upon that of the colonies. No *importations* are more beneficial than raw commodities, to be worked into manufactures; and no *exportations* fo pernicious to a manufacturing country as that of fuch raw commodities; for which reafon Britain fhould wifh to import wool from thefe colonies; and were the fyftem of policy I am now fketching thoroughly executed, fuch importation might very eafily be effected. Every particular of this fyftem is the link of a chain, and all equally connected; the more iron, timber, pot-afh, and madder were imported, the more likewife you might have of wool, for the more would the colony woollen manufacture fuffer, and confequently the lefs would be their demand for that commodity, and then the additional demand from Britain, at a time when the Britifh manufactures were poured into every market, would completely give her the command of all the American wool. This
impor-

importation might be made to extend to a very large fum annually.

" As to fhips, fome may perhaps think the benefit refulting from them to the mother country more equivocal ; but in a certain degree I fhould apprehend the fupply from the colonies highly advantageous. In many cafes it might be found advantageous to build men of war there. But leaving them out of the queftion, let us confider the repeated outcries and complaints that have been made in this kingdom for fo many years, of the want of timber for fhip building ; and that fuch complaints are not ill grounded, every body agree. Now would it not be a very prudent meafure, to referve the timber in this ifland for the ufe of the navy alone, and depend on America for that for merchantmen ? It is by no means advantageous to this country, whofe agriculture is of fuch immenfe importance, to have any land occupied by wood that is good enough to yield corn, and confequently no more fhould be raifed than is neceffary ; and fuppofing it neceffary to raife all that is requifite for the royal navy, that is certainly the moft ; for there is no occafion to extend it to all that is ufed in merchant fhips. The latter had

T 4

better

better all be built in America.   Nor would
there be any neceffity to lofe the manufacturing of the hemp with which fuch fhips
were rigged, fince we might import it
raw from the new colonies, and re-export
it to the northern colonies, manufactured
into fail cloth with as little expence as
much of the hemp lies under, now ufed
by New England, &c.   If Britain builds
annually 40,000 tons of fhipping (I am
only ftating a fuppofition), this at 3l. 10s.
per ton would alone amount to 140,000l.
a year.   Nor can I fee why the northern
colonies fhould not build for all Europe.
The building trade might eafily be carried
to the underfelling all other countries, and
efpecially when the culture of hemp and
the working the iron mines are carried to
perfection ; for then there is no country in
the world that will unite all the requifites
for building cheap fo completely as our
colonies in North America; and that at
the fame time while all the benefit re-
dounds to Britain alone, and without there
being the leaft danger to her from fuch natural advantages in them.   The danger
would be great, if at the fame time fhe fuffered them to be traders and fifhermen ;
but I laid it down as a rule to proceed upon,

that

that trade, fishing, and manufacturing were put an entire stop to among them. Now the trade of ship-building has not only the advantage of selling timber (a mere drug in America) to great advantage, but of obliging those who bought it, at the same time to purchase some quantity of our hemp and iron. Thus if we built 100,000 tons of shipping annually for foreigners in our northern colonies, it would make up the former amount 500,000l. and I am very well persuaded that this might be easily effected. Supplying other nations with shipping cheaper than they have it at present, would be no objection to this plan, since all the benefits they would reap therefrom are not comparable to those which we should receive from taking their money. Nor do I think in true politics it would be the least adviseable to refuse French gold for men of war thus built : for we may lay it down as a maxim, that the French will never want as many or more men of war than they can man; experience shews this; so that our enemy will not meet us with a ship the more for our selling them. And most assuredly we had better take his money than let it be given either to the Swedes or the Genoese,"

The

The reader will here obferve, that this point of employing the northern colonifts upon ftaples, or commodities which anfwer the fame purpofe, by way of enabling them to do without manufactures, would in the nature of things lower their fabrics, and take off all that eagernefs for making a progrefs in them which has of late been fo ftrong among the Americans. Give them employments more advantageous than manufacturing (which all that I have named would prove), and they will, in the nature of things, apply at once to them with as much avidity as ever they did to manufactures; for in the courfe of affairs in the colonies, it can only be the *furplus* of population that can found manufactories for fale.

And here it is necessary to obferve, that this fyftem of deftroying the fabrics of the colonies by buying up their raw materials, giving a bounty on the export of the Britifh manufactures, and employing the colonifts on ftaples, might be vaftly affifted by the meafures before explained of planting new colonies in better climates: this would draw off yet greater numbers than the above mentioned employment on iron, timber, fhips, &c. The population that is

to

to be commanded for manufactories can only be had when there is a surplus, which the lands do not take off. The northern settlements are very populous—the beft lands taken up—new grants only to be had in fpots which poffefs not the advantages which fettlers neceffarily are defirous of: when fuch difficulties increafe, and at the fame time the people vaftly increafed, it is the nature of things that the application to manufactures muft increafe proportionably; and the neceffity of counteracting the ill effect every day muft be more and more evident : that furplus of population arifes merely for want of lands worth taking up, as the very term implies, for no fuch thing can be found while land is fo plentiful as to yield an immediate and beneficial maintenance to every family that applies for it : hence it is that manufactories are eftablifhed, and hence the propriety of finding new employments on ftaples for the people, inftead of manufactures; the fame principles act in pointing out the neceffity of fuch new colonies. That every man without employment may meet with every poffible inducement to fettle as a planter rather than as a manufacturer : and while any fuch exift, we may be certain what choice

will

will be made ; the country life in America has too much independency, too much plenty, and too many conveniencies not at all times to be embraced in preference to the bufinefs of manufacturing, which in every circumftance is fo much inferior.

When land is difficult to be had, or not good, owing to the extenfion of the fettlements, or to the monopolies of the country, the poor muft be driven to other employments than thofe which depend on land ; manufacturing, commerce, fifheries, &c. muft then thrive in the natural courfe of things, unlefs fome fuch meafure as I have ftated is put in practice in order to provide other employment. Such meafures cannot be carried to the extent that is neceffary with fuch an increafing people: the plan therefore to be adopted is certainly to prevent the future increafe of the evil, by providing a motive for the frefh emigration of the people. Settling Canada, Nova Scotia, and Florida, is not providing any fuch motive, as it has long been found that the people of the other colonies will not go to them ; but colonies on the Ohio, Miffiffippi, and in the Ilionois, would have this effect beyond any other meafure in the world. The journey from New England,

New

New York, Jerfey, Penfylvania, and Maryland is by means of the rivers in the back country, the Ohio, the Miffiffippi, and the lakes, as eafy, cheap, and commodious, as can be wifhed : fo that the people in thofe colonies who cannot get good land at home, may, at a very fmall expence, provide as much as they can defire in thofe territories, which are in every refpect as excellent, in point of foil and climate, as can be wifhed. Water-carriage from the old colonies is abfolutely neceffary to fuch new ones as are defigned to draw off the people from them. The inhabitants of America are fo accuftomed to do without expence, that they would confider a long land carriage of their effects as an infurmountable obftacle to their removal ; I mean the lower ranks of the people, whofe emigration the fyftem of policy I have juft been ftating would moft concern. But the paffage to the tracts of country I have mentioned, is as commodious, efpecially by the Ohio, as they can wifh, and would not fail to draw off a very great number of the people.

Here I have traced that fyftem, the feveral parts of which could hardly fail of having the effects I have mentioned. In

the

the firſt place, buying up their wool and other raw materials would lay a tax on their maſter manufacturers, at the ſame time that it would be an advantage to thoſe of Britain. Secondly, giving a bounty upon the import in America, of ſuch Britiſh manufactures as the Americans had made the greateſt progreſs in ſetting up, would enable us to under-ſell them in all the towns in our colonies. Thirdly, buying up or giving a bounty on the tonnage of all ſhips that brought iron, timber, or naval ſtores from thence, would find employment for their people more beneficial than that of manufactures; which would not only prevent ſuch people as are now employed on them from falling into diſtreſs, but would prevent others from engaging in them in future. Fourthly, planting new colonies in fertile and healthy countries would draw off that ſurplus of their population, which has hitherto thrown them into manufacturing; it would leſſen their preſent numbers conſiderably, and be a drain to their future increaſe.

Theſe ſeveral points of conduct aim at the ſame purpoſe;—a purpoſe too important to admit of any delay; which on the contrary requires ſpirited endeavours, and

ſuch

such variations in the view as shall attack the evil on every side. One or two of these measures might do much good, but all of them are necessary, if a complete cure is intended; and prevention meant in future as well as present ease. Manufactures in these colonies have been owing to the increase of the people being beyond the proportion of fresh land to take off the surplus of population; nothing can either put them down or prevent their increase, but drawing off many of the inhabitants, by tempting them with a better country and plenty of land, and finding more profitable employments than manufacturing for such as stay at home. These are the grand objects: well pursued they would prove effectual in putting down all their manufactories for sale, and preventing new ones being erected; but if the work was not sufficiently executed thereby, the bounty on similar British fabrics would give the finishing stroke. The northern colonies under such a system of policy would no more have manufactures abounding among them of their own make, than the West Indies or the southern colonies, excepting what was the private work of families; an

object

4

object not of much jealousy to Britain, and even those would be much lessened by the same conduct. At the same time that this great and desirable effect took place, the manufacturing interest of the mother-country would be amazingly advanced more than by any other measure that could be devised ; for the export to America would be increased proportionably to the quantity made by the American manufactories for sale, and the import of naval stores ; so that instead of paying a vast sum in bullion to the Baltic for those commodities, they would be bought of the colonies with manufactures, a difference infinitely great. The trade and navigation of Britain would be greatly encouraged—and her American affairs would be thrown on a footing that would, if well pursued, be effectual in preventing those many evils which cannot but arise from the establishment of manufactures among the colonists. Such advantages are rarely to be gained without trouble or expence; but in this case both would be small in comparison with the benefit : the small bounties already in being shew that our legislature think the thing extremely desirable; but if they would ef-

fect

fect it, they muſt ſubmit to a larger
expence, in order to ſecure a profit of far
more conſideration than almoſt any expence.

CHAP. XXXVI.

INDEPENDANCY.

*Great errors in the accounts given of the pro-
greſs of population in America—Principles of increaſe — Dependancy connected
with ſtaples—Surplus of population—
Power of the colonies—Obſervations.*

THIS is one of the moſt curious and
interesting diſquiſitions that can at
any time demand the attention of this kingdom. The colonies we have planted in
America have ariſen to ſuch a height of populouſneſs, power, and wealth, that an idea
of their future independancy ſtarts into the
mind of almoſt every man on the very mention of them in converſation: ſome aſſert
the period near at hand, while others are
willing to believe it yet at a diſtance; to
enquire when it is to happen is not of importance; but to examine thoſe circum-

ftances, whofe tendency is either to accele-
rate or retard it, is an enquiry which is
equally interefting and ufeful, fince from
thence may be deduced the plan of conduct which it is proper this nation fhould
purfue, in order to fecure a continuance of
the advantages fhe at prefent enjoys, by
means of her fettlements in America.

Virginia, from its firft plantation, has
doubled its number of people every twenty
years : this fact, which is well authenti-
cated by actual enumerations, has led
many of our writers into a moft capital mif-
take concerning the progrefs of population
in America : they have transferred it from
Virginia to our colonies on the continent
in general, than which a greater blunder
could fcarcely be made. Virginia is a fettlement where the people are fpread all
over the country, quite to the mountains,
among the hills, and even over them ; and
have been fo for many years, owing to the
uncommon inland navigation all the country enjoys ; but in the colonies to the
fouth the people are confined to the unhealthy coaft for the fake of cultivating
rice, the moft unwholefome employment
under the fun. Tobacco and wheat, which
are the grand products of Virginia, will

6

not

hot grow in fwamps and marfhes ; though the former requires a rich moift foil, yet it muft be free from wet, and dry lands do for it, provided they are fertile ; rich wood-lands, for inftance, where oak, hiccory, and locuft trees are found: fuch lands in America are ever healthy; and as to wheat, it may be laid down as a maxim, that wherever it thrives the climate and foil are falubrious to the human body. Another circumftance is the climate of Virginia, which at fome diftance from the coaft is as fine as any in America ; it is the medium between the cold of the northern colonies, and the heat of the fouthern ones, as its fituation is between both. Further, Virginia is without towns, the people make fuch advantage by their agriculture, that all are employed in it, confequently all are on the increafe : they have neither merchants, manufacturers, nor fifhermen among them.

If the reader confiders thefe circumftances, he will find them extremely well adapted to increafe the number of a people. The healthinefs of the climate—the goodnefs, and at the fame time drynefs of the foil—the eafe with which every man finds employment on the foil—the profit

of

of agriculture exceeding that of any other profeſſion. Theſe are points which, when united with the plenty of land that moſt of our colonies enjoy, could not fail to occaſion a very rapid increaſe of the people.

That this increaſe is not to be extended in idea to the reſt of the colonies, will evidently appear from theſe circumſtances in them being very different : in the north the climate is ſo very ſevere, that it is impoſſible population ſhould thrive in the ſame degree as a more temperate one, for the neceſſaries of life muſt be had with more difficulty. In the ſouthern colonies, the heat is too exceſſive, in the low country on the coaſt, where the planters confine themſelves on account of rice, for the people to increaſe as they do in Virginia : in the northern colonies the ſoil is not comparable to what it is in the tobacco ones, conſequently proviſions cannot be had with equal eaſe. The ſame obſervation is applicable to the planted parts of the ſouthern ſettlements, and will continue ſo till the back country is cultivated. In the northern colonies agriculture, is far from being attended with that profit which reſults from the culture of ſtaple commodities ; the conſequence of which is, a large

pro-

proportion of the people applying to other professions, which are far from having that tendency to increase, which is found in classes maintained by the soil: thus the people gather into towns, populous cities are met with, the bane of increase, trade, manufactures, and fisheries flourish: and although such may be thought to increase the people, it is a great mistake; those employments only find business for the surplus of agriculture; where is a town full of those professions, in the most healthy climate, that doubles its number from its own increase in twenty years? Yet is this done in Virginia: on the contrary, all great towns would be presently depopulated, if they were not supplied by the country. Another circumstance is the considerable tracts of country in the northern settlements that are fully peopled, and where land is as dear as in the cultivated parts of Great Britain. In such there cannot be that increase which is found in Virginia, where the people are spread so much more over the country.

It is here necessary to attend particularly to the progress of population in a newly planted country, in order to see from what principles the increase of the people arises,

and

and what are the circumstances that draw them from the professions which depend on agriculture. The great increase found in Virginia has been owing to the plenty of good land in a climate that will allow of the culture of a staple. A man there who fixes upon a plantation, breeds his family of course to a knowledge of agriculture ; the sons marry early, because they no sooner form a connection with the daughters of a neighbouring planter, than they think of marrying : it is the same in England, but what puts it aside is the difficulty of supporting a family ; the young couple, as much as they may wish it, are obliged by prudence and their parents to wait till they can be settled advantageously, which often is till the chance of a numerous family is half cut off. In Virginia, and those parts of the other colonies circumstanced in the same manner, the connection is no sooner formed than the marriage ensues. The man takes up a grant of land, his father gives him a little stock, and assists him in building a house : money is wanting for but very few things, and a small sum all that is necessary ; the business is then done, and the future success of the family undoubted. Such a state of the case not only

brings

brings on marriages early, but also early courtships; for in thickly peopled countries men are retarded in their ideas of connecting themselves, for fear of that poverty they are always in danger of: an unmarried young man in parts of 'the colonies is a prodigy.

Here therefore we deduce the first principle, which is plenty of land to be had for asking, and under the payment only of some slight fees: the second is, that land being good, and well situated; if it is not good, too much expence and difficulty will attend the cultivation of it; for if subsistence for a family be not easily and speedily to be gained, with some surplus, by the sale of which other necessaries may be purchased more money must be had in readiness before a plantation is undertaken, and if the situation is not within a due distance of water-carriage, it will be in vain to raise products for sale, as they cannot be sold.

From hence we find there must be a difference in the progress of the population of different provinces proportioned to these circumstances; the land in Virginia is much better than in the northern colonies, and it is in general far nearer to navigation; these are points of superiority which can-

U 4

not

not fail of rendering the increafe much quicker in the former than in the latter.

The third obfervation to be made here is concerning the climate; the foil muft not only be good, but the climate muft be warm enough to yield products that are of a value fufficient to make agriculture more profitable than either manufactures, commerce, or fifheries. In Virginia the culture of tobacco is much more beneficial than any other employment; the crop yields a certain and ready value, by means of which they are able to purchafe fuch manufactures and neceffaries as their lands will not produce, and at the fame time afford a good profit to the planter; fo circumftanced they have no inducement to change their way of life—their fons have no other bufinefs before their eyes, by which they can better themfelves even in idea. But all this is different in the northern colonies; agriculture there is nothing more than the culture of provifions, which, though when prices are high, and a market ready, is very profitable, yet is it not that regular profit which attends a ftaple; this want of a regular market for commodities rarely to be fent to Europe, renders other means of getting money neceffary,

fuch

fuch as commerce, fifhing, and manufactures; and when once thefe are but partly
eftablifhed, they muft neceffarily draw off
many people from the culture of the earth.
The fuccefs which attends fome of thefe—
and the inclinations of individuals, which,
when there is a choice, will neceffarily ope-
rate with many, by degrees lead more and
more into purfuits entirely different from
agriculture; circumftances owing originally almoft entirely to a want of ftaple
products. When once there is a population formed independent of agriculture, the
people are divided; one part increafe proportionably to the circumftances above defcribed, but the other have no increafe, or
probably require the fupport of the country to keep up their numbers.

We find therefore that the firft requifite
is plenty of land in a healthy climate; the
fecond, fertility and a convenient fituation;
and the third, the climate's yielding a ftaple product: if we examine the reft of the
colonies with Virginia, we fhall find them
inferior to it. The plenty of land in the
northern colonies is not comparable to that
in Virginia, unlefs it be in places either
not fertile, or in inconvenient fituations;
the navigation of Virginia is infinitely fuperior

perior to that of any other colony: New England has very little inland navigation; and in point of fertility, the foil in the tobacco provinces much exceeds that of any of the reft. Refpecting the product of ftaples, the northern colonies have none, and therefore have been driven to every profeffion as well as agriculture. And in the fouthern ones, where there are both ftaples and good land, the rice culture has fixed the principal part of the people on the coaft, where the climate is fo unhealthy, that, inftead of breeding people, it is formed for deftroying them.

From thefe confiderations it is very evident, that the increafe of people in Virginia muft be far greater than in the reft of the colonies, and confequently, that thofe writers who have fuppofed the whole of our fettlements to increafe in people as quick as that colony, muft have erred very confiderably in their calculations.

This is a material point: it is a very good thing for Britain, that the colonies which have not ftaples do not increafe fo quick, for if they did, their manufactures, &c. would increafe proportionably; but that increafe in other colonies brings on a correfponding increafe of the ftaple products,

duéts, and alſo a proportionable conſumption of Britiſh manufaétures.

The independency of the colenies, whenever it may happen, muſt turn on this point, *the increaſe of people in thoſe ſettlements which have not ſtaples.* The increaſe in thoſe which have ſtaples, muſt always be for the advantage of the mother-country. It is therefore of conſequence to know the truth of ſo important a matter : the northern colonies are moſt populous, but it does not therefore follow that their preſent increaſe is equal to that of Virginia.

Dr. Mitchel ſays, the number of people in the tobacco colonies ſoon after the peace was 800,000 ; in the northern colonies near 1,500,000 ; and in all the colonies 3,000,000 ; the total I do not apprehend at that time to be ſo great. The melancholy circumſtance in this account, is the number in thoſe ſettlements which produce no ſtaples. If the total, as ſome authors aſſert, be 2,000,000 at the peace, the number in the northern colonies could not be above 1,000,000 or 1,100,000.

It is no difficult matter to explain how the danger of America's becoming independent does not lie in mere population,

but

but in the territories where that population is found. A people spread over a vast
extent of fertile country, and employed in
raising staples so valuable as to pay well for
the freight to Europe and distant countries
—the raising which is attended with more
profit than any other employment—such
a people, it is very evident, can find little
or no inducement to oppose the designs of
the mother-country. The latter finds a
ready and certain market for all the staples
of the former, and sells in return every
article of manufacture or other commodities that can be wanted, at the same fair
price she fixes on them in all other markets: at the same time that this friendly
and mutually beneficial intercourse subsists
between them, the mother-country is at
all times ready and able to protect the colony against all enemies and invaders. In
such a situation it is evident that both parties must remain satisfied with each other,
until one of them is guilty of some great
indiscretion or false politics; and we may
venture to assert, that such false steps, in all
probability, will come from the mother-
country, that is, from the active and superior party. This is the true description
of a colony founded upon just principles,

and

and the great object to be attended to is the people's employing themfelves in a bufinefs wherein they cannot interfere with Britain.

Now if we turn our eyes to the north-ern colonies, we fhall find that the cafe is extremely different. As the climate will not produce ftaples of value enough to pur-chafe manufactures, &c. the inhabitants are neceffitated to apply to other profef-fions; thefe are commerce, fifheries, and manufactures; the moment they get into this train, they engage in a rivalfhip with the mother-country; both are in the fame purfuits; they meet each other in the fame markets, and with the fame commodities; when once the mother-country *feels* the ef-fect of fuch a competition, jealoufies, heart-burnings, reftraints, oppofition, and a number of effects of rivalry arife, and are the fore-runners of that independency of which we are treating at prefent.

It is not that the northern colonies are without a confiderable and a profitable a-griculture; the diftinguifhing circumftance is the product of the agriculture. In the tobacco colonies, &c. the ftaple is a com-modity that is wanted in Europe, and yields a good price, confequently the

planters

planters can sell to the British merchants a product that regularly supplies them with a return of British manufactures. But the agriculture of the northern provinces, that is, of all the settlements north of the tobacco colonies yields only corn and provisions; valuable articles, it is true, but not sufficiently so to bear the freight to Europe, except in years when they are very cheap in America, and very dear in Europe: consequently the sale of them to the merchants of Britain must, in the nature of things, be a mere uncertainty, a contingency depending on accident: whereas the sale which is to pay for the import of manufactures must be regular, and absolutely to be depended upon.

Now the want of such staple products must have the consequence of obliging the inhabitants of such colonies to make those fabrics they cannot buy, or else to apply to such businesses as may have the effect which the agriculture of other colonies produces.

But, say some, why cannot these settlements apply to manufactures, commerce, and fisheries, without such an application bringing on their independency?—Because those employments, by whatever people

they

they are carried on, occafion wealth, military power, and that furplus of population from which armies may, on any occafion be raifed. When the general bufinefs of a colony is the fame as that of the mother-country to the degree of rivalfhip, difputes and quarrels muft arife; and when thefe become inflamed by a continuation of the fame difputes, the poffeffion of a great body of feamen, many fhips, with every fort of naval ftores, arms, and ammunition for the equipment of fleets, armies, and their attendants, with a great furplus of population for the recruit of both; manufactures in number fufficient to take off a dependence on others, and commerce for a general fupply; when this is the cafe, it muft furely be apparent, at firft fight, that colonies in fuch a fituation poffefs the principal means of becoming independent; in fuch a fituation they will have little compunction at difputes with their fuperior, and every day feel lefs and lefs dread at any open hoftilities.

The difference is extremely great between fuch and others that are in a different predicament; among whom we find no furplus of population, no fhips, no feamen, no magazines of naval ftores, nor

any

any great cities, to plan, direct, and head
the difcontents that may arife from the
caufes I have juft fet forth. While the
natural tendency of the foil, climate, productions, and navigation is to fpread the
people over a whole country, their increafe does not make them powerful; add
millions to Virginia, and fpread over the
Ohio, Ilionois, and Miffiffippi, they will
be no more powerful with four millions
than with one, becaufe, as long as frefh
land is plentiful, there will be no furplus
of population to gather into towns; without the fame furplus there can be no manufacture, nor any poffibility of raifing
armies or navies. A colony not a fourth
fo populous, but poffeffing a furplus of population apparent in its cities, and confe-
quent employments independent of agriculture, would be far more dangerous to
Britain. Hence we find how ill judged a
conduct that was in the Britifh government, which lead it to attempt to force a
capital in Virginia: every means were
ufed to lead the people to flock into
Williamfburg, and magnificent edifices
erected to adorn it; miferable want of fore-
fight! Inftead of which, had great reftric-
tions been laid on towns increafing, in the

infancy

infancy of Boſton, New York, and Philadelphia, this country would at preſent
have been in the poſſeſſion of perhaps
20,000 ſeamen more than ſhe now enjoys ;
and all the trade depending on them. A
modern author obſerves, " The navigation
than of our American colonies has been more
once exerted in actual feats of power, in
carrying on a war—againſt the enemies of
Britain indeed ; but the ſame power might
be exerted againſt her, and in the caſe of a
revolt moſt certainly would."   " We have
been here, ſays an American writer, but
little more than one hundred years, and yet
the force of our privateers in the late war
(that of 1744) united was greater, both in
men and guns, than that of the whole Britiſh navy in queen Elizabeth's reign."
What therefore muſt it have been in the
late war! Beſides ſuch a formidable naval
force, they have raiſed, paid, and armed
great armies.   During the late war they
kept an army of above 30,000 men on
foot. They have founderies of cannon, magazines of war, arſenals, forts, and fortifications, and even victorious generals amongſt
their own troops. They have a ſtanding
militia ; and conſtantly have the means of
raiſing and arming a formidable body of

forces. Let it not be imagined that I am drawing a comparison between the power of Britain and her colonies; far from it; I am only touching upon a few concurrent circumstances, which add to the grand ones of an independent agriculture and manufactures. Supposing that the latter are of capital importance to a people about to throw off the dominion of another, the former are likewise of vast consequence to the attempts, and would render the execution much easier than it could be without them: and how much likewise would depend on the situation of Britain at the time! For instance, whether she was in the midst of a successful or an unsuccessful war;—in the midst of a secure peace or a doubtful contest. A certain concatenation of events might give the colonies an opportunity of not only striking the blow, but preventing all future hopes in the mother-country of reversing it. The effect of external circumstances therefore must be great."

Seeing the principles upon which the danger of this independency lies, we may, without great difficulty, examine and point out the means of preventing it as long as possible: we have found that the situation
which

which moſt threatens it is the populouſneſs
of thoſe colonies which have no ſtaples :
hence therefore all thoſe meaſures I before
pointed out as a remedy againſt the manufactures of America are equally applicable
to the preſent caſe ; ſince in their operation
they cannot leſſen the fabrics of the northern colonies without either leſſening the
number of their people, or in giving them
employments which ſhall have the effect of
ſtaples. In proportion as theſe objects were
effected, the greater would be the difficulty
of their becoming independent; and in that
chain of conduct no link is more important
than the eſtabliſhment of new colonies in
ſuch a climate as will yield ſtaples, and in
ſituations which will admit an eaſy emigration from the northern ſettlements to them.
Such new colonies, among which that of
the Ohio will be foremoſt, would have the
effect of drawing off that ſurplus of population which in a country moſt of which is
cultivated, applies to manufactures, commerce, or fiſheries ; and as long as ſuch ſurplus could be made to flow in this new
channel, we ſhould be in no greater danger
of the independency of America than we are
at preſent, and perhaps not in ſo much.

I have ſhewn, that the general increaſe
of people in the colonies is not near what

                    the

the generality of writers make it: inftead
of doubling all their numbers in 25 years,
their prefent number will not probably be
doubled in 50 years; and then the next
doubling may take 120 years, and fo on; a
confideration too much overlooked by all
authors that have treated of American
affairs. But granting the increafe to be
quicker than I have flated it, yet it is not
the numbers, as I before obferved, but the
furplus of agriculture that we are to fear.

Suppofe the total fifteen millions, but
fpread over the continent fo much, that the
manufactures, commerce, and fifheries were
no greater than at prefent—in that cafe I
affert, that we fhould be in no greater danger of their independence than we are at
prefent. But on the contrary, if their numbers had filled all that part of the continent
which will yield ftaples, fo that frefh land
for a fmall expence could no longer be had
for new fettlers, then of courfe that furplus
of population which ufed to be taken off
continually by new cultivation, muft neceffarily have recourfe to other employments; then cities arife, commerce and
manufactures flourifh, the arts are introduced, and a mother-country eftablifhed
inftead of remaining a colony.

Here

Here we may make an obfervation, which, though at firft fight it may appear great'y diftant, yet deferves attention; whenever population has advanced to fuch a degree in our colonies: it is, that we muft then, at all events, make the acquifition of Louifiana, on the weft of the Miffiffippi, to fupply that neceffary quantity of frefh land which will be wanting to prevent the furplus of population applying to any other profeffion than agriculture: if the preceding principles are admitted, and they can hardly be rejected, then this obfervation will not have the appearance of wildnefs. The author above quoted gives an idea of Britifh policy fimilar to this: he remarks, " That fhe fhould abide by the boundaries fixed already to the old colonies, that of the rivers' heads; and all further fettling to be in *new colonies* wherever they were traced. —That fhe fhould keep the inland navigation of the continent, that is, of all the great lakes and navigable rivers to herfelf, and not fuffer any fets of men to navigate them, and thereby communicate from one part of the continent to another.—That fhe fhould never fuffer any provincial troops or militia to be raifed, but referve entirely to herfelf the defence of the frontiers.—That

X 3   fhe

she should throw whatever obstacles she could upon all plans of communication from colony to colony, or conveniencies from place to place.——That in proportion as any colony declined in staples, and threatened not to be able to produce a sufficiency of them, the inhabitants should receive such encouragement to leave it, as more than to drain its natural increase, unless new staples were discovered for it.——A people, circumstanced as the North Americans would be, if such a system was fully and completely executed, could not possibly even *think* of withdrawing themselves from the dominion of Britain until their staples failed them, and they were drove, in spite of all laws and prohibitions, to herd together in towns for the purposes of manufacturing those necessaries which their staples would not pay for. No matter what their numbers might be, they would remain subject to the mother-country as long as she could supply them with staples, and that principally would depend upon providing their increase with fresh land. It is true she would find an end of her territory at last, and then the natural course of things would form towns and manufactures of that increase, which she before took off by means of plenty of land.

land.   A connection would then arife between town and town and colony and colony ; *numbers* would feel that ftrength which refults from *connection* alone, and the influence of the mother-country would be too weak to oppofe the confequences."

If a contrary conduct in Britain fhould be purfued, which it muft be owned is but too likely, the independency of America may happen in no diftant period ; for as fuch progrefs has been made in the northern colonies towards general manufactures, and the poffeffion of great fifheries and an extenfive commerce, the effect will every day be an increafe of thofe employments proportioned to the furplus of population in the fettlements ; and this increafe muft neceffarily bring on a degree of power, which will enable them, on the firft fair opportunity, to throw off their obedience to the Britifh government.   Or affairs may gradually go on in fuch a train, as will bring on he fame independency by flow degrees, and at laft reft in the completion of it without any acts of violence againft Britain—by rifing into too powerful a people for the mother-country to think of controuling.

X 4   CHAP.

CHAP. XXXVII.

REPRESENTATION.

Of a union between Great Britain and her colonies—Objections which have been made—Answers—Difficulties—Observations.

THAT different parts of the same empire ought to be united as closely as possible by all the ties of political interest, is a maxim, which as it has never been denied, so one might imagine it would never be necessary to prove the cases in which it ought particularly to be applied. But in this of our American colonies such difficulties have been started, and such objections have been made that have made many persons to think truth no longer truth—or that a strong exception is here found to a maxim otherwise infallible.

Mr. Pownal, who resided long in America, and was supposed to be well acquainted with American affairs, started the plan of an union in a more direct manner than any other writer of credit had done before, shewing that an American representation might

might take place without very great difficulties: and the late Mr. Grenville went pretty much into the same idea when he planned the stamp act, but from that blundering execution which was seen in all his schemes, he totally defeated the plan by beginning at the wrong end.

A very able and lively author, in the *Observations on a late State of the Nation,* took Mr. Grenville's scheme to pieces, and ridiculed it with great severity. His objections turn chiefly, if not entirely upon the distance of America, and the uncertainty of that navigation, from length of voyage, shipwrecks, and war, which must bring the American representatives to Great Britain: in all which he displays much wit and great ridicule. But I am one of those who do not think that wit is reason, or that he who gets the laugh must infallibly be on the right side; since this would be nothing more than saying, that a man's conduct is always right in proportion to the wit with which he can defend it. We are not therefore to see nothing but impossibilities in a matter which at most abounds with only difficulties; and a resolution to conquer difficulties ought always to be taken

in

in proportion to the benefits which will result from the victory.

The difficulty of the distance, I think,
may be got over by several means, suppose
the members from America, who may be
there chosen either by the freeholders of the
provinces, or by the present representatives
in the provincial assemblies, should always
be elected for an uncertain duration; that
is, the member resident at London should
continue the sitting member either till another landed who was to succeed him, or
till his own re-election was noticed. I
think this plan would at once answer many
of the objections which the above mentioned ingenious gentleman has started. Nor
do I see to what material ones the plan is
open: if it is said that the member in England cannot support his interest in case of
new elections in America, I reply, neither
can the member of our own parliament, in
case he is abroad, which often happens,
and yet we see his friends exerting themselves near as effectually: but granting the
fact, of what consequence is it to either
Britain or America, whether Mr. George
or Mr. Thomas be the member? As long
as there must be a sitting one, the necessity

is fully anfwered by either; and if fome individual happens to be of fingular merit or popularity, he will of courfe be re-elected. This uncertain duration of a member's fitting may appear ftrange at firft fight, but upon a little reflection there will be found nothing objectable in it, as the term will be fixed by no minifterial artifice, nor by the artifice of any other man: if a member is not re-elected, it will of courfe be the bufinefs of his fucceffor to take his feat as foon as he can; and if on the way he fhould be taken by the Spaniards, and carried to Lima, it will be a difagreeable adventure to him, but public bufinefs will fuffer nothing by it.

But there is another circumftance which anfwers a great part of the objections which have been made to American reprefentation: Englifh counties elect Scotch members—Scotch towns elect Englifh members—and both of them Irifh ones; why not upon the fame principles elect Britifh members for America? They will be equally eligible. At prefent the provinces appoint agents, and give them falaries; why not elect the fame men into parliament; their feat will render a falary unneceffary, and they will be much more able to advance
the

the bufinefs, and defend the intereft of
their conftituents : it would be at the op-
tion of the electors of America either to
chufe fome perfon among themfelves, or
elfe upon the fame principles as they make
choice of their agents, to chufe fome perfon of reputation or knowledge in Britain.
There does not appear to be any infuperable
objections to any part of fuch a bufinefs.

As to the arrangement of the electors in
America, it would have no more difficulties in it than that of the fame thing in Scotland :—it would only be neceffary to take
care that the increafing population of that
vaft country fhould be reprefented, which
would be well enough fecured by decree-
ing all freeholders, whofe freeholds were
above the value of ten pounds fterling—
fhould have a vote, both fuch as were in
being at the time of the union, and alfo
fuch as fhould be gained or erected afterwards.   And if the reprefentation of towns
was entirely dropped, it would be fo much
the better, and be taking a proper hint from
the experience of electors in England.

Objections have likewife been raifed
upon the fcore of difficulties in contefted
elections, from the tedioufnefs and expence
of trials at the bar of the houfe, when wit-
neffes

neſſes are to be brought, and all their attendants, acroſs the Atlantic ocean : but as well might we object to the repreſentation of the Highlands of Scotland, becauſe ſuch evils were infinitely greater than with Middleſex :—there are boroughs in Scotland from whence it is near as difficult and expenſive to get a tribe of people to London on ſuch a buſineſs, as it would be from parts of America. If objections againſt extending legiſlation throughout the empire are ſtated merely from the extent of the empire, it is ſo weak a plea, that one might almoſt reply to it by ſaying, you ſhould get rid of what you cannot govern. You can ſend governors, deputies, ſurveyors, marſhals, regiſters, and placemen of every denomination to America; it is a pretty joke to imagine they cannot as well return us repreſentatives.

Concerning the general expediency of this meaſure, I recollect nothing material that has been urged againſt it. On the contrary, very many reaſons have been offered to ſhew that it is not only proper but neceſſary. It ſhould be conſidered, that the danger of the American colonies throwing off what is commonly called the yoke of their mother-country, turns principally
upon

upon points of government in which the one party is supposed to be aggrieved by the laws enacted in the other. Nor can we well state a case in which there is any probability of a revolt, but what arises from this circumstance.

If the union was to take place, and all the provinces of our American dominion represented in the British parliament, there would be a tye and a connection of a very different nature from what at present subfists between them. Acts of the legislature would then be acts to which themselves had given their consent; a point of vast importance, and by no means treated in a satisfactory manner, by speaking of a virtual representation.

Let us suppose the administration of our government to be so unexceptionable in regard to all American measures as to prevent any open revolt among that part of the subjects in our empire, in what manner then could America become independent? I reply, by the connection gradually falling off, until it became of no consequence—this connection is merely commercial. Its declension would be proportionate to the colonists supplying their own markets with manufactures, after which, the remaining

connec-

connection would be too inconfiderable to deferve a thought: hence therefore we find a natural and eafy death to every advantage which can refult from America to Britain. But if the former was reprefented in the parliament of Britain——and if that reprefentation formed an entire new legiflative power, to which they gave unreftrained obedience, the *connection* between them, which has been found of fuch importance, would be properly perpetual—— as fecure as the connection between Scotland and England.

If in any future time the population and importance of America become, what we have reafon to fuppofe they will be, then it might be expected that a change in the place of parliamentary meetings might enfue, and America become the head of the empire, as far as the refidence of government could make it fo; a revolution which might be much more advantageous to this country than a total feparation would be, under many circumftances which might attend fo great a change. But as this idea is in reference only to a period extremely diftant, no arguments to be drawn from it can be conclufive in the prefent enquiry.

INDEX.

I N D E X.

A

AMERICA, sea coast marshy, i. 218—
    ii. 47
    Value per ton of the commodities
    of, 259
    Population of, rightly managed, no
    cause of jealousy, ii. 93
Anguilla, climate, ii. 174
    Farming in it, 175
Antigua, climate, ii. 163
    Soil, 164
    Produce, ibid.
    Improvements, 165

B

Bahama Islands, climate, ii. 199
    Healthiness, 200
    Soil, 201
    Improvements proposed, 202
    Navigation, 204
    Afford the most pleasing retreats, 205
    Most agreeable and beautiful spots, 206

Vol. II.   Y   Bar-

INDEX.

Barbadoes, climate, &c. ii. 151
    Soil, 152
    Progress of its culture, 152, 153
    Present state, 154, 156
    Profit from it to England, 155
    Proportion of export to soil, 157
    Culture of sugar in, 158
    Improvements proposed, 160, 162
Barbuda, climate, ii. 170
    Product and property, 171
    Farming there, 172
Bounties and premiums, advantages of, ii. 36
Buckwheat, culture of, i. 135
Buffaloes, ii. 88

C

Cabbages, culture of, i. 164
Canada, climate of, i. 16
    Soil, ibid.
    Husbandry, 20
    Exports, 25
    Importance, 27
    Defects in the agriculture, 31
    Compared with that of Great Britain, 37
    People in, 38
Cape Breton, i. 13
Carolina (North), climate, i. 330
    Products, 331
    Soil, 332
    Lawson's description of in 1700, 333
    Advantages of the planters, 337
    Cattle, ibid.

Caro-

I N D E X.

Carolina (North), hufbandry, 339
    Fruit, 341
    Tobacco, 342
    Rice, ibid.
    Products of a plantation, 345
    Exports, 346
    Defects of their agriculture, 348
    Improvements propofed, 352, 358
    Advantages of the back country, 353
Carolina (South), climate, i. 367.
    Surprifing degrees of heat and cold, 368
    Products, 376
    Timber, ibid.
    Fruit, 381
    Soil, 384, 387
    Back country, 388
    Rice, 391
    Indigo, 397, 400
    Expence and profit of a plantation, 407, 414
    Situation of the people, 432
    Exports in 1748, 434—in 1754, 440—in 1761, 441—in 1764, 443—in 1771, ibid.
    Improvements propofed, 446
    Madder, 467
    Hemp, 468
Carrots, culture of, in England, i. 210
Cattle, great ftocks of, i. 167, 337
    Ill conduct of, i. 350
Ceded Iflands, ii. 177
    Obfervations on, 196

Y 2

Chartres

INDEX.

Chartres (Fort), ii. 104

Cherokee country purchased by Sir James Wright, ii. 33

    Fertility of, 34

    Propositions for improvement, 35

Christopher's (St.), climate and extent, ii. 165

    Soil and produce, 166

    Account of a plantation in it, ibid.

Codrington, (Christ.) account of, ii. 171

Colonies, importance of, ii. 208, 217

    Reasons for planting, 210

    Political management of, 213

    Regulation of commerce, 215

    Products of the British, 216

    Principles on which they should be planted, 222

    Number of people in, 299

    Manufactures of, 255

    Independency of, 289

    Power of, 305

Cotton, culture of, ii. 84

Country gentlemen in England, state of, i. 68

D

Dominica, climate, ii. 177

    Soil and products, 178

    Sugar, 179

E

Egmont, earl of, his plantation in Florida, ii. 50

Emigrations, ii. 210

I N D E X.

Export of corn from colonies, i. 88, 182
    Ill confequences of, ii. 246

F

Farming, profit of, in England, i. 202, 204
    Labour and teams to land in England,
    311
Fences, i. 167
Fifhery (Newfoundland), does not de-
    pend on planted fettlements, ii. 245
Flax, culture of, i. 21, 55
    Native fort in Penfylvania, 162
Florida (Eaft), hiftory of the accounts that
    have been given of thefe countries,
    ii. 42
    Different accounts, 44
    New defcription, 45
    Climate, 46
    Soil and face of the country, 48
    Products, 50
    Plantations, ibid.
Florida (Weft), coaft of, ii. 51
    Miferable country, 52
    Climate, 54
    Hiftory of fettling, ibid.
    Political confequence of the Floridas,
    57

G

Georgia, climate of, ii. 1, 6, 8, 9
    Soil, 2, 5, 10
    Back country, 3
    Productions, 4

Georgia, forests, 13
    Account of a plantation near Augusta, 14
    Great advantages of living in, 18
    Agriculture of, 20
    Cattle, 23
    Profit of agriculture, 25, 28
    Silk, 26
    Hemp, 27
    Planters in, 30
    Exports of, 32
Grant, Mr. his plantation in Florida, ii. 50
Greenville, Mr. George, his preposterous regulations, ii. 58
Grenada, climate and extent, ii. 182
    Character of, 184
    Products, 185, 187
    A plantation in, 188
    Errors in culture, 189
Grenadines, ii. 186

H

Hemp, culture of, in New England, i. 54
    —in New York, 102—in Jersey, 137—in Pensylvania, 161—in Virginia, 257, 260
    Profit of, not equal to tobacco, 152
Horses, ill treatment of in colonies, i. 89
Hudson, river, account of a plantation on, i. 105, 108
    Great profit, 113
    Compared with husbandry in England, 116

I N D E X.

I

Jamaica, ii. 111
    Climate, 112
    Hurricanes, 114
    Extent, ibid.
    Soil, 115
    Productions, 116, 143
    Sugar, 116
    Plantation in, 139
    Improvements propofed, 144
    A great improvement by Mr. K. 145
Jerfey (New), climate, i. 132
    Soil, 134
    Defects in the hufbandry of, 142, 146
    Timber, 141
    Fruit, 139
    Improvements recommended, 149
    Inhabitants, 152
Illionois, fituation and defcription, ii. 99
    The fineft country in the world, 100, 101
    Beautiful tracts, 102, 104
    Settlements near Fort Chartres, 105, 107
    Climate, 105, 106
    Products, 108
    Advantages which may be made of it, 109
Imports, Britifh, from other countries, which might be had from the colonies, ii. 37, 38, 40
Independency of the colonies, ii. 289

On

I N D E X.

On what turning, 299, 304
Progreſs of, 301
Connection with agriculture, 302
Prevention of, 306, 310
Indigo, culture of, i. 397, 400
John, St. iſle of, i. 13
Joſeph river, St. country on, ii. 103

K

Kaſcaſquias, French ſettlements there, ii. 107

L

Labour, price of, i. 73, 169
Leeward Iſlands, ii. 163
Louiſiana, Eaſtern, climate and extent, ii. 62, 64
Soil, 66, 67
Propriety of planting it, 68, 91, 93
Foreſts beautiful, 70
Timber, 70, 74.
Vines, 72
Grapes and wine, 73
Mulberries, 74
Products, 75, 77
Hemp, grows naturally, 76, 79
Flax, 76
Maize, 77
Indigo, 78
Tobacco, 79
Of excellent quality, 80
Silk, 82
Cotton, 84

Olives,

INDEX.

Louisiana, Eastern, olives, 86
    Immense herds of cattle, 87
    Deer, 89
    Fruits, ibid.
    General advantages, 90
    Manner in which it ought to be settled, 94
Lucerne, i. 453

M

Madder, culture of in England, i. 211, 305
Maize, culture of, i. 77, 99, 134, 160
    Horse-hoeing, culture of, 51—ii. 76
Manufactures in the colonies, ii. 255, 257, 265
    Difficult to know the amount, 259
    Proportion to people, 262, 263
    For sale, 264
    Difficulties under which they labour, 265
    Means of reducing them, 267, 271, 276, 282
    To what owing, 287
Mississippi, navigation of, i. 292
    Its consequence, ii. 60
Mitchel's *Contest in America*, i. 286
Montserrat, ii. 169
    Produce, 170
Mortgages in England on American estates, i. 66
Mulberry trees in Pensylvania, i. 165
Myamis, French settlements on, ii. 107

Naval

INDEX.

N

Naval ftores from the colonies, ii. 273
   Freight of, compared with Baltic, 275
Negroes, treatment of, ii. 138
Nevis, ii. 168
   Produce, 169
New England, climate, i. 45
   Soil, 46
   Settlements lately made, 48
   Hufbandry, 50
   Timber, 56
   Exports, 59
   Inhabitants, 61
   Country gentlemen, 64
   Farmers, 66
   Their happy ftate, 68
   Errors in rural management, 74
   Compared to Great Britain, 86
   Gentlemen of fmall fortune much
      happier in New England, 91
   Tillage, 81
Northern colonies, peculiar circumftances
      of, ii. 235
   Great commerce of, 238, 240
   Ill confequences of, 241
   Illicit trade of, 243
Nova Scotia, foil and climate of, i. 1
   Hufbandry, 4
   Characteriftic of the country, 12

O

Ohio, climate of, i. 278

Ohio,

Ohio, settlement of, 279
    History of, 280
    Circumstances in favour of a colony
      there, 283
    Soil and products, 288
    Tobacco, 289
    Communication with the ocean, 291
    Hemp, 295
    Vines, 297
    Silk, 299
    Cotton, 301
    Indigo, 302
    Madder, 304
    Comparison with Britain in that cul-
      ture, 308
    Expences and profit of a settlement
      there, 319
    Compared with husbandry in Bri-
      tain, 327
    Junction of the Mississippi impor-
      tance of that situation, ii. 69
Orchards, i. 103, 139
Orleans, New, strength of the Spaniards
    there, ii. 97, 98

P

Pens, confining cattle to, excellent hus-
    bandry, ii. 120
Pensylvania, climate of, i. 154
    Soil, 155
    Productions, 156
    Timber, ibid.
    Husbandry, 157

Penfylvania, labour in, 169
     Improvements propofed, 171
     Defects, 179
     Silk, ibid.
     Vines, 178
     Exports, 181
     Inhabitants, 184
     Method of living, 186
     Fruits, 187
     Plentiful living, 188
     Hufbandry and living compared with
       that of England, 201
Philadelphia, price of land near, i. 174
     Society of agriculture there propofed,
       180
Pine land, i. 384
Pitch, i. 342
Plantations, progrefs of fettling them, and
     the expences and profit, i. 109
     Firft attention in fettling one, 316
Poa anguftifolia, in Canada, i. 22
Population of colonies, progrefs of, ii. 290
     On what depending, 292, 294, 296
Potatoes, culture of, i. 100—ii. 22, 173
     Great products in Barbuda, 173
Proclamation of Oct. 1763 condemned,
     ii. 63
Providence, ifle of, imports from, ii. 200

R

Rain, the lefs there falls the more whole-
     fome the country, ii. 46
                   Reeves,

Reeves, planter in Bay of Fundy, i. 6
Reprefentation of the colonies, ii. 312
        Reply to the difficulties ftated, 314
        Propriety of, 317
Rice, culture of, i. 342, 391
        Product and profit of planting, 395
        Dry, 463
Rice colonies, import of, ii. 224
Rolle, Mr. his plantation in Florida, ii. 50

S

Saffron, in New Jerfey, i. 138
Scotch grafs, ii. 133
Settlement, beginning of, and progrefs of a
        new one in Penfylvania, i. 190—in
        Georgia, ii. 15
        Account of one, 192—another, 198—
        another, 319
        Profit of, 325—another, 414, 424
Settling in America, advantages of, i. 116,
        194, 245, 325, 427—ii. 16
        Compared with Britain, 197, 207,
        213
Ships from colonies, of, ii. 279
Silk, i. 268, 354
Silk-grafs, i. 274
Soils in America, figns to Judge of, i. 313
        —ii. 47
Sporting, perfection of fifhing and fhooting
        in Penfylvania, i. 186
Staples from Penfylvania, i. 183
        Importance of colonies producing, ii.
        235, 253
                                Stores,

Stores in America, what, i. 227
Sugar, culture of, ii. 116, 118, 125
        Description, 116
        Soil for, 117
        Manuring for, 119
        Holing, 121,
        Weeding, 122
        Boiling, 124
        Rum, 125
        Buildings, 126
        Errors in culture, 127
        Improvements proposed, 129, 130,
          131
        Objections answered, 132, 135
        Negroes, 138
        Expences and product of a plantation,
          139
        Profit, 141
        To absentees, 167
        Culture in Barbadoes, 158
        ————— St. Christopher's, 166
Swamps, i. 387

T.

Tar, i. 343
Taylor, Mr. his plantation in Florida,
        ii. 50
Tobacco, culture of, i. 222, 246, 247
        Sorts, 225
        Inspection law, ibid.
        Product of, 227
        Profit, 229
        Necessity of fresh land, 230
        Nature of a tobacco plantation, 231

INDEX.

Tabacco, improvements recommended, 231
    Expence of culture an acre, 233
    Expences, and profit of settling a
      plantation of, 235
    Why the planters are not rich, 237
    Life of the planters, 242
    Superiority of the lands on Mississippi
      for, ii. 80
    Importance of, 227
Tobago, climate, &c. ii. 190
    Spices, 191, 192, 193
    Soil and timber, 191
    Products, 192

V

Vincent, St. climate, ii. 179
    Soil and products, 180
    Inhabitants, 181
Virginia and Maryland, climate of, i. 216
    Soil, 217
    Products, 218
    Timber, 219,
    Animals, 220
    Face of the country, 221
    Tobacco, 222
    Advantages of settling in, 243
    Comparison between a Virginia planter
      and a British farmer, 250, 251
    Exports, 256
    Hemp in, 257
    Husbandry of, 263
    Improvements proposed, 267, 272

Vir-

I N D E X.

Virginia and Maryland, filk, 268
    Vines, 270
    Hemp, 274

W

Wafte lands in Great Britain, 249
    Not to be fettled, 250
    Advantages of landlords farming
       them, 252
    Propofal to the legiflature for fettling,
       254
Watering meadows, i. 166
Water-melons, i. 140, 102
Weft Indies, peculiar importance of, ii. 220
    Supply of, with corn, 250
Wheat, culture of in New York, i. 98
    New Jerfey, 136
    Penfylvania, 157
    An univerfal grower, 182
Wine, from the colonies, i. 463
Wool in Penfylvania, i. 167
    From the colonies, ii. 269

Y

York (New), climate, i. 94
    Soil, 95
    Propofals for improving the hufban-
       dry of, 126
    Vines, 129
    Timber, 101
    Culture of grain, 98

F I N I S.

www.ingramcontent.com/pod-product-compliance
Lightning Source LLC
Chambersburg PA
CBHW021807110726
47902CB00006B/1685